New England Mysteries

Book #1 - *A Cold Morning in MAINE*

published in October, 2014.

ISBN 978-0-9962397-0-7

Book #2 - *A Quiet Evening in CONNECTICUT*

published in April, 2015.

ISBN 978-0-9962397-1-4

www.nemysteries.com

A Bad Night in
NEW HAMPSHIRE

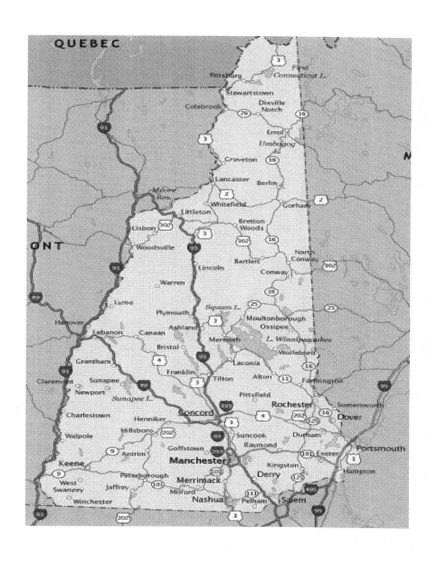

A Bad Night in

NEW HAMPSHIRE

Terry Boone

ISBN   978-0-9962397-2-1

First Paperback Edition: November 2015
10 9 8 7 6 5 4 3 2 1

Published by
THREE RIVERS GROUP

Cover photo by the author.

A Bad Night in

NEW HAMPSHIRE

This is a work of fiction. Names, places, events, timelines, distances and other information have been adapted or created entirely by the author. While some aspects of the story were inspired by career experience as a broadcaster, far and away much of what you will read in this book is made-up. Any similarity to real people and real events is mostly coincidental.

Published by **THREE RIVERS GROUP**

Contact: threeriversgroupvt@gmail.com

For Rick Miller

One

We were walking from the lake back to the cottage, wooden steps that went from the dock up to the screened porch 60 feet ahead.

It was going on midnight, the remnant of a full moon on the far side of Lake Winnipesaukee. Solar garden lights along the path made it safer in the dark. We each carried a flashlight, switched off, and empty wine glasses.

Considering how cold it had been a week earlier, the air was pleasantly warm. Well, at least not cold. I had my right arm around Bonnie's shoulder, she had her left arm around my waist. We weren't drunk, but walking slowly.

There was a scream. It came from the far end of the island, maybe a quarter-mile to the east. We both stopped and looked in that direction. Bonnie looked at me. "Tonight is Halloween, Michael" she said.

"Right." We stayed put. And there was a second scream, definitely a woman.

"Come on," I said, putting my wine glass on the ground next to one of the lights. I turned on my flashlight and began to jog toward the scream.

A footpath ran along the edge of the lake between cottages set back from the water. This section of Bear

Island had older cottages, all facing west and 150 to 200 feet apart. Most were empty this late in the fall. Those with their own dock all had steps, either wood or stone, that went to the lake.

Bonnie turned on her flashlight and was a few feet behind me, walking quickly to catch-up. The moonlight made the trunks of tall pine trees and the ground ahead of us easier to navigate.

There were no more screams, but we could make out voices. Some lights came on ahead and I could see a man come onto a porch as we approached. It was an older guy named John O'Neil whom I'd met earlier in the day. Then a second man came out to join him.

The sound of the water lapping against the shoreline was soft and rhythmic. The voices ahead were now more like loud stage whispers, as though everyone speaking just realized how late it was and didn't want to disturb anyone.

"Oh, Christ," John said.

We were closer now and I could see the second man. I was pretty sure I'd seen him before dark coming across the lake in an old wooden boat with an outboard motor.

"Damn kids. Out partying. Someone fell overboard and they don't even miss him," O'Neil went on. He was talking to a young man and woman standing at the bottom of the steps to his cottage. The couple had just come up from the water. They each wore headlamps, now turned off. They looked up at the two older men on the porch. Several outside lights were on now.

"It's a man. He's under your dock," said the young man standing on the ground. The couple turned to face me as I came closer.

"Evening," I said, holding my light toward the ground.

"Hello," the man said. The woman stood with one foot on the steps up to the porch. Bonnie came up behind me.

"Everything OK?" I asked.

"There's a body in the water," the woman said. Her voice was flat. She appeared to be maybe mid-30s. The guy with her looked the same approximate age.

"You sure it's really a *body*, not a joke. A mannequin? Tonight's Halloween," I said.

"It's real," the man said, his voice tense.

"I'll call Marine Patrol," John said, turning to go back inside. The other man stood in silence.

"It's a real person," the woman said, looking back toward the lake. They guy put his arm around her.

"His eyes are open," she added softly, placing her hand to her mouth and looking right at me. She was obviously frightened. The guy looked a little shaken, as well. Bonnie clasped my left hand in both of hers. I looked at her for a second, then started moving toward the dock.

Across the lake were a few lights still on in houses on the mainland, Meredith Neck Road that ran along the shoreline. There were two street lights near the public parking area at the boat access and dock where visitors to the islands loaded and unloaded. This time of year, only a few boats made the trek. The tourists were long gone for the season.

Bear Island, the largest of more than 30 islands on the lake, was only a 5 minute ride across the lake. Our trip yesterday was in a small aluminum boat that came with the cottage. The place was ours for the weekend.

We walked out onto the dock. I shined my flashlight into the water and there it was. Not really under the dock, more to one side. And not a mannequin.

Two

The body was partly tangled in orange, plastic fencing submerged in the water about 2 feet below the surface. As the woman had said, it was a man's body. Eyes open, one arm and hand seemed to be clawing at the plastic fence. You might've believed that he was about to come up.

On the far side of the twin docks was the wooden boat with the outboard. Tied to the inside of the closer dock was the classic 1948 Chris Craft Sportsman Sedan, the *Donna Sue*, owned by O'Neil. He'd been working on it earlier in the day when I stopped to talk with him.

I looked back as though I really expected the man to rise from the lake. But it was a *body*, not a living, breathing person. He wasn't coming up. Not of his own volition.

The young couple had gone inside with the two older men. Bonnie was standing at the edge of the dock. Turning to join her, we walked back up the path and I glanced at my watch. It was five after twelve, which made me wonder what the couple had been doing out so late. Surely not jogging in the dark? Not here on the island. But maybe they knew all the paths. They wore headlamps. I hadn't paid attention to their shoes. Maybe like us they were just out to look at the moon and its reflection on the lake.

We went up the steps to the porch. It was similar to the cottage we were renting; screened enclosure on the front of the structure, facing the lake. Some padded, wicker chairs, a metal glider, and one old rocking chair with ragged, stuffed cushions that had seen better days.

John O'Neil and his visitor were just inside the door, talking with the man and woman. I gave a light rap on the door and pushed it open. O'Neil motioned for me to come in. He arched his bushy eyebrows at me.

"Anybody you know?" he said. I shook my head. He half-cackled and turned toward the fireplace. In contrast to the pleasant temperature outside, probably mid-50s, the living room felt like a sauna. It had to be above 80.

"People just don't pay attention," O'Neil said, shaking his head and reaching for a poker to tend the fire. "Lots of folks have no damn business being on the water. Especially after dark." He gave the logs a couple of good pokes and closed the screen on the hearth.

"You've forgotten when you were young, Johnny boy," the other guy said. "My memory has it that you had one or two adventures. Least according to Betty."

O'Neil waived a hand in dismissal at the comment.

"Betty had quite the imagination," he responded. "Lot of things she remembered never really happened," he added, placing the poker back on a stand next to the fireplace.

"I'm sure," the other man cracked. "She made it all up, no doubt."

Bonnie had stepped inside the door behind me. I was watching the other couple. I looked down at their feet and, sure enough, both were wearing running shoes.

The guy was maybe 6 feet, thin, black hair combed straight back. The woman was also tall and thin, with short blonde hair. They looked to be late 20s, early 30s. Both also wore the runner's outfit, matching pants and top. His outfit was black, hers was a blue heather. I knew that serious runners referred to these get-ups as R-gear; lightweight, warm, functional, yet stylish. OK.

The other old guy, O'Neil's friend, stayed near the fireplace while John eased himself into a sagging club chair that looked as if it had come with the cottage nearly a hundred years ago. Both guys appeared to be in their late 70s. John could be older.

"The marine patrol boys'll be here pretty quick," O'Neil said. "Not in a good mood, I'll bet."

"I'm surprised you got 'em. Late on a Saturday night," the other guy said. Listening to the tone of these two codgers, it was apparent they snipped at each other at any opportunity. And they sounded well practiced at it.

O'Neil rubbed his eyes with both hands then seemed

to remember something as he sat upright and started to get out of the chair.

"Dana, get these folks something to drink," he said to his friend. "Put some water on for tea." He looked toward the kitchen. "We have some nice Irish whiskey," he added, looking at the couple, then to Bonnie and me.

The other man, now we knew his name was Dana, moved slowly to the kitchen and turned on a burner of a gas stove. He lifted a tea kettle to check that it had water, then placed it back over the flame.

"Might as well get comfortable," O'Neil said, still looking at those of us standing inside his cottage. "Nobody's getting' any sleep 'til all the fuss is over."

Three

Warren Lapierre only partially regretted the loss of his younger friend. The man had become too much.

What gave him more worry was the manner in which the "accident" occurred. While he knew that once the body was found and examined, accidental drowning was almost certain to be ruled as the cause of death. Almost certain.

Yes, they would find the blow to the head. Then they would eventually find a small boat gone to ground farther down the lake. In fact, they were likely to find the boat before the body showed-up. No, Lapierre didn't know who might have stopped at the dock to talk with the victim.

That's exactly what he would tell anyone who asked. He repeated the story to himself over and over. Now it was after midnight and he was going to bed.

Charles Pollard Reilly, Chaz to some, CPR to his old prep school pals, was boyishly handsome, extroverted beyond reason, both smart and smartass, at ease with men and women – he preferred men – and he had become a 'rapidly going over the edge' alcoholic.

But now he was dead, so that no longer mattered.

Why he died did matter.

How, when and where he died would eventually come together. New Hampshire may be a rural state with a frugal approach to many things, but the law enforcement folks were much better than the media often portrayed them.

"Live Free or Die" was a motto that was awfully close to becoming a cliché. You read it and heard it all the time, especially during election cycles. More than one candidate too quickly incorporated it into a stump speech that made the locals yearn for reruns of *The Lawrence Welk Show*.

Only recently celebrating his 40th birthday, Chaz was perhaps bipolar. There certainly were incidents throughout his life pointing in that direction. His mother openly and often talked about psychiatric issues among members of her husband's family. A not so subtle joke had been about cousins marrying cousins. But Charles' father was long gone from his life. He never found the interest to do any genealogical research.

Now Charles was dead. And this unfortunate news most likely would kill his mother as well.

Tragedy befalls most of us sooner or later.

Sipping tea and listening to the verbal ping pong match between John O'Neil and his friend Dana, we learned that his last name was Martin. Bonnie and I, along with the joggers, Charlotte and Ben, had almost settled into a collective mood of late night Quaker meeting, each speaking softly and using few words with our stories and replies to what the others said.

Mostly nods, a few knowing smiles, not much more.

We only came back to the present when I heard the motor on the lake, looked down and saw the lights on the bow of a boat that stopped short of the dock and was shining a bright spot light into the water.

"The marine patrol is here," I said, putting my hand on the door knob.

O'Neil pushed himself up from the old chair, Dana moved from his spot standing next to the fire, Bonnie and the other couple all made movements in preparing to go back outside.

"Maybe best if not all of us go rushing down to the dock," O'Neil said, pulling his coat on and looking at Bonnie, then at Charlotte. He was of an age that probably thought women perhaps should not get involved in something like this. Leave it to the men.

"I'll stay here with the ladies," Dana offered. Bonnie smiled politely, Charlotte did not. But neither made any movement to the door. So it was just me, John and Ben going to meet the marine patrol.

I looked at my watch; ten after one. As we walked off

the porch, the clouds had cleared out and the sky was clear, illuminated by the moon now rising higher.

We let John lead the way to his twin docks below, lights on posts at the end of each that he turned on from the cottage. The body was in the water on the outside of the dock on the left.

The idling boat had reversed its engine and was now moving slowly to the dock on the right, closer to the old Chris Craft tied-up on that side.

I could make out the red and blue vertical slash stripes on the bow, along with large blue letters, MARINE PATROL. The boat came around, maneuvered so it could pull to the end of the dock and a man swung one leg over the side stepping off the boat. He wore a dark colored life vest over a state police issue parka. His baseball cap had the NH Department of Safety emblem on it.

"Evening," he said, turning to us. The guy was stocky, maybe mid-40s. He carried a flash light in his right hand. O'Neil, at the head of our greeting party, stepped up to meet the officer.

"You boys may be headed for a record this year," O'Neil offered. "Still a couple months left."

"You Mr. O'Neil?" the patrol guy asked.

"Yep."

"You called in the report. You the one who spotted the body"

"Nope."

O'Neil half-turned and pointed back to us. "Young

man here. Came up to my cottage when he saw the man in the water."

The officer studied us for a couple seconds. I moved aside to allow Ben to step forward. The boat stayed in position at the end of the dock, but another man was preparing to get off and join us.

"I'm Sergeant Condon," the officer said. "You two discovered body?"

Ben shook his head. "My fianceé. She's up at the cottage," he said, pointing up the path. "She saw it first." He was rubbing his hands together as though they were cold.

"We were jogging. Stopped to walk out on this dock and look at the moon."

Sgt. Condon gave a cursory glance back at the moon about the same time the other man came onto the dock. He wore an orange and black diver's wetsuit, oxygen tank strapped to his back, flippers on his feet and a mask pushed up on his forehead. He stepped up behind Condon.

Condon shined his high-powered LED flashlight across the water between the two docks.

The body hadn't moved. From this angle we could see that the right arm, in fact, *was* caught in the plastic fence under the dock.

The guy in the wetsuit pulled the mask over his eyes, adjusted it, put the oxygen mouthpiece in and stepped off the dock like someone stepping across a big mud puddle.

The splash threw water onto the dock all around us.

Rolling himself forward, the diver kicked his feet once and was instantly next to the submerged body. Another bright light came on from the boat and pointed to the area where the diver was.

John O'Neil turned his back to the lake and walked off the dock back onto the shore. I watched him for a second. He was mumbling to himself. Ben turned to watch him as well. The man just stood with his back to us. I couldn't make out what he was saying.

Four

Another three months in New Hampshire covering the political doppelgangers of *Snow White and The Seven Dwarfs* might be more than Bruce Lyndon could take.

This would be the fifth Presidential Primary of his stint with The Associated Press, plus the occasional foray to the Granite State way back when he was a newbie reporter for The Courier-Journal out of Kentucky. Too many miles to think about.

Lyndon checked in at The Red Hill Inn. It was after midnight. The middle-aged woman at the desk was not a happy camper. She looked as though she'd been asleep and was clearly annoyed that the buzzer had awakened her. No, she was annoyed at the guy who had pressed the buzzer.

Five minutes later, Lyndon schlepped his bag up to the third floor, no elevator, pushed the unlocked door open and went into the room. It suddenly occurred to him that surely there could not be many people staying at this place this time of the year. Why in hell am I on the third floor?

Never mind. Deal with it in the morning. Sleep now.

He was out of the bathroom and in bed in less than 2 minutes and asleep instantly. A long fucking day.

An hour south of Lake Winnipesaukee, other reporters were going to bed, too. Some alone, some not.

Most of the media types stayed at the mainstream, national franchise hotel chains in the Manchester area, near the airport. A few of the veterans would slip off to more remote lodgings, usually a place they knew from previous trips.

It was doubtful that anyone covering this period of the campaign would drive as far north as Lyndon had, to the Lakes Region.

None of the reporters, including Lyndon and other more seasoned observers, had quite figured out *why* so many of the presidential candidates had agreed to appear at a joint "Town Hall Meeting" the following week. Other than the fact that it would mark precisely one year until the real election, the scheduled event was unlike anything they'd ever seen. And that went for the press, the public and the candidates.

But no fewer than eight presidential wannabes were scheduled to be here. Good for the economy, maybe good for some of the candidates, almost certainly good for some laughs on the late night TV shows.

Perhaps.

The diver pulled the body free of the plastic fence as we watched from the dock. He got one arm around the waist, made a stroke with his other arm and moved away from us, pulling the man toward the Marine Patrol boat. The boat's engine had been at a low idle since the diver went in the water. I presumed that it had also dropped an anchor. Now, a third person on the boat was preparing to help lift the body. Sgt. Condon was back at the end of the dock shining his light on the diver.

In a procedure that gave the impression they'd done this before, the diver lifted the body at the same time the other man took it under the arms and pulled it dripping onto the boat. It was one smooth, steady motion that reminded me of someone pulling a roll of carpet onto the bed of a truck.

While we were watching the two men on the boat move the body, Condon was puzzled by the snow fence under the dock. He shined his light back on the orange fence.

"Mr. O'Neil," Condon said, stepping off the dock to where John was standing. "What's the fence for?" He twitched his head back toward the dock. The fence appeared to be stapled all the way around only the far dock, away from O'Neil's antique Chris Craft.

John let out a long sigh and shook his head.

"Neighbor's grandson put it up. Thought he was going to corral a bunch of fish." Condon arched his eyebrows. O'Neil went on with the explanation.

"Apparently he saw something like this down in Florida last winter with his parents. They were at a tourist trap where somebody rigged up a pen to hold fish that came in for food. He thought he could do the same thing."

The guys on the boat had positioned the body on the deck out of sight from us. I turned to listen to O'Neil talking to Condon.

"Of course, a nine year old has lots of ideas. It took him a couple days to figure out most of the fish were small enough to swim through the fence. And any larger ones were going out the bottom." He shook his head. "It was entertaining for his gramp and me."

Five

The clock on the microwave showed 2:07. Warren Lapierre was not going to get any sleep tonight. Maybe adrenaline, maybe too much caffeine. Maybe a double latte mix of fear and uncertainty.

There were times, in fact most of the time, when Warren was not only comfortable but very pleased with his decisiveness and speed. Analyze it, do it. That's how it had played with the determination that Charles had become a major liability in too many ways. Unfaithful, needy, reckless, often drunk and always lying. And completely ungrateful.

Columbus Day weekend. That was when he knew it was over. Knew they would not have another winter together. No more parties, no more trips to Boston, no more summers on the lake. Time to move on. Alone.

With his quick mind, sharp analytical skills and resourcefulness, Warren had long ago learned the real importance and absolute effectiveness of delegating. As in delegating unpleasant tasks. Bump on the head, boat accident? Simple. There were people who could handle these things.

Once the decision is made, call in some chits. After 30+ years dealing with and helping all types of people around the Northeast, Warren knew he had bags and bags of chits out there. And he knew that he could call some in when necessary.

Assuring that Charles Pollard Reilly was not likely to really fuck things up had become totally necessary.

Still.

Warren's mind already had started playing the flashbacks, like a highlights reel on some TV show. No sleep tonight.

"Give me a few minutes, Wayne," Sgt. Condon said to the diver and the other man on the boat. He looked over at us, then turned back to John.

"I'd like to come up," Condon said.

O'Neil turned to face him. He nodded and held his right arm up in a gesture toward the cottage.

"We're open," he said, leading the way. Condon followed, Ben and I fell in behind.

When we stepped inside, Bonnie and Charlotte were both seated on the sofa. Dana was seated in an old wicker rocking chair directly opposite them. They all went silent as we came in.

Condon took his hat off and nodded to the women

and Dana.

"Evening," Condon said. "Or guess I should say good morning." He looked at his watch. "I understand that one of you was first to see the body in the lake," Condon went on.

Charlotte lifted a hand from her lap in a timid acknowledgment.

"Could you tell me what you saw?" Condon said.

Charlotte looked at Ben, then back at Condon.

"We walked out onto the dock. We turned off our headlamps to look at the moon. After a couple of minutes, I was checking the batteries on my light. It had gone off and back on while we were jogging."

Ben nodded as he listened to her relay what happened.

"Apparently the bulb was loose. When I tightened it, it was fine. I was shining the light in the water next to the dock. That's when I saw something. It was the arm."

Condon didn't reply. He seemed satisfied with her account of how they spotted the body. He turned to John.

"Mr. O'Neil. You have some paper we could use to get everyone's name and phone number?"

O'Neil went to an old desk on the other side of the living room. It was an oak, drop-front secretary style, with letter slots and drawers inside. He opened a drawer, removed a sheet of paper and brought it to Condon.

Condon took a ballpoint pen from his shirt pocket and clicked it. He wrote something on the sheet of paper.

"If I could ask you to write down your names and contact information," he said. He held the pen first toward Ben, who took the paper and pen and went to the dining table to write. Charlotte got up from the sofa and walked to the table.

"You folks visiting the island?" Condon said to me. I suspected that he already knew that. He certainly wasn't as old as John O'Neil, but my hunch was that he knew most of the people around this end of the lake. At least those who'd been here for a while.

"Yes. We're staying at the Miller cottage." I said. "This is my friend, Bonnie Mackin," I added. Bonnie gave a slight tilt of her head at the introduction. As soon as I said it, I knew that I was likely to hear later about "this is my friend."

Charlotte was now at the table and writing on the paper. When she finished, she turned to me and offered the pen. I went over and wrote down our names and phone numbers, then gave both the pen and paper to Condon.

"Thank you," he said. He folded the paper and put it in his pocket with the pen.

As Condon opened the door to leave, O'Neil walked slowly behind and followed him onto the porch.

Six

"**That's three since July. Not a good year,**" O'Neil said when he came back inside. He rubbed his eyes with both hands, turned toward the fireplace, took the poker off the rack, opened the screen and poked at the logs. We all watched him, not saying anything.

"First Betty. Then Woodrow," O'Neil went on, almost as though he was talking to himself.

"Now this. Bad night." He placed the poker back on the stand, shook his head and moved slowly toward his chair.

Dana got up from the rocker and started for the steps that led upstairs. "Pretty late, folks. Think I'll hit the hay," he said, foot on the first step. "You might want to try some sleep, too, John."

Charlotte and Ben, Bonnie and I all started to move at the same time. Ben opened the door.

"Thank you for the tea, Mr. O'Neil," Bonnie said.

"Yes, thank you," Charlotte echoed.

"We're here until Monday morning," I said. "I'd like to take you up on the offer to go out on your boat" I said.

"Good night." He gave a half-hearted wave to us. Dana was still at the bottom of the steps as we went out. O'Neil had gone into stone silence.

"Go to bed, John. Nothing to be done now," Dana said.

"I'll go up in a bit," O'Neil replied. He leaned forward in the chair, clasped his hands together and rested his elbows on his thighs. And continued to watch the fire.

It was 2:30 when Bonnie and I got into bed. She turned off the lamp on her side of the bed and was asleep a minute later. I leafed through an old issue of *Wooden Boat* magazine before turning out the light.

The curtain was open and I could still see the light of the moon out on the lake. Quiet. No loons in the middle of the night. No late night boats coming back from parties this late in the year. Nearly all the summer residents on the island were long gone.

I thought about the body pulled from the water. You couldn't really determine the age of the man, but he was on the young side, probably younger than I. Guess we'll learn more tomorrow.

Moving to my left side, I snuggled a little closer to Bonnie. She didn't make a sound. I closed my eyes. As I began to drift off, my thoughts shifted to John O'Neil. I wondered how many times since his wife died he'd sat in front of that fire place, rubbing his eyes, replaying the memories.

It probably helped that he had Dana to come spend some time with him.

Sunday, November 1st. Bright, clear and a bit on the crisp side. Good day for a hike.

After breakfast, we walked up to the old church at the center of the island. A small structure maybe 30 x 80 feet, services were held only May thru mid-October with different visiting pastors. I'd attended once on a previous visit.

Coming back down the path to the lake I spotted John O'Neil shuffling out to his boat. I tapped Bonnie's arm and pointed. We headed that way.

"Good morning," I said. O'Neil turned. He hadn't seen us coming.

"Maybe. Too early to tell," he replied.

"Did you get some rest?" Bonnie asked. He stared at her for a second.

"I don't normally sleep more than a couple of hours," he said. He looked back at his cottage. "Not like Dana. He takes some kinda' blood pressure pills. He'll sleep 'til noon if you let him."

O'Neil was now looking at me, as if he were assessing something about my clothes. Jeans, sweater, down vest, hiking boots. Pretty standard, I thought. Then Bonnie's observation about my wardrobe – predictable – zipped through my mind.

"Care to take a little ride on the *Donna Sue*?" he asked. "Have to make a run down to the marina."

"Sure," I said. We followed him to the boat.

O'Neil climbed aboard, waited, then held his hand to help Bonnie. I stayed on the dock until he started the engine. I glanced over at the other dock where they had pulled the body out of the water last night. After a minute, O'Neil pointed at me.

"You can untie that line," he said. I did, then stepped aboard his beautiful, classic old boat. Wow.

As we slowly backed away from the dock, I rubbed my hand along the polished gunnel. Bonnie sat next to O'Neil in front. I stayed in the stern.

My guess was that the boat was about 25 feet long. The engine had a throaty rumble, but ran smoothly. The seats were dark red leather. The chrome trim was polished to a bright luster and all the deep mahogany made it just one outstanding work of craftsmanship. I had no idea what a restored boat like this would cost.

When he had the boat turned from the dock, O'Neil opened the throttle a bit and the bow lifted from the water. We were headed northwest toward the cove at Brown's Marina. I saw no other boats out on the water and only two tied up along the mainland.

A gas fill up, a copy of the New Hampshire Sunday News, we were back at O'Neil's dock 30 minutes later.

Seven

What a waste of talent. Not the first time this thought occurred to Warren.

Good genes, a privileged upbringing, educational opportunities not available to most people. And good looks. Which, of course, opened even more doors.

But Charles had just had a way, more of a penchant, of slamming doors at almost every opportunity.

When did that start? When he was spoiled as a child? When he cavalierly strolled through college, then law school? Something in his genetic make-up, perhaps like the pre-disposition to alcohol addiction?

At this point, it simply didn't matter. Charles was dead. Yes, tragic. But Warren knew that the waste was not unique to his former lover. Just pick up the paper on any given day and you read some story about someone wasting his life.

Warren also knew that he had a few things to sort out before his own life got back into any kind of normal routine. Initiating action is one thing. When it involves a crime, in this case, a murder, tidying-up is a little more complicated.

A month earlier, standing in this same living room, in

very near the same damn spot, Lapierre had scrolled through the contacts on his phone. He had stopped and stared at one name. The name was of a man he'd worked with in the past and who once told him, "whatever you need, call me."

It was a Sunday morning, just like today. Warren had been up early studying the preliminary, not yet official schedule of public and private political events in New Hampshire for the next 90 days. Things were at the point in the campaign where more people were starting to pay attention. At least that's what the pros told themselves. Who really knew?

The distraction that day a month ago that had him looking at names on his phone was that, once again, Charles had launched into this rant about "the sleaze and the slime" of virtually every political hack he'd ever met. Nothing Warren countered with would get him off it.

Charles spouting off with his half-assed opinions in private was nothing new. It was the increasing frequency of snide, often revealing accusations that Charles made in the company of others that both elevated and cemented Warren's resolve.

Warren had placed the phone call, explained the urgency of the situation and told the man what he needed. The man asked a few questions, got the address and said the matter would be dealt with.

And here we are 4 weeks later, and it's done.

Warren now used his land line phone to call the

Meredith, New Hampshire police. He knew they would immediately contact the Lake Winnipesaukee division of the marine patrol.

He told the dispatcher that he'd already left messages with a couple of other residents on the island in case Charles had somehow shown up at their home. But he also said that this late in the fall it was not likely those folks would even be there on the lake.

And, in fact, he did make two of those phony calls to houses that he knew were unoccupied at the moment.

The focus now for Warren Lapierre, a 60-year-old veteran of mostly behind-the-scenes and not always above-the-table fundraising and political fixing, was to get into the role of a worried, distraught friend and mentor to a man gone missing.

Eight

"You have any plans for supper?" O'Neil said. Bonnie looked at me and shrugged. We had food at the cottage but had not yet decided what we would fix.

"Not really. I was thinking about grilling a steak," I said.

"I'm making a big pot of chili," O'Neil added. "You're welcome to join us. Dana and me. Two old farts might benefit from something new to talk about."

Bonnie and I exchanged the 'you go first' look.

"That's very kind of you, Mr. O'Neil," she said. "I can make a salad. And we have some fresh, home-baked bread." Guess she did go first.

"Chili's one of my favorites," I said.

O'Neil handed me the newspaper and placed his left hand on Bonnie's shoulder.

"Mr. O'Neil was my father," he said. "Tough old bird. Been gone nearly 50 years. Call me John."

She gave him the smile. I wondered if guys his age still had the spark for attractive young women.

"You can read that paper first. Bring it over when you finish." He turned to go up the steps.

"Yo, Michael. It's Bruce Lyndon, intrepid AP sleuth looking for a little down field coverage on the NH Primary festival," the voicemail said.

"Got in late last night. I'm at the Red Hill Inn. Give me a call when you hear this."

The message was from an old friend now based in New York. A reporter now working for the Associated Press, we had met on the NH Presidential Primary trail maybe 20 years ago and always made a point of getting together at least every 4 years when he came north.

It was the only message on my phone during the two days on Bear Island since we had arrived Friday afternoon. I knew Bruce was coming up. We had exchanged email and I had told him to call when he got here.

Placing the cellphone on the table, I refilled my coffee cup. Bonnie was in the shower. I sat on a kitchen chair next to the woodstove and began reading the *New Hampshire Sunday News*.

The first section of the paper had a story on the continuing campaign efforts of the various candidates jockeying for a win in the Presidential Primary in just 3 months. The story included a schedule for the following week and listed which candidates would crisscross the state for a novel series of Town Meeting forums.

There was nothing in the paper about a body being pulled from Winnipesaukee the previous night. No surprise, the paper had gone to press before the body was discovered. I suspected there would be something later in the day on radio and TV.

The boat was spotted by two men on their way across the lake. They circled back and came closer.

Drifting along the western shore of Bear Island, the 16 foot fiberglass runabout was empty. The men assumed it had come loose from a dock somewhere nearby.

Pulling up to the starboard side, one man got hold of a bow line and they slowly towed the boat closer to shore and tied it off on a tree at the edge of the lake. They made a note of the registration number on the side of the boat and they could report it at Shep Brown's Marina.

Positive ID of the body had not been determined. The preliminary cause of death was drowning. Approximate time of death and other details would come with the medical examiner's report in the next 24 to 48 hours. Finding the next of kin, absent someone contacting authorities about a missing person, could take longer.

Then a call came into the Meredith Police Department out on the Daniel Webster Highway. The dispatcher was aware of the body pulled from the lake the previous night.

"Do you have a recent photograph that you could

bring by or fax to us?" the dispatcher asked Warren Lapierre.

He did and he would. Lapierre asked for an email address for the police and said that he would immediately send a photo taken in the last month. In actuality, he'd anticipated doing just this before the tragedy occurred.

"**You could drive over to Wolfeboro** and walk around with a sign that says 'I'm a reporter'. Somebody will feel really sorry for you and invite you in," I said.

"No doubt. Tell 'em I know Mitt, huh?" Bruce replied. "That oughta do it."

"So, how long are you over here?" he asked.

"We're headed back to Vermont tomorrow morning. I could meet you for breakfast."

"We? I? Who you traveling with these days?"

"I'm not sure that's required information. Besides, she is *not* a New Hampshire voter."

"Even better. You could stop here for breakfast. Or, we can meet somewhere," he suggested.

"Yeah. Actually there's a good breakfast place right in the center of town, George's Diner. It's a block off Main Street, back from Aubuchon Hardware."

"I'll find it. 8:30 too early for you?"

"Better make it 9," I said. "By the time we get across the lake and load the car, we're still 10 minutes away."

"George's Diner. 9 tomorrow morning. You are

locked-in to my calendar."

"Good. I look forward to seeing you." I clicked off.

I took the newspaper down to John O'Neil and confirmed that we would show-up at 5:30. He'd said that he had some port that we could have with crackers and cheese before the meal. I normally associate port as an after dinner drink, but what do I know?

"Just an excuse to get Dana tellin' stories," he said. "And the chili needs to simmer awhile."

"Great. We'll be here," I said, turned and went back to the cottage.

Nine

Meredith Police Chief Ken Storrow studied the photo. The man looked vaguely familiar, but Storrow had *not* seen the body recovered last night. Hard to say where he might have seen this guy before.

He forwarded the email with jpeg attachment to Condon at Marine Patrol. Then he phoned to tell him that it was on its way. Pretty good chance Condon was watching the Patriots on a Sunday afternoon.

Ten minutes later, Condon called back.

"Looks like the same guy," he said. "I sent the photo to the lab. They'll get right back to me."

"You saw the name and personal info in the email," Storrow asked.

"Yeah. Reilly, Charles. What's his relationship to the guy who phoned in the report that he was missing?"

"I haven't talked with him. He told our dispatcher that they were close friends," Storrow said.

"OK. Let me get the confirmation it's the same guy. I'll call soon as I know." Condon put down the phone and went to his computer. While he waited for the call from the lab, he would do his own search of both names and see what came up.

The dinner with John O'Neil and Dana Martin was not what I expected. While both men were older and gave the initial appearance of grumpy curmudgeons, O'Neil proved to be thoughtful and considerate, while Dana was quite amusing.

Bonnie sipped wine and stayed in the kitchen with John as he stirred the pot of chili, shredded some cheese and prepared the table for our meal. I was in the living room hearing Dana's stories of visiting John and his late wife at the lake for nearly 50 years.

"Betty was a sweetheart," Dana said. "She made him a better man," he added, nodding his head toward the kitchen.

"How long have you known each other?" I asked.

"Went to high school together. Laconia, Class of 1948."

I did a quick calculation that pegged them to be in their mid 80's. O'Neil looked that old mostly because of how slowly he moved. Dana could have made you believe he was 10 years younger.

"Were you married?" I asked. Dana averted his eyes for a second.

"Forty-one years," he replied. "My wife died back in '96. Cancer. Pretty unpleasant."

"Do you have children?"

"Our only son was killed in Viet Nam," he said.

"I'm sorry."

Dana shook his head. "Not much different from today. Young people going off to defend the actions of old men. Guess it's always been like that."

More conversation during dinner revealed that John and Betty had both been school teachers, with John becoming a principal at a Middle School. Dana had run a small insurance agency and both men had been fully retired for nearly 20 years. They clearly spent a lot of time together and enjoyed wry humor at each other's expense.

Bonnie and I talked about our work; she as an Admin Assistant to a man who ran a large Vermont construction firm. I explained the shifting of my career from radio broadcasting, to media relations and consulting, now evolving into private investigation and some security background checks. O'Neil picked right up on the broadcasting.

"Seems to be a lot more yelling on radio than the old days," he said. "Lot of the announcers sound angry, or, *pretending* to be angry."

"You must listen to news and talk radio," I said. He nodded.

"When I can stand it," he quipped.

Dana asked about our families. I offered that I had an older sister living in California, also a school teacher.

Bonnie reported that she was the youngest of three daughters from a fifth generation Vermont family.

The phone rang and O'Neil went to the kitchen to answer it. We continued swapping small talk about the chili and trying to guess all the ingredients. John came back into the room, sat and remained silent for a few seconds. Dana looked at him and waited.

"They think the body was a man from Meredith. Reilly, a young lawyer. Not one of my students," O'Neil offered. Dana shook his head and gave a sigh.

"Worked for Wehner & Garlow. Sort of a flashy, free spirit," he said.

"You knew him?" Bonnie asked.

"Only to say hello. I'd seen him around town. Fancy dresser, drove an older model Mercedes around. Stood out pretty good."

O'Neil was rubbing his eyes as I'd seen him do last night coming back up from the lake when the body was taken away. The gesture was like someone fighting off sleep.

"Don't know anything about a family," Dana said. O'Neil placed his hands on his lap and took in a deep breath. He looked at Bonnie, then at me and shook his head slowly.

"A bad night," he concluded in a soft voice, the same thing he'd said the previous night.

Dana's expression matched the bewilderment we saw on his old friend's face.

Ten

Lapierre anticipated that it would be hours, if not days before any sign of the body. This was not an improvised plan. He was confident that the sub-contractor known to others but new to him, had done exactly what was required; drop the body in the lake a good distance before putting the boat adrift.

He looked at his silver and gold Rolex yacht-master watch; four minutes before seven. Shave and shower and he would be ready to leave for Manchester by 8 o'clock. The meeting, arranged by a former governor and two of his long-time business pals, was important. The unanswered question was, would it lead to more 'funny money' as he liked to think of it. That money could buttress the media campaign budget for his guy.

Just over two months before the NH Primary and a full year before the 2016 General Election, the candidates and dozens of special interest groups were about to open the floodgates. Early projections for just the primary cycle, with 15 Republicans and 4 Democrats running, forecast record expenditures in the Granite State. The total ad campaign in 2012 was over $25 million, ranking the state at number 8 in the media money marathon. Warren Lapierre had been around for a long time and knew the state's 10 counties about as thoroughly as one could. He knew where they voted and where they didn't, where money was effective and where it could be wasted, and he knew all the different sources of rounding up the cash. Legit and not so legit.

What Warren didn't know was just how well he could manage his emotions and explanations that were likely to stay near the top of his daily routine for the foreseeable future. The tragic drowning, with an assist, was a new experience. Still way too early to know if it would prove to be a boat length too far.

Bonnie and I left the Bear Island cottage at 8:15 on Monday morning. The short boat ride across to what is known as the "cattle landing" – the dock on the mainland near a public parking area – took just 5 minutes.

We'd come over 3 days ago in separate cars as Bonnie was going straight to her job in Springfield, Vermont while I planned to make a couple of stops on my return home. The first was meeting Bruce Lyndon for breakfast.

"We'll figure something out," I said, hugging Bonnie and holding the embrace before she got into the car. Her look told me that she wasn't sure that we would.

She gave me a quick kiss, put her bags on the back seat, got in and started the engine. She lowered the driver's window and looked up at me.

"Call me tonight?" she asked.

"Yep." I leaned over for another kiss. She slowly pulled out of the lot and raised the window.

As I made the short drive to Meredith to meet Bruce, I thought about "we'll figure something out." In fact, I wasn't sure either.

But it was about the best I could muster after a late night discussion. We'd been in bed for a while and before going to sleep, the conversation became strained as we talked about the idea of marriage and a family. It was the second such conversation since the end of summer. It was clear that Bonnie was eager for children and I was not.

She was a lovely person, we seemed to have good chemistry and a stimulating physical relationship. She was smart and a lot of fun. But, perhaps without clearly articulating it, I was reluctant for another try at married life. At least at this point. I knew also that our age difference – I am 16 years older – bothered me more than it did Bonnie.

My thought process was clouded with a little guilt. While I was recovering from a gunshot wound to my left shoulder over the past few months, Bonnie had looked after me like a personal nurse. The intimacy was a bonus.

Different scenes and snippets of conversations played

in my head as I drove. Maybe I needed some amateur shrink time with my buddy Ragsdale? He would not be shy in offering suggestions on my personal life.

I laughed at the thought that I could send a text message that might begin, "Dear Louie. My partner doesn't understand me..."

There was a parking space directly in front of George's Diner. I backed in, got out of the car and went inside. Bruce had already found a booth. He was reading the *Union Leader* and drinking coffee when I rapped my knuckles on the table.

"Hey, champ. Thought you'd be reading your tablet and scanning the internet," I said. He looked up, gave me a grin and reached across the table to shake hands.

"I would never miss a chance to read this," he said, tapping the newspaper. "It's come a long way in the past few years."

"Who do you think they'll endorse?" I asked, taking a seat across from him.

"Too early. But by January, I'd bet on Marco Rubio."

"Really? Not Jeb Bush?"

Bruce took a sip of his coffee, folded the newspaper and placed it on the table.

"We'll get a better idea after the debate season winds down. But I'm thinking Rubio," he replied.

A waitress appeared at the booth, poured coffee for me, then took our breakfast orders. I went for eggs and corned beef hash, Bruce ordered blueberry pancakes.

"I thought you would have a guest with you," he said, looking around the diner behind me.

"She had to get to work over in Vermont. And I'm not sure how much political gossip she would tolerate," I said.

"Too bad. You piqued my curiosity on the phone."

"So what the hell do you make of this Candidates Caravan that's starting today?" I asked. He laughed and shook his head.

"Some of the state organizers with the Republican National Committee had the idea that with so many candidates, especially in a small state like New Hampshire, they could leverage as much exposure as possible in a week long blitz across the state," Bruce replied.

"And how is this supposed to work?"

"It started last night. They packed in close to 500 people at Southern New Hampshire University. Eight candidates were there," he said. "Two other candidates are arriving today. They're all heading out in buses to visit 26 towns and cities over the next week," he added.

I raised my eyebrows. "Of course, a candidate, a couple staffers and 20 friggin reporters on each bus, right?"

"Something like that."

"Whose bus are you on?"

Bruce gave me the grin and shook his head.

"I took a pass. We've got one of our newbies jostling for a seat. I'm driving a rental, thank you."

"Smart move," I said.

"Yeah. I have the itinerary for the week. I know a lot of people from past elections. My focus will be trying to get a read on what voters think a year before the election."

"I suspect you'll find a lot of 'em are dreading the media onslaught. That surfaced pretty early 4 years ago," I said.

"Yeah, there's some of that. But it's always different. Some of it depends on the town, the venue. And which candidate somebody's favoring," he said.

The waitress was back with our breakfast and more coffee. After she left, we resumed the talk.

"26 towns," I said, pouring hot sauce on my eggs and hash. "How many buses?"

"Maybe 10. Split up on different routes through the week," Bruce answered. "I'll be surprised if every candidate is there every day at every stop."

"Surely they'll do it in waves. You're not gonna have 10 buses all rolling into Rumney at the same time," I said.

"I'm not sure Rumney made the cut," he said, taking a bite of pancake. "Maybe Wentworth, though. And yes, as I understand it, 2 or 3 buses will arrive at one time, those candidates and their media groupies will traipse around, then back on the bus."

"Traipse. That's probably a good word for it. Are we talking full size, 50 passenger buses?" I asked.

Bruce shrugged. "I'm not sure. Guess we'll see when

they hit the road. First stop today is over in Nashua," he said.

"Do you know when they're going to be in Lebanon and Hanover?" I asked.

"Saturday. Part of the tour, apparently, is to catch the Dartmouth football crowd Saturday afternoon."

"Can't wait," I said. "Maybe they can recruit some of the clown cars from the Shriner's summer parade."

"Don't be a cynic, Michael. This is democracy and a chance to see our best and brightest."

"Or not," I said.

Eleven

Lapierre entered the Manchester office building from the lower level parking garage via an elevator for tenants and staff only. It was 9:25 and he was expected in a fourth floor conference room in 5 minutes.

A veteran advertising agency associate from previous campaign forays had arranged for Lapierre to use the conference room. He would be meeting with two men and a woman representing a lower tier presidential candidate. That candidate, like all the others, was hoping for an impressive showing in New Hampshire.

Not a surprise, this particular candidate's team got a quick read on most of the money guys in the state. The guys who find and deliver media funds on short notice.

The funds most often came from independent groups not affiliated with any candidate. Long before the 2010 US Supreme Court ruling in Citizens United, organizations seemed to find ways to support or oppose particular candidates. You would hear the name of the organization at the end of a radio or TV spot.

In the 10 New Hampshire counties over a period of more than 35 years, Warren Lapierre had learned where to shake loose some money for political ads. Since the court ruling, some of the funds coming from out of state made it easier. The newest challenge was where and when to spend it. That was almost always on radio and TV.

"Nice morning not to be on a bus," Lapierre said by way of greeting the trio already seated in the conference room. He closed the door behind him.

The woman at the head of the table looked up from her tablet and offered a tight smile. One man was on his cellphone, the other stood and greeted Lapierre with a handshake.

"Thanks for coming," the man said. He was short, marginally disheveled and a tad nervous.

"My pleasure," Lapierre replied. By contrast, he wore tailored, casual clothing that cost more than your average political staffer made in a month. The other man, taller, younger and wearing a shirt and tie without jacket, put his phone down and stood to shake hands.

The short guy made the introductions.

"Warren, say hello to Rob Belcher. Rob's going to manage the media buys here through the primary." The younger guy offered a quick nod as he released Lapierre's hand. The short guy, Warren knew his name was Bill - Wissinger, maybe Wittiger, something like that - turned to the woman.

"Lisa Randall, meet Warren Lapierre," Bill said. Again the handshake.

"Pleased to meet you," the woman said. "Would you

like coffee or a pastry?" On a buffet at the side of the room were 2 coffee dispensers – one marked decaf – several coffee mugs of different colors and a tray of pastries and fruit.

"Thanks," Lapierre said, taking a mug and placing it under one of the coffee thermoses. He skipped over the pastries, took his coffee to the table and sat to the left of the woman, across from the men.

"I've heard that you could find money at the bottom of a granite quarry and be buying radio commercials before the day is out," the woman said.

Lapierre's face brightened and he offered a modest smile.

"Did you also hear that the biggest granite quarry in the state is on Rattlesnake Hill not very far from where we sit?" he replied.

The woman laughed, the younger man chuckled, short Bill gave a snort.

Lapierre made a quick calculation in his head that they were probably going to ask for a quarter million. He knew that he could find it if they made a good pitch.

Twelve

"**Family from Philadelphia,**" Ken Storrow said. "I just spoke with Chuck Wehner, one of the partners where the guy worked."

He was on the phone with John O'Neil of Bear Island, owner of the dock where the body was pulled from the lake. Storrow had known O'Neil since he was a kid and O'Neil was one of his school teachers.

"You said his name is Reilly?" O'Neil asked.

"Yep. Had a place here in town, out on Barnard Ridge Road. Came from old money, according to Chuck."

"What the hell was he doing out on the lake that time of night?" O'Neil said.

"Don't know yet. We do know that he apparently had a friend who owns a place in Moultonborough. Ever hear the name Warren Lapierre?"

"Know who he is. Never met him. Has one of the fancy places on Moultonborough Bay."

"So I'm told. State Police are gonna talk with him. The empty boat the father and son found is registered to a summer home owner from Massachusetts," Storrow added.

"Never underestimate how stupid people can be when they have too much to drink. But you've never run into that, have you Kenny?" O'Neil said to the police veteran. There weren't many people that still called the chief Kenny, at least not to his face. But he was not about to correct Mr. O'Neil.

"I just wanted you to know. Sgt. Condon said you seemed pretty upset at all the accidents on the lake this year," Storrow offered.

"Been over here most of my life. My grandfather built one of the first cabins on the island. Can't remember as many people drowned as this year."

Known as Chipper when he was a toddler, later as Chaz which lasted all the way through college, he'd insisted on using Charles once he earned his law degree.

There were still those who called him Chaz and he, for the most part, took it in good nature. But when he moved to the Lakes Region of New Hampshire to join a small law firm that specialized in family trusts and estate planning, it was always Charles. "Like the river in Baws'ton" he would say, usually when he was drunk.

After too much time doing not much of anything besides drinking, partying and spending months abroad as a younger man, Charles enrolled in Vermont Law School at 34. Smarter than most and with recall that amazed his fellow students and professors, he seemed on his way to a promising career initially as an environmental lawyer. But the alcohol wouldn't let him go and he wouldn't let it go.

He was not one to flaunt his homosexuality and, in fact, had had his share of flings with women in years gone by. It was the way he dressed and the way he talked that generated much of the gossip after he'd arrived in the small town of Meredith.

A guy who looked as though he just came off a photo shoot for *Gentleman's Quarterly*, or maybe a sales rep for some high-brow British clothier, and then laced his conversations with words - that were not in the everyday vocabulary of most people in town - it was often too much. People either laughed behind his back or perceived him as someone constantly auditioning for the lead role in a local community theatre production of *The Great Gatsby*.

If he could have gotten up from the cold slab and walked out of the Medical Examiner's lab, Charles might have offeredd his own thoughts on the New Hampshire Presidential Primary. In recent weeks, he'd certainly heard more than enough to gag an elephant or a donkey. And it all had become very tedious. He'd not been shy in sharing that opinion.

Before offering any thoughts on people running for the highest office in the land, Charles would have been more likely to launch into a scathing lecture to those enabling the process by funding the candidates and their egos.

It was highly probable that his recent penchant for "outing" some of the activities of Warren, his on again, off again partner, was what had ultimately led to Charles not being available to say anything to anyone. Not the media, not the New Hampshire Attorney General, not the younger and still hopeful candidates for some of the lower level offices. Nobody. Charles would not be issuing a statement in this or any future campaign season. One of his old frat buddies might have said that he'd cast his last ballot. But the truth was, Charles had not voted since he was 21.

Now he was dead. That fact was likely to color local gossip for a couple weeks, along with the absence of his old Mercedes-Benz driving around town. But there were other eccentrics and bons vivants around and the amusement for some would continue.

Just not for those who drowned.

"**Maybe the Trumpster,**" Bruce said. We were standing outside the diner next to my car. I was shaking my head and he was laughing.

"You know, I have this friend," I began, "kind of a progressive guy, reads a lot, not shy with his opinions. He thinks that Trump really is a stalking horse for Hillary. And he's got it in his head that if Trump winds up running as a third party candidate – maybe like Nader back in 2000 – that Jeb will win the election."

"Wouldn't rule it out," Bruce said.

"My mother was a real go-getter with political campaigns. Worked with the county and state Democratic committees, worked the rural polling places 12-14 hours every election day."

Bruce looked bemused as I began the recitation of my mother's political field work. "Should I get my recorder for this?" he said.

"Maybe. Anyway, one of her favorite stories was about the first time Adlai Stevenson got the nomination, 1952 I think."

"That's correct. Alabama Senator John Sparkman was his running mate. Ike and Nixon blew 'em away," Bruce added.

"The story was that after Stevenson's acceptance speech for the nomination, some woman delegate told him that it was a wonderful speech and that surely, every thinking American would vote for him."

"And he said..." Bruce knew the story. He gestured with his hand like he was introducing me to deliver the punch line.

"Unfortunately, we need a majority." I held my hand out for Bruce's half-hearted high five.

"Give me a call when you get to Hanover on Saturday. I'll buy you dinner," I said.

Bonnie Mackin certainly liked Michael Hanlon. A lot. And while they danced around using the term "love", the physical relationship was very good. They were at ease with one another, despite the age difference, and she admired and respected him as a person.

However, and it was a pretty serious however, his reticence to seriously explore the possibility of marriage and a family, was to use one of his metaphors, rising to the top of the charts. Bonnie had picked up the vibe over the summer as Michael was recovering from a gunshot wound and they'd spent a lot of time together.

Every time she thought they were getting to the heart of the discussion, he found some way to step back. He rarely spoke of his previous marriage. Bonnie was trying to determine if it was her, specifically, or, just a real reluctance on his part to make a new commitment, to get beyond the dating and "having fun".

Then there was clearly the interest he had in an older woman, his new neighbor, recently transplanted back to Vermont from New York City.

Driving to her job in Springfield, Vermont – two hours from Lake Winnipesaukee – Bonnie made a decision. She would give it another two months. New Year's Day, to be precise. Her birthday.

If they were going to move forward with this relationship, that would be a critical evaluation date to begin making plans. And they were are not moving forward, they should be clear about that, too.

She put in the new *Midnight* CD by Grace Potter.

Thirteen

There are eight important radio markets in New Hampshire for buying political ads. That doesn't count the larger market Boston stations that reach a sizeable audience in the southern portion of the state.

Lapierre looked over the map. He took out a pen and, working north to south, drew circles around towns: Berlin, Littleton, Lebanon/Claremont/Newport, Laconia, Keene, Dover and Portsmouth, Concord and Manchester, then Nashua.

"In the north, they're smaller towns and you lump them together. Pick the top two stations in each market, saturate the airwaves for a solid week," he said. The woman nodded, the two men studied the map.

"Do that right now, while all the attention is focused here on the candidate bus tours," Lapierre went on. "If you wait until Thanksgiving, forget it. It'll be wall-to-wall. You won't find thirty seconds available on most stations. It's the big run-up to Christmas advertising."

Lisa Randall pulled the map closer to her and began writing figures inside the circles. Lapierre leaned over to see the dollar amounts she was writing on the map for each market.

"We think that we to have to have an immediate blitz, and repeat it the week leading up to the primary," Randall said. "We're counting on some free exposure with news reports, radio call-ins, talk shows, whatever we can get," she added.

"Two important questions," Lapierre said. He pointed at the map and the figures Randall had written down. "One, how much are you planning to spend on this first flight, right now?"

Randall looked back at the map before responding.

"Minimum of a hundred-thousand. One-fifty or two is better." She tapped the map with her pen. "Just for these markets. Start in two days, run it out for a week, like you suggested."

Lapierre looked at the map again, then sat back and took a sip of his coffee.

"That's a lot of cash for one lower tier candidate. And you know it's all up front. Payment before any spots run."

Randall nodded again. "It's the same everywhere. Media outlets always require pre-payment when ads are scheduled." She paused and looked back at the map before adding, "And your second question?"

Lapierre uncrossed his legs and pulled on the creases of his pants. He leaned forward in the chair so that he was closer to her. Neither of the two male sidekicks had said a word. One was now studying his phone.

"I can get the money. But we wouldn't be here if you

didn't already know that." Lapierre watched Randall's face as he prepared to make his decision on whether he would fool with these people. "The second question is really the first question, regardless of the money." He watched her eyes and knew that Randall was probably as good a liar as anyone. She didn't just climb on this train last week.

"My," he hesitated, then went on, "donors, shall we say. They're going to ask me straight-out, so let me hear your best answer." Randall didn't flinch as Lapierre milked it a bit.

"Yes," she said. "I think I know your question."

"Do you really believe this cracker, with just two years in the US Senate, actually has a chance of winning the New Hampshire Primary?"

"No. Third place if he's lucky," she answered. "As you very well know, this is just the beginning. There are a lot of miles and a lot of opportunities between New Hampshire in February and the convention in Cleveland next July."

Lapierre smiled at her, sat back in his chair and clasped his hands together.

Randall held his gaze and showed no sign of being intimidated by the "go to guy for quick cash" in New Hampshire politics.

"Get your media schedule lined up. And by all means, write down the legal name of the PAC where the contributions are going," he concluded.

The drive back to Moultonborough was just under an hour. Lapierre stopped in Meredith, pulling into the lot of a shopping mall. He placed three calls on his smart phone. At the end of the third call, he had commitments for $150,000, all from out of state donors who had ties to the Granite State. Two had vacation homes in the Lakes Region, the other man owned multiple franchises of a national business with locations throughout the Northeast.

Sitting in the car with the engine running and the heater on, Lapierre thought about going home to an empty house. Normally this time of year, he and Charles would watch Monday night football. Charles would cook dinner.

A month ago, drinking non-alcoholic beer while watching the game, things began to change between them.

It was a peak foliage weekend. Charles had gone uncharacteristically quiet. Moody, no traces of his normal, sometimes outrageous, humor. No ribald remarks about the players on TV. Within a couple pf days, a dramatic shift in attitude appeared and he began criticizing and challenging Warren on his "sleazy and questionable" political activities, the sharpest dig being Charles blurting, "I'm really surprised that you haven't gone to jail by now."

That comment set off the first alarm. It got worse the following weekend when, in a heated exchange on Sunday morning, Charles said that Warren was engaging in "disgusting and unethical" behavior simply to benefit a few, mostly undeserving and unqualified individuals, who were seeking public office. Then he left the island abruptly and they didn't talk for three days.

Although Warren was able to persuade Charles to come back, things did not get better. The criticism began to sound more like accusations, veiled threats. It was completely unpredictable.

The gay community in New Hampshire, like other states, wasn't the same as it had been 30 years ago when Warren had gone to great lengths to obscure his homosexuality. Back then, it was a liability too often and too quickly employed in smearing political candidates or their associates.

Even if he were able to embrace the "loud and proud" attitude of other gays he observed on the national scene today, Warren Lapierre could never envision himself marching in a parade, going on a TV show, speaking with the media, doing anything that put a light on his life, either the past or the present. He simply couldn't imagine it. Personal experience in losing a race for the state legislature when he was in his early 20s had convinced Warren that others would use any tactic, any means to beat you.

Today it was money. Lapierre discovered this earlier than most and was now one of the best "dark money" guys in politics in the Northeast. It helped that he viewed his work as being a facilitator, getting rich people to channel large donations to organizations that supported a particular cause or candidate.

As far as Warren was concerned, the 2010 *Citizens United* ruling by the US Supreme Court, simply expedited the process. At least for him and those inclined to hand over the cash.

He completely dreaded the idea that anyone would expose both his sexuality and his "questionable activities." It became a fear that consumed him and, quicker than he thought possible, led to the decision and actions that ended in the death of Charles Reilly at the age of 40.

Finding a person to "facilitate" the act was not that difficult and also a relatively quick process. Warren only had to contact one man who would take care of "anything you need." A couple more phone calls, plus $25,000, the plan was hatched and executed. No muss, no fuss.

Now Warren was driving home. He would play the role with the police, expressing concern that he had not heard from his friend. Could he juggle the acting and keep up the appearances of a concerned friend, yet avoid a lot of unwanted attention? Maybe not.

Not for the first time in his life, Lapierre could hear the lyrics from the *Song from MASH* playing in his head. He was only ten years old when he saw the movie, first heard the song. Suicide is painless.

Fourteen

Back home in Vermont, the air was clear and my head was anything but.

The promised intensity of a long-term commitment to someone I really liked; vivid recall of the good and the bad from a previous marriage; mixed emotions and memories of chasing political candidates with a recorder, getting the interview, listening for the "authentic" sound bite; then a weekend observing a couple of old guys at the end of their days. Plus, the body of a young man pulled from the lake. Not stuff to put one on top of one's game.

Then there was that question. What the hell is my game? My friend Ragsdale's voice pecking at me, "Let's go, Radio Rick. Which is it, private eye or reporter?" Louie often found it difficult not to slip in the Radio Rick sarcasm.

That prompted me to text Ragsdale. We hadn't talked in nearly two weeks. I knew that he was somewhere in New Hampshire doing undercover work for a federal/state anti-drug task force. I also knew that he used at least two different cellphones, so it was not certain that I would hear back immediately.

'Buying a ticket for the Bahamas' I lied, typing the

message into the phone. 'Bonefish, beer and, so I am told, beautiful women. What are U up to?' Send.

I put the phone down, changed into jeans, an old sweater and work boots and headed across the back field to help my neighbor stack her firewood.

Virginia Jackson had arrived in the spring, moving back to the house she grew up in after her mother died. The sight of her in the driveway with a recently delivered load of firewood caught me a little off guard and inspired me at the same time.

"Kind of close to the season, don't ya think?" I said as I walked up behind her. She turned around and gave me a smile.

"Close to the pocketbook, too," she replied. Tall, I guessed 5'10", trim and attractive, Virginia gave the appearance of a woman at peace with herself. Her faded, worn corduroy jeans and a man's heavy wool shirt might have positioned her for some staged photographer's shot of life in the country, not Martha Stewart style.

"How much did you have to pay for this load?" I asked, admiring the pile of wood, clean and uniform in length, probably two cords.

"What would you guess?"

"Eight hundred bucks."

"Close. Seven-fifty. But that's only because I went to school with his mother," she added.

"It's good looking wood. Some oak, a lot of beech."

She pulled her work gloves off and brushed her hair

back. Cut just above the shoulders, her hair was dark with streaks of gray. No make-up and fortunate to have nice skin. I knew she was in her late 50s, but you could believe she was ten years younger.

"I was lucky to find some dry wood. Should've done this back in the summer. Or last spring."

"But you found some. Don't have to burn as much oil this winter," I offered.

"I'm not convinced of the economics. I've just always loved the warmth and the smell of a wood fire. I missed it all those years living in the city." She put her gloves back on.

I started picking-up 16 inch chunks of the wood and carrying them to her porch where she'd already stacked a couple of rows. One section of the porch was enclosed and would protect the firewood from the weather.

"How's the shoulder coming along?" she asked, a reference to my recovery from the gunshot wound a few months earlier.

"It's a lot better. The physical therapy helps. I'm glad I was able to avoid the second surgery." I stretched my left arm out parallel to the ground, slowly raised it to a vertical position and then very slowly rotated it forward to show the progress.

We stacked the wood for a little over an hour, working without much conversation. It only took a couple minutes for us to figure out a rhythm of alternating steps up and back to the porch, sort of like two people bowling at a faster than normal pace.

"Let's take a break," Virginia said, pulling off her gloves and placing them on the steps. "How about some fresh apple cider?"

She brought two glasses to the porch and we sat in wicker chairs drinking the cider. It was really fresh.

"Wow. This is good," I said. "Where'd you get it?"

"Andy Taylor, the kid who delivered the firewood. His parents have a small orchard in Hartland." She took a drink of the cider and laughed.

"He'd be pissed to hear me call him a 'kid'. Has to be almost 30. His mother sent the cider. She and I were friends growing up."

"Yeah, I know. Half the docs I saw at Dartmouth Hitchcock look like they're in high school."

The sun was dropping. I looked at my watch; twenty after three. I finished the cider and put the glass down. Virginia drank hers in a more civilized manner and still had some left. She didn't move from the chair, seeming to soak in the crisp air and autumn fragrances of the outdoors.

"Are you following any of the coverage of the New Hampshire presidential stuff?" I asked.

"A little. Some of the students at the law school are talking about it. Of course, all those years living in New York City, I find the idea of Donald Trump becoming President about as likely as me becoming the next ambassador to The Court of Saint James."

"I'm still trying to get an image of all these buses driving through the small towns," I said. "Stopping to unload the candidates, the staff, the press. Locals are probably hiding under cars."

Virginia laughed. "Not unlike tour buses. You know, people getting out to look at the sights, go in stores."

"Yeah, but they're not walking up to shake hands, push a flyer at you and saying, 'Hi. I'm Percy Shedlacker. I want to be the next President of these United States.'"

Virginia stood and took the empty glasses back into the house, returned and we stacked wood for another hour. The sun had set and it was getting colder.

"I'll finish this little bit tomorrow," she said, waving her hand at a smaller pile of logs still in the driveway. "Thank you so much for coming over to help."

"You're welcome. I like the exercise."

"I owe you dinner. Maybe a couple of dinners." I looked at her when she said this. Come on, Hanlon, tone down the domestic security alarm.

"That would be great," I replied. "We can coordinate our calendars and I'll come back over some evening."

"Nah. I'll take you out somewhere. Even spring for a bottle of good wine." She gave me a smile. And a wink.

Removing her work gloves, she shook my hand and gently patted my left shoulder.

"Really, thank you. Take care of yourself," she added.

I walked back across the field to my house. Is she asking me for a date?

Fifteen

The third bus pulled out and the show was back on the road. Next stop: North Conway.

Thank God, it would be the final stop of the day. Rooms at four different hotels and motels had been reserved for candidates and accompanying staff members, along with way too many reporters. But, it was good business for the state's economy. In fact, there was wide speculation that the party organizers of this great road trip were working closely with the state's Chamber of Commerce.

Starting at 6:30, less than an hour from now, the local Republican committee was sponsoring an informal "Meet and Greet" event at the Kennett High School gymnasium. More than 300 people were expected to attend, which would place the ratio of reporters to potential voters at 1 to 6.

Bruce Lyndon had a copy of the week long itinerary and was happy not to be locked in to the bus brigade. He would pick and choose the events, subject to clearance from organizers, and would find his own prospective voters to get at 'who do you like and why?' He was trying for interviews that went longer than two minutes.

New Hampshire State Police Detective Sergeant Will Costello waited for his fellow officer, Sergeant Rob Condon, to get into the cruiser for their drive to Moultonborough. It was only a 15 minute drive from the Troop E barracks in Tamworth. Condon had pulled together the information that prompted this little excursion and he hoped that it would shed light on the last hours in the life of the drowning victim, Charles Reilly.

The veteran law enforcement officers were headed to the home of one Warren Lapierre. And, based on some online photos listed with a real estate firm, it was an impressive waterfront post and beam house with a dock. Costello tapped the address into the cruiser's GPS unit.

They drove without conversation, Costello focused on the highway and Condon scrolling through pages on his laptop. There was little traffic as they turned west on Route 25. It would be a short trip.

Condon looked at the photo on his computer. A young man, 40 years old the report said, looked back at him. Smiling, handsome, confident. A real contrast to the face he had seen on the Marine Patrol boat less than 48 hours ago. Closing the laptop, he watched the light fading to the west.

In a two century old home in a nice, quiet suburb of Philadelphia, a mother made herself busy writing a list of names of men who would be asked to serve as pall bearers at her son's funeral.

Margaret Atwood Reilly knew grief better than most. The death of her older sister when they were in their 20s, the loss of an infant daughter before she was a year old, the plane crash that claimed her husband when he was not yet 50. Countless friends gone in recent years.

Now Charles. That sweet, lovable little boy that she had protected all those years. All through his confused and frequently disturbing adolescence, the brilliant sparks of promise during his days in college, then later in law school, his never ending fight with alcohol. It all ran together now. She would sort out the segments after the funeral.

As she wrote the names on the stationery in her lap, Margaret broke down with the name of Johnny Fenwick, Charles' childhood friend who had come to their home often during the holidays.

Three nights ago, just before she retired for the evening, Charles had called his mother. They had talked for nearly half an hour. He sounded the best she had heard in months. And he promised that he would come home for Thanksgiving.

Sixteen

The Senator was as obnoxious as they came. He regularly belittled his staff, showed only minimal respect for other members of his own party and oozed an odor of insincerity when he spoke with regular prospective voters. It was completely baffling to many who knew and disliked him; how and why he'd arrived in Washington? And after just two years in the Senate, with an ego completely out of proportion to his talents, skills and intellect, here he was running for President.

Or was he? Was it all just part of an act to grab headlines at any opportunity, in any venue, on you-name-the-topic, just to ratchet-up public awareness of his face and name? More TV exposure, more ghost written books, more speaking engagements and outrageous fees. Was that the end game?

No, Senator Tad Shipp was not that shallow. He actually believed most of what he espoused, knew that he and his most vocal supporters were right, and he was convinced that he had a once-in-a-lifetime opportunity to save America.

It was time to go shake some hands.

Louie Ragsdale threw his jacket on the bed, pulled off his boots and collapsed in the chair. The furnishings for this house were not the most comfortable.

But Louie was not unfamiliar with less than desirable accommodations. You work undercover, you frequently interact with low life types, you learn to suck it up and do what you need to do. As one of the key agents for the Joint Northeast Counterdrug Task Force, Louie did not let temporary discomfort throw him off track.

Now on his tenth assignment in four years of working mostly in northern New England, Louie had pretty much covered all of Maine and New Hampshire. This gig, a new effort to corral the latest group of drug trafficking bad guys on the New Hampshire coast, might be his last. It was getting old, he was getting tired of the routine and life was just too fucking short.

He undressed, turned on the shower and let it run for 30 seconds before stepping in. Please, let there be hot water. There was. And 15 minutes later, feeling marginally better and a lot cleaner, Louie picked up his phone and called Hanlon. It was 8:45 on a Monday night.

"Bahamas, huh?" Louie said when Hanlon answered. "The bonefish there will chase you across the flat, take your rod, sunglasses and designer shirt and shove them up your ass."

"Oh, it's the Bahamian Ambassador. Nice to hear from you," Hanlon replied. "You sound in top form."

"About as ducky as it can get. All I need is a case of

Rolling Rock and a large pepperoni pizza."

"You still out there, or headed home?" Hanlon asked.

"Been here for two weeks and get to go home for 36 hours this weekend." Hanlon let him talk. "You think you've seen it all, what people will do to get their hands on another fix. Not much different from the last time I was here."

"You're on the coast?" Hanlon said.

"Yeah. Different spot than two years ago, but some of the same crowd."

"You're not pulling that backwoods Maine greaser role are you?" Ragsdale was a man of many roles, subject to locale, wardrobe and the vehicle he was driving at the moment.

"Nope. That wouldn't cut it here. I'm going for the edgy, ex-vet, hard-ass stare MO. Usually keeps people from bothering you and asking dumb questions."

"I could maybe get you a stint shadowing some of my reporter friends. One or two of them may have some knowledge of recreational drugs," Hanlon cracked.

"Who's got time for that shit? It's all gonna' be legal soon anyway. We're just trying to stay even with the scumbags pushing the hard stuff. ODs every time you turn around." Ragsdale yawned, then shifted the conversation to Hanlon.

"What's going on with you? You're not really going to the Bahamas." he said. Hanlon laughed.

"I wish. Hurricane season's over. I bet they have some

really good fishing right now."

"Wouldn't know. I've seen a couple of the cable shows about one of the smaller islands, Walker's Cay. Looks pretty nice."

"I'm sure. But, nothing quite like Vermont and New Hampshire in November. Gray, dreary skies, dark at 4:30, early, slushy snow. I love it."

"You freelancing with the Radio Rick stuff? Chasing candidates again?" Louie asked.

"Not yet. I still have my Press ID. Haven't had any cause to use it in a while."

"You know all the local party activists. Be a shame to spend your evenings at home watching MSNBC. You must know some of Bernie's people, right?"

"Yeah, one or two of the old staffers. But he's brought in some newbies to help with the campaign."

Ragsdale laughed. "Back when you were covering this stuff every day, did you ever imagine that Vermont's Junior Senator would get this much traction on a national level?"

I'd thought about this very question in recent months.

"Nope," I replied. "But, what you're seeing and hearing from Bernie is consistent. He's been talking about these issues since he was elected to congress back in 1990."

"Yes, Hanlon. You forget that I've had a few years in Vermont, too. Bernie's about as progressive as they come."

We yakked about some of the other candidates for a

few minutes, Louie groaning about all the people converging on small New Hampshire communities with the Candidates Caravan underway. He said he was glad to be out of the path of the media and the hype, comparing it to a late fall hurricane coming up the coast.

By the time we were ready to get off the phone, I suggested that we do a stealth dinner or breakfast if I got over to the coast during the next few weeks.

"Yeah, I can probably do that. Depending on the day and which of the bozos I'm watching. Send me a text."

Before clicking off, he couldn't resist offering some always ready personal advice.

"Keep up the shoulder exercises. And be nice to Bonnie." Then he was gone.

I instinctively raised my left arm as far as I could and slowly waved it over my head as if I could reach my right shoulder. I held it for a few seconds. The pain was fading, not nearly what it was back in the summer after the gunshot wound. I repeated the exercise. Better.

My thought went to Bonnie. Being nice was not the challenge. Being in it for the long haul was the real test. The line from the old song *Did You Ever Have to Make Up Your Mind* played in my head.

Seventeen

Warren Lapierre stared at the two New Hampshire State policemen. He answered their questions for nearly an hour. They were preparing to leave his home.

Sgt. Rob Condon stood from the sofa, hesitated, then turned back to face Lapierre still seated across from him. Sgt. Will Costello was already at the door.

Condon tried a variation on a question he asked earlier. "You're confident that Mr. Reilly did not meet anyone before he went out on the lake last Saturday night?"

Lapierre shook his head. He got up from the chair where he had sat throughout the interview.

"I'm confident. But that doesn't mean I'm right. He said that he needed to walk and would be back in half-an-hour. I never saw him again. It's possible that he met someone, I guess." Lapierre held the gaze of the cop, neither adding to the exchange.

"Thank you for your time. We'll take a look at the car before we go. You said it's unlocked?"

Lapierre nodded in the affirmative. "Will you need to tow it in?" he asked.

"That's unlikely. We'll take a preliminary look before we leave. Maybe send one of our techs out to go through it. If we decide that it needs to come in, we'll call." Condon joined his partner and they went out through the same door they entered, which led them down stone steps to the driveway. Lapierre closed the door behind them and remained standing where he could watch them.

The faded blue, 1973 Mercedes-Benz 4-door sat on the far side of the crushed stone parking area, away from the double garage doors under the house. Costello went to the police cruiser to retrieve a flashlight and the two men walked around the vehicle shining the light through the windows but not touching the car or opening the doors.

A minute later, both cops were back in their car and leaving Lapierre's driveway.

"Some place," Costello said, turning the cruiser back onto the pavement that would take them up to the main road and west to Route 25.

"Indeed. A few of them on this part of the lake. Maybe not up to the same level as those over on Governor's Island, but pretty nice. I'm guessing a couple million."

They rode in silence until they reached the highway, Condon pulling out his laptop and typing in notes from the interview with Lapierre. Condon had asked most of the questions, Costello took the notes. He stopped typing and looked out through the windshield at the darkness and the oncoming cars.

"It has to be nearly 15 miles by car from here to where

we pulled the body out. Maybe a couple miles less by boat, but not much," Condon said. "The guy goes out for a walk and winds up way over in Meredith? And that little boat they found. Unlikely that someone cruised all the way down the bay, around the islands and up to that section of the lake."

Condon scratched the side of his head just above the left ear, then made a quick glance at Costello before adding, "The dead guy worked for a firm in Meredith?"

"Yes," Costello replied. "Meredith PD is talking to his boss and some other people who knew him." He continued. "Maybe a friend gives him a ride. They drive back to Meredith, he somehow winds up going out on the water by himself. If he's been drinking, who knows what could've happened. Next thing you know, you guys are pulling him out of the lake in the middle of the night. A little strange, huh?"

Condon was skeptical that this was an accidental drowning. But that would be resolved with medical examiner's report.

The crowd dispersed from the high school gym. All the candidates, their hangers-on and the media had left an hour earlier. As with many volunteer organizations, only four women, one man and two high school students stuck around to do the clean-up detail.

All of these people had some connection, interest or

enthusiasm for the Carroll County wing of the Friends of Better Politics, a New Hampshire based organization promoting the Candidates Caravan touring the state before the Presidential Primary.

"Who would you vote for?" asked Jennifer Moore, one of the students picking up campaign literature from tables. She was standing next to her class mate, Dylan Lambert, also a senior at the school. He shrugged at the question and continued placing used paper plates and empty plastic cups into a recycling container.

"I won't decide until the week before the election," he replied. "I can't vote in February and I don't turn 18 until next summer. I have lots of time before the real election next year." Jennifer rolled her eyes and went to help her mother at a nearby table. Dylan was pleased with his answer.

Senator Tad Shipp did not get back on the bus headed north. He would rejoin the others the next morning. Instead, he went with two other men who had attended the reception earlier at the high school. He would ride with them to a private residence in Bethlehem, New Hampshire, for a private meeting with a very private man, a man in a position to offer generous and ongoing financial support to the senator's campaign.

While Shipp had repeatedly shown self-confidence and bravado since he had joined the race nearly a year ago, the truth was that his fundraising efforts were simply not measuring up.

Even if he continued to receive media and voter attention going into the end of the year, especially in the most conservative districts of the so-called "red states", without serious campaign funding, or the miracle of finishing in the top three in New Hampshire in just 90 days, Shipp could very well be out of it before the South Carolina Primary at the end of February.

Shipp was determined to stay on the big stage of national politics. No matter the outcome of his brazen run for the top political job in the land, he repeatedly told himself, his wife and his most trusted friends that he had "zero interest" in running for a second term as the junior senator from Oklahoma in two years.

If this meant travelling to small towns in a small state, 18 and 20 hours days, listening to the opinions of those you considered to be vastly inferior, OK. Bring it on. He could and would do that.

Eighteen

Walking across a motel parking lot, Bruce Lyndon caught-up with one of the other reporters, Jack Fleming. The two men had covered previous campaigns together and shared mutual respect for each other's reportorial skills and work ethic. Like Lyndon, Fleming also had had a stint with The Associated Press Radio network in his early days, and liked to swap stories. He was glad to see Lyndon.

"Thought you might be covering the secret plans for Obama to join the professional golf tour when he leaves the White House," Fleming said as they shook hands. "Where the hell have you been?"

"You don't think they'd let me on the bus with you guys?" Lyndon replied. "I don't get that kind of treatment anymore. Too old."

Fleming knew this not to be the case and that Lyndon could get press credentials for practically any event or campaign bus anywhere. But he laughed and went along with the dig.

"You have that right. I'm one of the oldest farts in the crowd. We weren't like that were we? Looking at our elders like they should be doing commercials for senior diapers."

"I think you were," Lyndon said.

They walked into the lobby of the motel. It was after ten and the place was quiet. A middle-aged man behind the reception desk took Lyndon's reservation information while Fleming waited. He'd been checked in earlier with some of the others on the media bus.

"So, you gonna' be with us tomorrow?" Fleming said when Lyndon got his room key.

"For a couple of hours in the morning, here and when the buses head south to Littleton."

"That's it? You drove all this way for two stops?" Lyndon shook his head and picked up his bag.

"No, I'm working on the one voter's perspective angle. Spending a couple of hours with different people around the state. I started on it back in 2012 and want to expand it this time around."

"So you're skipping all the scheduled events and stump speeches?" Fleming said.

"I may be at the gathering in Durham on Friday evening. And hope to get to the Dartmouth event in Hanover the next night."

"Well, if I miss you in the morning, let's catch up later. I'll save you a seat at the senior table."

"Thanks," Lyndon replied. "Will that get me two drinks, or is it all decaf at this point?"

"Certainly two drinks. But I'm only buying the first one."

The official report from the state police lab said the victim had, in fact, not died from drowning. Preliminary results from the autopsy showed the man died from a blow to the back of his head before the body was in the water. The information would be shared first with the victim's family, then the investigation would officially begin.

What had appeared as a two paragraph, lower inside section of a few newspapers in the state, New Hampshire's 15th drowning of the year would now be ruled a homicide. And that would shift the story in more ways than one.

But the first step was breaking the news to the victim's family. That responsibility would fall to a Philadelphia police detective working in conjunction with the New Hampshire Department of Safety and the State Police.

The second step, or more likely a simultaneous action, would be the shift in the investigation. State and local police, possibly New Hampshire Fish and Game, would all contribute resources and personnel to the effort. During the last ten years, there had been seven unsolved homicides or suspicious deaths in the state. Over a longer stretch, going back to 1990, there had been a total of 50. Going back still further, there had been more than 100 unsolved cases dating to 1966.

Sgt. Rob Condon knew the statistics as well as anyone in New Hampshire law enforcement. He would do all that he could in order for this case not to be added to those columns and summary reports issued at the end of the year. Of course it would be reflected in the statistics; the issue was in which category.

Chuck Wehner, founding partner of the firm Wehner and Garlow, was very distressed to learn that his young protégé had been a murder victim, not a drowning victim. In the two short years that Charles Reilly worked for him, he had been thoroughly impressed with the young man's gift for grasping the nuance of complex legal questions pertaining to trusts and estates. Charles could get there as fast as anyone Wehner had ever known.

And it was Wehner who had convinced his partner that they should take the gamble on Reilly, even though both men suspected a serious "drinking problem". There was a problem, Wehner stayed on top of it and eventually, Reilly stopped drinking and excelled at his work.

After receiving the news from the Meredith Police Chief, Wehner sat looking out the window of his office. It was a crisp, clear day with the first serious hint of the New England winter temperatures to come.

Chuck Wehner felt the cold in his bones. It was a feeling he had experienced more than once in the past, most notably a long time ago with the multiple deaths of young men he had served with in Viet Nam. Like them, Charles Reilly was gone. Forever.

Nineteen

The call from Bruce Lyndon came out of the blue. I was surprised at his suggestion that I might want to tag along for a couple days.

When we had had breakfast together two days earlier, we agreed that we would try to meet again the following Saturday when he would be in Hanover. Now, he was asking for help and he seemed to want some company.

"You know the roads up here, the towns, you probably still have some contacts, right?" he said. "Locals see a rental car and a guy with a notebook, that won't make it any easier."

"Tell me more about your plan," I responded. "Where exactly do you expect to go, and what's your timeline for getting back to this part of the hot campaign trail?"

"I wouldn't call any of it hot. More like a warm toaster oven at this point. And my schedule's pretty flexible."

"Didn't you tell me that you were going to connect with some voters you interviewed four years ago? Where are they?" I said.

"Yeah. There's a woman in Plymouth, a retired foreign service guy now living in Durham, and an old college prof over your way, used to be on the faculty at Dartmouth."

The thought of driving in northern New Hampshire in

November, swapping bullshit stories or twiddling my thumbs while Bruce spent time talking with voters, was not getting me excited. Maybe one day, two at most.

"I have some things that need attention here for a couple of days," I said. "If you can juggle your schedule to turn in the rental car after you've been to Plymouth, I could meet you and do the Durham/Dover/Portsmouth leg, then bring you back here on Saturday. The candidate round-up at Dartmouth is Saturday night, yes?"

"Yes. You think I can get a shuttle out of Hanover on Sunday to the airport in Manchester?"

"Bruce, it's election season. I think you could get a shuttle to West Ossipee."

We worked out a tentative plan that had me meeting him in Manchester on Friday morning, then on to Durham and the coast that same day, back to Hanover on Saturday. He was to call to firm it up on Thursday.

That gave me a full three days to maybe get up to speed on the candidates, the media stories of this caravan thing, and to try to put my mind in a "do you think he has a real chance of being elected" mode. But then, I wasn't anticipating doing any actual interviews. For the moment, I was only agreeing to be another reporter's driver. Thrilling.

After thinking about the phone conversation and the prospect of going over to the coast, the bell went off: Ragsdale.

Louie was always yanking the chain about my liberal friends, "media types who live in a fantasy world with no real appreciation of what normal people do and think about everyday". I wondered when, if ever at all, he'd had a substantive conversation with a reporter? Much of our verbal jousting was mostly superficial, but from our first encounter I always sensed that Louie really placed little trust in or had any use for people who worked in the media. If he met a guy as smart, thoughtful and as solid as Bruce Lyndon, maybe he'd lighten up a bit.

Dinner with the Undercover DJ. Why not?

If there is something you really need to do, just do it. That had always been the sound advice of Bonnie Mackin's mother, long before it became an advertising slogan for some shoe company.

Bonnie's constant problem, however, was that too often she spent an incredible amount of emotional energy trying to figure out the best way to actually implement her decisions. It made her mother crazy.

This was different. This decision, if it turned out to be wrong, would change the rest of her life. Of course, if it turned out to be right, it would change the rest of her life.

She was convinced that Michael Hanlon did not have any interest in starting a family. While he was willing to discuss the idea of marriage when she brought up the subject, he went quiet when the conversation drifted toward children.

Bonnie would be 35 in two months. She knew of

women who had had children after the age of 40, that was not for her. Adoption was certainly a possibility if it came to that. But one way or another, Bonnie was eager to become a mother. What she was less eager to do was to stay in a relationship that idled along for years, only to make a late break and try to start again with someone else. She did not want that kind of urgency as the foundation of starting a family.

Right now, she needed to stay focused on her job. She could work out the thoughts about Michael before she saw him again. Maybe on the weekend.

At least she told herself she could.

Twenty

Margaret Reilly would not shed another tear. Not right now. The anger cut too deep and froze her heart to allow the grief to consume her. There would be time for that later. When the Philadelphia detective left her home after delivering the news about the real cause of death for her only son, Margaret was determined to do all that she could, spend whatever it took, and devote all her waking hours to see someone pay for this crime.

She went to the Rolodex card file in her study, found the phone number of her cousin in Boston and placed the call.

Blair Watson, age 81, was still a formidable attorney and a man with connections throughout the world. He would guide Margaret through this. As children, the cousins were more like siblings, Blair acting as the older brother she did not have. And she knew that his resolve now would be every bit as strong as her own.

Lapierre's mind stumbled again. In hastily ordering the elimination of his friend, lover and recently avowed detractor, his arrogance had fused with panic and that had gotten the better of him.

In repetitions like the stupid clock on his office wall, every 15 minutes his brain would run through the conversations and behavior that had led to the decision that Charles was a real danger to all that he'd done for the last 30 years. Where his mind hesitated was the part about being rejected both as a mentor and a companion. Lapierre's ego could not take that.

All the time Charles was drinking, he was dependent on Lapierre. Their lives together mostly revolved around Lapierre's acquaintances, not anyone from Charles' work or life away from the Lakes Region of central New Hampshire. Over time, that had all become tedious and not much of a challenge for the bright, cynical lawyer.

When he stopped drinking, his personality took on a new edge in a matter of days. Bordering on evangelical behavior, Charles had begun to step up the pace of criticism about how Lapeirre made his living and purchased all the trappings of their life together - all the unsavory actions that Lapierre often boasted about.

A repeated phrase Charles had used was "the total depth and stench of the sleaze you perpetrate on society." None of Warren's counter arguments that this was just politics, things that had been going on long before he came on the scene, seemed to carry much weight.

The arguments became more serious and it became clear that a real schism was developing. Charles would plant his flag in the sand and refuse to budge. Lapierre could still hear the echo of the words Charles had uttered in one of their final confrontations a month earlier.

"It's not right. You don't have to keep doing it. And I want nothing to do with you if it continues," Charles had said, before driving off the Tuesday morning after Columbus Day weekend.

Hasty, mean thoughts; a couple of phone calls; some cash handed over to someone else. In less than a month, the problem goes away.

No more arguments, no more a threat.

Now Warren Lapierre was coping with something he was completely unfamiliar with: guilt.

Twenty One

The three buses rolled into Berlin and stopped at the back corner of the IGA grocery store parking lot.

The plan called for six of the candidates and all their attendants, along with at least 30 reporters, camera people and photographers, to start at this location and move up to Main Street once they had made contact with people out buying food for the week. At this very same moment, it was believed, two other buses carrying four candidates were touring the southern end of the state.

One man, who obviously knew nothing of this rolling caravan of smiling politicians stood at his car in disbelief. A female reporter, with a young camera man at her side, approached the man.

"Excuse me, sir," the woman said. "Could we talk with you for a minute about who you support in the upcoming election?"

The man looked directly at the reporter, then at the kid aiming the camera at him. The man shook his head. "If that's the same crowd I been watching on TV," the man gestured at the candidates moving toward the front of the super market, "probably none of them." He gave the woman a dead-on gaze which seemed to fluster her for a few seconds. A nervous laugh and she looked back at her camera man, then recovered.

"May I ask why?" she said.

"You may ask anything you like, miss," the man retorted, moving plastic bags of groceries from a cart into the back seat of his car. He showed no inclination to engage with the reporter. She rolled her eyes at the camera guy, who apparently was digitally recording all the time he accompanied her, no matter who or where.

The old guy closed the car door and tuned back to the woman. He gave her what might pass for a half-hearted smile. "No disrespect, young lady. It's not your fault most of 'em are self-serving clowns trying to sell their next book, or get on some more TV shows." Again he waved his arm in the direction of one female and three male candidates greeting shoppers at the front door of the IGA.

"I heard a couple of them on that debate last week say they were proud to serve their country," the old guy continued. He held his gaze on the reporter, with only a brief glance at the camera. The man spoke in a soft, slow manner without much inflection or emotion.

"If they really meant that, best way to serve the country right now is go back to Washington, do about two weeks work that they generally stretch into an entire session, then go back to their home state and see what's really going on."

"You don't sound like you think congress accomplishes

much," the reporter said.

The old guy's smile returned, maybe a little stronger than 30 seconds earlier.

"Oh, no. They accomplish quite a bit. Trouble is, it's mostly for themselves. And a bunch of wealthy and privileged folks who pay real good attention to seeing their friends get reelected." The man opened the driver's door of his car but didn't get in immediately. He appeared to have more to offer.

"I'm sure back in their home state," he said, arm again pointing at the candidates, "they must be pretty popular or they couldn't get elected." He looked at the reporter for acknowledgement but received none, so he continued.

"I've been around a long time, miss. Been voting for presidents since Eisenhower, the first time. You ask me, the last really honest person to serve in the office, and I use that word purposely, served, was Carter. I'm afraid it's been all downhill since then." Now he slowly lowered himself into the driver's seat, but didn't close the door.

The reporter stood next to the car, the camera guy kept his lens on the man who looked back at them.

"But I'm an old man," he added. "You need to go talk with my granddaughter and some of her friends. They might give you a different view." He closed the car door, started the engine and eased forward from his parking space.

In front of the IGA, no other shoppers were in sight and the candidates and staff assistants talked among themselves. The other reporters circled around them. It was a pretty slow, ordinary Tuesday morning in Berlin, New Hampshire. The only thing not ordinary was the crowd of 50 people gathered there not for shopping. The store manager could have told you that they didn't get this many people on double-coupon days.

Twenty Two

"He was certainly dead before the body went into the water," said Dr. Andy Thomson, Chief Medical Examiner for the state of New Hampshire. He shifted the phone to his left hand.

"Best guess on how long before? And maybe how long you think the body was in the lake?" Sgt. Condon asked.

The two men were familiar enough with one another that Condon could get away with informal banter. He knew there was no guessing involved and that, ultimately, Thomson would nail down the time of death to within minutes.

"When the report is finished," Thomson went on, "it will specify the exact time frame. At this moment, I'm saying the man stopped breathing between 5 and 7 PM and the body was in the water for less than 6 hours."

"We got the call just after midnight Saturday. The couple who first spotted it said it was approximately 11:55 when the woman saw the arm next to the dock."

"There you go," Thompson said. "You can read all the detail in the report. But cause of death was blunt head trauma. Base of the skull."

"No chance the guy fell. Hit his head on a rock. Or a boat dock?" Condon asked.

"There is a 'chance' for almost anything, Sergeant. But, photos and information from the autopsy will clearly indicate that it was a blow administered from an object moving against the head with great force."

"Ideas on what that object was?"

"Something with a dull edge," Thomson said. "More likely than not a piece of some type of metal. Perhaps a flat wrecking bar, or, simply a strip of smooth steel. Very little blood. All internal. Guy was probably dead instantly."

When the phone call with Thomson was over, Condon waited a beat before calling Meredith Police Chief Ken Storrow. He would not share everything at this point, but would rely on Storrow and his department to help identify good sources who knew the victim.

It was Condon's career experience that the more people you talk to, generally, the better the profile you developed of a victim, getting a handle on what kind of person one might have been before becoming a victim.

He tapped in the numbers for Storrow and listened to the three second call signal.

I spent over four hours online reading and watching clips from the most recent Presidential Election debate, various candidate appearances and three lengthy opinion pieces from veteran columnists I liked and trusted.

The process was coming back to me. A lot of media attention early on for the entire field of candidates, and at 14 Republicans and 4 Democrats so far, this was an unusually large crop. A couple of them would be out of it even before the New Hampshire Primary.

But what I recalled from previous elections was that for the main contenders, perhaps two or three in each party, their campaigns would go all-out with public appearances, advertising and rallies before the February voting. Then once New Hampshire was over, everything would shift to the south.

The so-called Candidates Caravan that was underway this week apparently was the brilliant idea of a young marketing woman working with a media/communications firm in Manchester. The story was that she conceived the plan after watching the 2012 election and was able to convince party power brokers to pull it together for this cycle.

Not everyone bought in to the scheme. But, they had 10 candidates out there travelling together in a week-long blitz that was getting a lot of attention. And those 10 were scheduled to come together for what was being billed as an "informal" discussion on what they had heard and seen in their travel around the granite state.

This wrap-up discussion event was scheduled for one of the auditoriums on the Dartmouth College campus in Hanover. Without question, there would be multiple TV satellite trucks, the campaign buses, security and law enforcement personnel, and enough reporters to cover every last quirky detail and sliver of political minutia imaginable. Maybe a wardrobe or fashion analyst.

And, it would be held on the Saturday night of a home football game - Dartmouth vs. Yale. There would be some money in town. Perhaps even some that was not yet allocated in support of any particular candidate in the Presidential Election.

"Oh, Hanlon. You are such a cynical turd," the voice in my head chuckled.

What the hell. A chance to visit with some old acquaintances and maybe learn something. In fairness, there really were some bright, engaged people covering the campaign. If I kept my mouth shut, I might actually learn something.

Twenty Three

Blair Watson's phone call to the New Hampshire Attorney General's office was returned within the hour. He fully expected that it would be.

Kelly Alexakis, in her first year of the four year appointment to head the state's Department of Justice, was eager to respond. She had met Watson through her father, who was also an attorney and politically active in Massachusetts. She had no idea what the call was about.

"Thank you for calling back, Kelly," Watson said.

"Certainly. How are you?"

"Not well, I'm afraid" he replied. She had not seen Watson for at least a year and was unaware of any news of his present health.

"There's been a tragedy in my family. A young cousin was murdered over the weekend."

"That's horrible. I'm so sorry, Blair."

"I just got news this morning. You will hear about it very shortly, I'm sure. His body was found in Lake Winnepesaukee early Sunday morning."

She instantly flashed on the news of the recovery of what was believed to be a drowning victim, the 15th this year which set a new state record, followed by the call her office received this morning that it was now being treated as a homicide.

"We just heard," she said, fumbling through the notes on her desk. She found her scribbling of the victim's name.

"Charles Reilly," she said.

"Yes. He is a second cousin. His mother and I are very close. Neither of us have siblings and we've been like brother and sister since we were children."

"That's just so terrible. I am truly sorry." She looked at her notes to see if anything else was written down about the incident. Only that it was Sgt. Condon and State Police Troop E out of Tamworth. She had not yet received the ME's report on cause of death.

"What have they told you?" she asked.

"Not very much. Margaret, his mother, had a visit from police in Philadelphia, where she lives. Then a phone call this morning from someone with your state police. She then called me and you are my first call." His voice had a cultured, articulate quality, each word enunciated with the smooth flow of an experienced public speaker.

"I would appreciate if you could call Margaret personally. Reassure her that there will be a thorough investigation of Chipper's death," he added.

"Of course, Blair. Please. Give me her number."

Two men with little concern for the lives of others sat in a bar in Lowell, Massachusetts. They were flush with cash and good to go with both a substance of choice and a preferred drink; heroin and double-shots of tequila. It was noon on a dreary Tuesday.

Recent activities on behalf of their main supplier had brought them to this temporary state of completeness. The only thing missing, they agreed, was a good night with some uninhibited women.

"I'm workin' on it," John Dervil cracked. "Soon as we take care of the, uh... liberation of that Airstream, we'll take a whole fuckin' week of down and dirty." He held his shot glass up and touched it to the one held by Eddie Walker, seated next to him.

"Mostly down," Walker said as he knocked-back his shot, not looking at his friend.

Dervil was the self-appointed arranger for the pair. He arranged getting the smack and other drugs. He arranged for getting the little side gigs that gave them cash. And he most recently arranged for a quick trip to New Hampshire to handle a job for somebody else, who was handling a job for somebody else. Everything should be this efficient, he thought.

The real truth was, even though Dervil might be reluctant to acknowledge the fact, was that the two of them had readily become little game board pieces being moved around at will by a person who really didn't give a shit for their lives, either.

Twenty Four

Bruce Lyndon sat in a comfortable chair in a living room in Plymouth, New Hampshire. It was the home of Barbara Brown, a visiting nurse and active citizen in this town of just over 7,000 people.

During the election four years ago, Lyndon met Brown at a local event for then candidate Jon Huntsman, who later came in third in that primary and dropped out of the race.

As the current campaign was picking-up steam, Lyndon contacted Brown and told her that he was planning a series of interviews with three or four individuals and asked if she would consider being one of his sources. She said yes.

At 52, Brown was married, no children and a New Hampshire native. She'd grown up in nearby Bristol, enrolled at Plymouth State and then switched to Colby-Sawyer where she earned a BS in nursing. She'd also served for six years on the town Select Board.

Now, Brown had yet to declare support for a specific candidate. She told Lyndon that, "None of them seem to have gotten serious yet. It's just a lot of jockeying for position. On any given day, you get the sense that anyone of them might say anything just to get ahead in the polls."

"Do you think that's a problem with their campaign, or the way it's being covered?" Lyndon asked.

"Probably both. I know that the major parties run training sessions for promising candidates early in their careers and teach them to speak in short sound bites. Now we have social media and instant messaging. Seems that it is harder and harder to get to any substance."

"What about your husband? I recall last time that he sat out the election, didn't like anybody. Any change for him this time around?"

Brown laughed. "Oh, Matthew might bring himself to vote this time. I've worked on him a little," she said.

The small talk continued a few minutes longer, then Lyndon told her he had a series of questions that he planned to ask each of the people he interviewed. He explained that it might take two sessions, he would record the interview and by the time he finished writing the piece, it could run 10,000 words or more.

"Let me start by asking, with all the media fluff, if you will, all the campaign slogans and the never-ending criticism of opponents, is there one issue that you believe stands above all others, the major challenge for the next president?"

"Hard to rank just one. There are several. But I truly believe that two of the most important are, education and the country's deteriorating infrastructure."

After working the phone all afternoon, Lapierre was ready for a break. Enough with the bad jokes and the petty sniping at every candidate but the one that particular donor happened to support.

"Hi, Bill. It's Warren Lapierre." Christ, he would hear it in his sleep. The stapled sheets on his desk had more than 100 names on them and he'd called 27 people and had 22 conversations in just four hours.

But, he also had commitments for over a hundred grand. All this was off-the-books, no campaign finance reporting on this money.

No one in the state of New Hampshire knew better than Lapierre that there were many people ready to give cash on the side to activities they deemed important. He'd come to think of it as analogous to people who spent cash on lottery or scratch tickets. Nobody reports that money.

What Warren had managed to do over the years, in addition to helping you get through to a particular office holder or person of influence, was to make you feel like an important, behind the scenes player. And he cultivated a list of people who liked that feeling. They were always prepared to chip in.

While he was not the only practitioner of the "How much can you help us with" this week solicitations, Lapierre was pretty certain that he was the best compensated. One of the reasons for that was that he completely controlled his take. Any given week during an election year, raise a hundred thousand, keep 20 per cent. Four years ago, nearly a quarter-million off the books.

A dark thought that had crept into his mind after the recent interview with the two New Hampshire state policemen, was that in all likelihood it would be necessary to dip into his slush fund. While $25,000 addressed the "problem" with Charles, Lapierre didn't kid himself. In the end, he would not get off with that little. He wasn't exactly sure how, when or where, but he was certain that more money would change hands.

Twenty Five

Senator Tad Shipp looked at the people gathered in the living room of a modest home in the northern end of the state. In his eyes, these people were true believers in his brand of single-minded, simplistic – and often blustery rhetoric – that excited his base even if there was no chance in hell that he could deliver on his repeated promises of all that he would do on his "first day in office."

When all the participating candidates agreed to be part of the bus caravan around the state, it was with the clear understanding that they would only be committed to the buses for a few hours each day.

Breakfast meetings, late afternoon and evening functions could be on their own schedule, as long as they showed some sign of a united effort at the stops along the way. All of them signed on for three public evening events; the initial appearance at the high school gym in North Conway, and two more forums scheduled on Friday and Saturday in Durham and Hanover, respectively.

Senator Shipp was going for the jugular at every stop. Just above single-digits in most polling, he was desperate for attention to his campaign. He was too smart to attack those in his own party this early. If he survived New Hampshire, Iowa and maybe one of the southern primaries, he could always go after any of the other challengers.

For the moment, and in nearly every claim or promise that he made, he focused on the "failures" of the last eight years. More than a few in the press corps could lip-sync with his stump speeches and frequently unsubstantiated claims about what the current president did or did not do.

Louie Ragsdale put the newspaper aside and shook his head. The all-consuming media circus that cycled through the state every four years was nearing the main act, a primary election three months away that would have approximately a half-million people – or 40 per cent of this small state's population of 1.32 million – vote for one of maybe 15 people to be the next president.

But that is democracy. We get to vote. No matter how shallow or frustrating the system might seem at times, he still believed that in the long run, we have a freedom and a privilege that too often is either taken for granted or completely neglected.

The article he'd just read was projecting possible turnout for the primary. It speculated that with multiple candidates in both parties, some 530,000 citizens might actually vote and that most of those would be: a) over the age of 45; b) vote with the Democrat ballot and c) be a toss-up as to whether more women than men voted. His vote in Vermont wouldn't come until March.

Ragsdale got ready for an evening out looking for scumbags. He had his eye on several and would make a determination, subject to guidance from his boss, which of these assholes was most deserving of his close attention. As he walked to the car, he was humming *Born in The USA*. He thought that he'd like to see that Boss in concert again.

My short phone conversation with Bonnie was a bit off. I sensed when we left Meredith on Monday morning that something was amiss. Now I was pretty sure that it was going to become more difficult before it got settled.

Smart, young, attractive, wants to start a family. Could almost be a personal ad online or in the newspaper. Likes to have fun with guy 16 years older, will tolerate dumb jokes and esoteric references to music from another time. Well, maybe less of the dumb jokes.

An old radio friend had suggested back in the summer, when I was doing the physical rehab with my shoulder, that I could do a weekly stint on one of the local stations. He went on about how much things were changing and that call-in shows covered just about any and every topic. Personal advice, keep it clean, make it relevant? Maybe not.

My focus at this point was discreetly getting my name

out to companies and individuals who might consider my services in the security/background checks and private investigation. Two quick situations in a few short months over the last year persuaded me that I could do the work and actually enjoyed it, at least when I got results. Mixing the new PI work with previous experience in media and communications didn't hold much promise. Do one or the other.

So I took some classes, got a license from the state of Vermont, went through basic firearms training and got shot on my second job out.

Probably didn't want to include that part in my pitch to prospective clients. But then again, wasn't that sort of earning your stripes? I'm still here and still showing up.

By 10:30 I was beginning to fade. I took a glass of port and a book to bed. The book's title was *Zoobiquity: The Astonishing Connection Between Human and Animal Health*. OK, where's the part about the behavior of apes?

Twenty Six

Engine idling, they sat in the pick-up truck smoking. Dervil was behind the wheel, Walker across from him.

"Good you got the truck," Walker said.

"Couldn't hardly pull it off without it." Dervil looked at Walker. He wondered what the idiot would do on his own.

"You said you already went to the place where the trailer is. Nobody there? You think we can get it in just 10 minutes?" Walker was getting anxious.

"Less. We scoped it out, no one around. I don't expect a problem."

There was an IT guy who regularly stopped at the bar. Dervil managed to borrow a Ford F-150 from him. It had a trailer hitch. He gave the guy $200 and said he would have it back before the guy's shift ended at seven in the morning.

"That'll work," the guy said. Now, they sat outside an employee parking lot off Apollo Drive. It was a 30 minute run to where the trailer was parked, 25 miles round-trip. There would be a slight detour for the return, leaving the trailer at a designated drop spot. If they made it that far, another two-grand and maybe a bonus pack.

By 1:30 in the morning, they had quietly backed the truck to hook up to a nearly brand new Airstream Flying Cloud travel trailer. They waited in silence to see if they'd attracted attention. Lights out and being directed by an accomplice with a flashlight, it took less than 10 minutes to connect the trailer and begin the trip back.

The accomplice, really the guy running the whole show, removed the protective vinyl tire covers, rigged the wiring harness for the lights and even furnished a stolen New Hampshire license plate. He watched them pull away. He would follow them to the remote spot for the trailer's new destination.

If all went as planned, never a sure thing, nobody was going to find this trailer anytime soon. Not even aerial surveillance would be able to spot the shiny, brushed aluminum body. A lot of thought, careful timing and some added forest cover would assure that this theft went off without a hitch, so to speak.

Twenty Seven

Wednesday – and yet another overcast morning in all of New Hampshire. One of those early November days that could go either way. But the forecast called for rain and a high temperature around 40. Not pleasant.

And Senator Shipp was not in a pleasant mood, something his top campaign assistant, Bob Horner, was all too familiar with. He could put on the smiles and phony back-slap and handshake routine with the best of them. It was Horner and other staff members who got the shit treatment, regardless of how well they did their jobs.

"Assholes. Think if they make a donation, I'll jump through any hoop they put up," Shipp said, exiting his hotel room. Horner knew better than to respond. Besides, he hadn't been at the small gathering the previous night. He had no idea who the new group of assholes was.

Shipp looked out at the parking lot, the buses, one of the other candidates and some of the reporters already there. He braced himself for another day of his own brand of "patriotism and prattle," as he'd come to think of much of the campaigning. Perhaps he wasn't as suited for politics as his ambition and ego dictated.

"And which scenic burgs today?" he said to Horner.

Margaret Reilly listened without reaction to the comments of Chuck Wehner. He'd called to inquire about any plans for a memorial service for his young associate, her son.

As soon as she replied that it would be a private, family service, details still to be worked out, Wehner had launched into a recitation of all the promise that Charles had shown, especially in recent weeks. He danced around any reference to the fact that Charles had stopped drinking. Wehner didn't know this woman and was having a difficult time finding the right words.

Finally, desperate to be off the phone and stop having to listen to someone she didn't know talk about her dead son, she found the abrupt words for ending the call.

"Mr. Wehner, you are very kind. I will be in touch soon. Thank you." And she was gone.

Wehner stared at the phone.

At the very same time one phone call was ending, a call that I was not aware of, I placed my own call to John O'Neil.

When we had left Lake Winnepesaukee two days ago, O'Neil had told me that he normally stayed on Bear Island until Thanksgiving, later than almost anyone else on the island. As I was making other calls and beginning to focus on political news from New Hampshire, my mind came back to the drowning and my observations late Saturday night and then at dinner on Sunday with O'Neil and his friend Dana Martin.

Nothing in the local paper about the identity of man they pulled out of the water. O'Neil seemed to know just about everyone around that area, so I suspected that he was up to date regarding the man's identity and any other news about the accident.

After five rings, I was about to hang up just as he answered. Considering his age, I was quick to remind him who I was.

"I'm fortunate, Mr. Hanlon. Names don't usually leave me for a while. And your young friend, Bonnie, isn't that right?" he said.

"Yes, Bonnie." Now I felt a little dumb that perhaps I'd offended him, or implying that he might not recall meeting us. "Nothing in the news over this way about the drowning victim. Curious if you've learned anything?" Silence at his end of the phone, then he spoke.

"I imagine it will be in the news pretty soon. Word that I hear is that the state police will announce that it is a suspicious death," O'Neil said. "Not sure they'll come right out and say murder. Least not at first."

"Huh. Have they released the name of the man?" I said.

"Charles Reilly. Young lawyer here in Meredith. Only

been around a year or two. Fact is, information I heard was that he went to your law school there at the University of Vermont." I wondered where he was getting his information.

"Actually, the Vermont Law School is independent of the University. UVM is up in Burlington, the law school is down here close to where I live."

"Didn't know that," he responded.

"Yeah. The law school's only been around since the 70s. Started out as Royalton College about 50 years ago. Similar, I think, to your former Belknap College over in Center Harbor."

"Well, no matter where it is or how long they've been awarding degrees, this dead man got one of them."

I detected the same wry humor we'd observed over dinner at his cottage Sunday evening. I could most see the twinkle in his eyes as he played it straight.

"Did you speak with Sgt. Condon again" I queried.

"Mr. Hanlon, didn't you tell me that you used to be a reporter? Are you fishing for the name of my source?"

Amusing old coot. Now he was playing with me.

"Not at all," I lied. "You've been over there since Benning Wentworth was handing out land grants. I suspect you know who's behind on their property taxes, what the chances are for passage of the next school bond issue and who's gonna' win the primary election?"

"All of that. And more," he chuckled. "But, as long as you don't put it on the radio, the Meredith Police Chief was one of my students about the same time you were in middle school. Not much happens," he went on, "that I can't get some information before it goes public. Even some of the things that never go public."

"Good for you. I'm sure the chief trusts you. Or, he's still afraid of you."

"Kenny's a good boy. Being serious, now, if that body hadn't been at our dock, not likely that I, or anyone else who didn't need to know, would hear much about it until the police were prepared to release the name."

"It's not going to leak from me."

"No, like I said, it will be out pretty soon. The Union Leader will probably have a story tomorrow," he went on. "Doubt they're going to have much about how the man was killed. But it was not a drowning. So the state record is safe. At least for a few more weeks."

"So, who is going to be our next president?" As soon as the words were out of my mouth, again I heard the chuckle.

"Isn't it going to be your Senator Sanders?"

"Bernie's my guy. He's is the real deal. Been that way his entire career. But I seriously doubt that he could ever get 60-million votes across the country a year from now."

"Surprising things happen," O'Neil said. "I'm an old Yankee moderate Republican and I feel bad right now, especially for you younger folks. This country really needs some help."

Twenty Eight

I managed to make some sense of the Candidates Caravan schedule of events for the rest of the week. The dates and locations of interest to me, anyway, were the Friday and Saturday legs. The route, as shown on the Live Free and Drive website, was pretty much what Bruce Lyndon had explained on the phone. A zig zag from southwestern New Hampshire over to the coast, back to the western side of the state in Hanover, then ending on Sunday at noon in Manchester with a rally.

With my own route in mind, to accommodate Lyndon's planned stops for interviews, I sent a text to Ragsdale about Friday night in Durham.

'Can you clean-up? Will buy dinner. Meet one of my liberal mainstream media friends. Fri night?' Send.

Not five minutes later he replied.

'Hoo-ah. Maybe. Back to you later.'

The hoo-ah was thrown in for my amusement. I'd also been eager to tell him about the body from the lake. He would know someone who knew something.

Lyndon was back to conclude the interview with the nurse in Plymouth. Now her husband agreed to share his view of the candidates, as well.

Matt Brown, also a native of the state, had a slightly different take on the New Hampshire primary than that of his wife. Where she came across as serious and thoughtful about all levels of government, frequently commenting on elected officials' responsibility to uphold the trust given them by voters, her husband was less enthralled with the system. He thought it was broken.

Once they settled in for another round of questions, this session at the couple's kitchen table, Lyndon started with the husband.

"A few minutes ago you said that you thought our system of government, at the federal level, was broken. Can you expand on that?" The man looked at Bruce, smiled and shook his head.

"You guys must see more of it than we do, covering this stuff every day. I used to watch C-SPAN a lot. It got to be more than I could stomach. Way too much posturing." He looked at his wife, who remained silent. Lyndon had made a note with his pen. Matt Brown went on.

"The incumbents almost always win. No matter what the rest of the country thinks of a particular member of congress or the senate, they've rigged it so the money keeps flowing to their reelection. Far and away, most challengers don't have any chance at all. Plus, they've figured out how to play to the media and the folks back home. If they keep opposing everything the other party proposes, and they're only in Washington, what, less than 40% of the year, how can they accomplish anything?"

"Any thoughts on," Lyndon began to ask, hesitated, looking at Brown, then completed his question, "on steps we might consider to improve the things?"

"Term limits, for a start. And the money," Brown rolled his eyes and raised both arms toward the kitchen ceiling, "it is way out of control. It's just crazy how much we spend on elections. Personally, I think it's obscene."

This session went on with both husband and wife answering questions and offering thoughts, stopping short of two hours. When he was ready to leave, Bruce Lyndon had more than enough material to work with for his first segment of the essay to be published later.

Next stop: Durham, seat of the University of New Hampshire with 15,000 students. And the home of at least one retired US Foreign Service officer, a man who, as far as Bruce was concerned, had displayed refreshing candor in 2012 when talking about the qualifications of presidential candidates. But the list was longer now. How would he size them up this time around?

Lapierre was in his car and headed to Nashua. It would be a "kiss the ring" visit for him, a yearly visit with one of the political power brokers in the most densely populated county of the state.

Very much like himself, probably more so, the man Lapierre was going to see was strictly a behind-the-scenes kind of guy. Not really secretive, just getting things done without any need or desire for public attention.

Before the phenomenon of internet fundraising and the opening of the floodgates after the Citizens United ruling by the US Supreme Court, most states had had at least one network of individuals that knew where to chase down the money. That was certainly true in New Hampshire.

With 234 cities and towns spread over 9,283 square miles, the core group of this network could be recorded with the names of fewer than 20 people. If that list of names existed anywhere on paper, it was not at the Federal Election Commission, nor was it in the New Hampshire Secretary of State's office in Concord.

Warren Lapierre was in the top five of the network. He wasn't certain that would help him now. Moving past 72 hours since the discovery of Charles Reilly's body, Lapierre was experiencing increasing flashes of guilt, sadness and fear. It had been a long time since he felt anxiety. He would have to find a way to deal with it.

Kelly Alexakis knew the statistics the way she knew the alphabet. And it was certainly one of the reasons she was appointed Attorney General at the young age of 36. She was smart, thorough and not only read more than most of her contemporaries in the legal community, she was almost encyclopedic in referring to any particular area of law as it applied to the citizens of her state.

Consumer and environmental protection cases, civil law, medicaid fraud, transportation, drugs, all part of the job for the AG and her staff. Alexakis could pivot on a dime when addressing any of these.

But nothing got the headlines and TV time like the cases that came through the Homicide Prosecution Unit. With 104 names currently on the list of Suspicious Deaths and Unsolved Homicides, covering a period that dated back to 1970, none were added to the list during her first year in office. An accidental drowning switched to a homicide had the potential to put another victim's name on that list.

Not if she could help it.

Twenty Nine

Piecing together information for an obituary was not something any mother should have to do. Yet it happened every day all across industrialized countries of the world.

Margaret Reilly knew very well that her family was more fortunate than most. At 76, she enjoyed good health and daily contact with friends. Widowed 29 years earlier, there had never been a serious interest in remarrying. And nearly 50 years after the fact, she still grieved for the daughter who died in infancy.

But she'd always had Charles. Was always proud of him, even during trying times. His homosexuality, or bi-sexuality, was something she accepted a long time ago. She was horrified at stories of families who disowned their offspring when they learned they were gay or lesbian. It made no sense. How could you disown a son or daughter?

Using a pen and paper, she began writing a summary of Charles' life. Blair told her that she only needed to include the important dates, schools and a short list of any particular achievements or affiliations that she wanted to acknowledge. The funeral home would handle the rest, Blair said. They would get it to the newspaper and their online listing with other obituaries.

She filled five pages before she stopped writing. Too much information. The memory of her husband's obituary came back to her. Her now deceased brother-in-law had handled most of the funeral arrangements then. Staring at the sheets of paper on the desk in front of her, she tapped them together and placed a large paper clip at the top, then placed them inside a brown 9 x 12 envelope which she would turn over to a representative of the funeral home later that afternoon.

Few reporters routinely paid attention to what the candidates said in brief exchanges with individual voters when they were campaigning. Unless it appeared as though there might be some confrontation, however, most of the energy and effort was reserved for organized events, stump speeches and the occasional banter between candidates as they traveled together.

Generally, reporters gave little merit to the quick handshake exchange or words of support from people in a supermarket parking lot or at a factory gate. So when a young woman leveled a short, emphatic response to Senator Tad Shipp when he reached out to shake her hand, only two reporters heard what she said and only one of them got it on camera. But that was enough. The video was on the internet within minutes and, as they say, went viral immediately.

What people saw was a woman who looked to be in her late 20s or 30s, walking to her car and holding the hand of a small, pre-school age boy. Senator Shipp approached the woman and extended his hand in greeting. The woman stopped, looked directly at Shipp and did not shake his hand. He held it there momentarily. Finally the woman spoke to him.

"I have seen you on television several times, Senator. You are an embarrassment to our country. I can't imagine how you possibly fooled enough people in your state to actually get elected." She turned away from the politician and continued walking with the little boy. Shipp, flustered for a second, also turned in the opposite direction.

The reporter, a young man from a college newspaper, caught-up with the woman. "Excuse me, may I ask why you said that to Senator Shipp," he said, holding his iPhone camera to record her reaction. The woman stopped again and turned to face the reporter.

"I find political opportunists like him despicable," she answered, waving her right arm back toward the retreating not-so-presidential candidate. She was still holding the little boy's hand. The woman, right arm pointing in the direction of Shipp, continued. "He is a demagogue of the worst kind. Speaker Boehner said that some of these men are 'false prophets'. And that man, I believe, is poison for his own party and the entire country." She lowered her arm and held eye contact with the reporter.

"I work for The Equinox. Can we use this? I would like to post it on the web," the reporter said.

"Yes. You may use it." She began to move away.

"Could I get your name?" The woman hesitated before responding, then spoke clearly and deliberately.

"My name is Linda Snider." A pause, then, "I am a native of New Hampshire. I'm not a volunteer for anyone's campaign and I am not a 'plant' by another candidate."

"Cool," the reporter said. "Thanks." He turned to catch-up with Shipp and the others.

The woman and the little boy continued to a car parked a few feet away. She strapped the boy in the back seat, got in and drove off. The car had NH plates.

Of course, the only clip of the video that made it to YouTube was the "I have seen you on television several times, Senator" edited through and including the portion of "poison for his own party and the entire country."

The reporter was savvy enough not to use the woman's name and not to show the face of the young boy. But the clip, edited to under a minute, would get hundreds of thousands views in the days ahead. It was not going to help Shipp win friends and influence voters during this party unity week. And it most certainly was going to fuel criticism from the other candidates.

"Poison for his own party and the entire country."

Just too good to pass up. It probably would show-up in more than one TV spot, too.

Thirty

How do you get a story? Keep asking questions, pay attention, follow-up.

That was my thinking as I picked up the phone to call Virginia Jackson. Of course, 'the story' wasn't likely to go anywhere, at least not from my end. I wasn't working for anyone and had no place, yet, to submit any information I might find. That didn't stop my curiosity.

"Hello," she said after three rings.

"Virginia. It's Michael Hanlon."

"Hey. Ready to stack some more wood?"

"You didn't get another load?"

"No," she laughed. "All done. You're off the hook."

"If you have a minute, I have a question. Actually, a couple of questions. About your work."

"O-kay." Her voice had a tinge of uncertainty.

"You're getting settled in at the law school, yes? Been there, what, a few months?"

"That's right. May 1st." Still the uncertainty.

"There's a story that's about to get some coverage over in the Lakes Region of New Hampshire. A guy drowned. But now they think it might be a murder, and

I'm told that he was a Vermont Law School graduate. "

"I'm sorry to hear that. The murder, I mean."

"Not sure when that's going to become the official story, but I have it from a pretty good source. I didn't say anything when we were stacking wood the other day. But I was there Saturday night when they pulled the body from Lake Winnepesaukee."

"What?" she exclaimed.

"Yeah. Kind of strange. A couple was out jogging late at night, spotted a man's body in the water. The woman screamed. Bonnie and I were staying at a cottage close by and we got there two minutes later."

"That's awful."

"The Marine Patrol came across the lake awhile later, it was after midnight, and pulled the body out from under a boat dock." I still had the image in my mind, could still see the boat slowly moving away after they loaded the body.

"You say the man was a VLS alum. They must have identified him, then," she said.

"Yes. Charles Reilly is the name I have. But, I don't think the media has the word yet that it's now been ruled a homicide." We had a couple seconds of silence before I went on. "The story is going to break pretty soon. Maybe on the news this evening. Hard to say who will have it first."

"So you want me to see what I can learn about him while he was at the law school?"

I shouldn't have been surprised at her getting to the

point of my call. I was pretty sure that lawyers called it 'discovery' when they were pulling together information about a case.

"If you could do that, great."

"I have a class this afternoon at 3:30. Later, there's a budget meeting with some admin people that a few of us have been invited to attend. Let me see what I can find out," she said, then added, "Reilly you said?"

"Yes, Charles Reilly."

"Any idea of his age? That might give me a time frame of when he was a student."

"No. My guess is that he was probably in his 40s. So would that put him there 16, 17 years ago?"

"Not necessarily. A lot of people going to grad school these days are older. Often they've done something else for a few years before the go back to the classroom. That's especially true of a school like ours."

"If it's any help, my source says the guy was working with a firm in Meredith, New Hampshire for the past two years." I looked at my notes from the call with John O'Neil.

"Wehner & Garlow is the name of the firm," I said.

"That could make it easier. The Alumni Affairs and Development people keep pretty good tabs on graduates and their careers. I'll call you this evening."

"Thanks."

Thirty One

Ragsdale drove slowly along the coast on Ocean Boulevard, just beyond the Seacoast Science Center. This time of year there were few cars on this stretch of road, unlike the occasional bumper-to-bumper traffic in August. He was on the lookout for a particular vehicle, an older model, yellow Nissan Pathfinder. A tip from one of the cops in the nearby town of Rye had it that there were reports of possible drug dealing by the person driving said yellow Nissan. He was skeptical.

Driving a pretty beat-up car – a 12-year-old gray Ford Taurus with mediocre tires, a considerable amount of rust and 178,00 miles – he parked at a scenic pull off spot just above a stone wall and the beach. The water looked cold. The sky was the same color as his car.

He cracked the driver's window and let the engine idle. On the radio, 92.1 FM, *MacArthur Park*.

"April, 1968. Richard Harris," Louie said to himself. "Made it to #10." He watched the ocean and a lone gull that landed on a rock near his car. He thought about the story of songwriter Jimmy Webb reportedly having composed the song after the breakup with his girlfriend.

Webb claimed that the unusual lyrics were inspired by

things he actually saw while having lunch with his girlfriend in Los Angeles' real MacArthur Park. He wanted The Association to record it, but they declined because it was too long and they thought the lyrics and structure were not suited for their style.

Years later, Donna Summer had a disco cover of the song that reached # 1 and reportedly sold multi-million copies. It was also covered by The Four Tops. And the country singer Waylon Jennings.

Louie chuckled at the memory that by the time he worked in radio many years later, Harris' original version, running more than seven minutes in length, was referred to as a 'bathroom record.' When dee jays played these long singles, it gave them a chance to go to the bathroom, get coffee, call their girlfriend.

"Whatever," Louie said to himself.

No yellow Nissan. No mysterious boats hovering just off shore. Gray sky, gray day, gray gull on a rock waiting.

"*Ain't no sunshine when she's gone...*" on the radio.

"Bill Withers, 1971. Classic."

The gull didn't fully appreciate Louie's trivia. Didn't matter. He would stick around for maybe another 30 minutes listening to the radio, then get ready for an evening of watching the yahoos.

Is this exciting or what?

Thirty Two

The phone call from Sgt. Condon came at 6:02 PM. Warren Lapierre was not surprised. He knew when the state troopers left his home on Monday night that things were likely to change.

Now, and he was pretty sure of this, it would just be a matter of days, if not sooner, that they would pull together all they needed to place him in a no win predicament.

"The ME report is conclusive," Condon said. "Cause of death was a blow to the base of the skull from a blunt object."

Lapierre attempted a desperation pass, not expecting it to be caught.

"Is it possible that he was drunk? Fell and hit his head on the gunnel?" he said.

"The blow came from something that struck him with great force, not from falling. No, he did not strike his head on the side of the boat."

Lapierre covered his eyes and nose with his right hand and lowered his head. His mouth closed, he took in a deep breath through his nose, held it and then blew out like he was inflating a balloon.

After a couple seconds of saying nothing, he heard

Condon's voice speak again.

"Mr. Lapierre, we'd like you to come to our office to go over this again. I can send a trooper."

"That really won't be necessary," he responded. "I can drive. You're in Tamworth?"

"Yes. Off Route 16, a little north of The Yankee Smokehouse. It's a left just after you pass the used car lot with all the banners. Our sign is right at the highway."

"I know where it is." Lapierre looked at his watch. "I can be there by 7:30. Is that OK?"

"That's good. I will be here," Condon said.

I'm sure you will, Lapierre thought. "Right. Thank you. See you shortly," he said, then put the phone down.

A group of reporters sat in the lobby of The Fairfield Inn and Suites in downtown Keene, NH.

A long day travelling to the southwest corner of the state and there were no events scheduled for the evening. Waiting for one other person to join them before heading to a bar a block away, the conversation was all about the YouTube video of Senator Tad Shipp's close encounter with a blunt, non-supporter earlier that morning.

"One of these days, you guys will remember what it was like to be a rookie. That kid was eager and he was on top of it. And you were playing Angry Birds on your phone," said Eliot Page, laughing at the group.

Page, one of the oldest reporters in the pool covering the Candidates Caravan, was referring to the college newspaper reporter who caught the exchange between the woman and the least likable candidate.

"She'll have her own blog before the election in February," said Don Eli, a radio guy who usually kept to himself. He glanced up from his phone only long enough to see that he was getting no attention from the others.

"What's her name?" asked Tom McMillan, another reporter.

"Linda Snider," piped up Beverly Foster, the only woman in the group. The others remained silent.

"Eliot's right," Foster added. "We need to pay more attention to the people out there and maybe a little less attention to every burp and fart from the candidates."

The men all looked at her, not the first time she had admonished them for the all too frequent pack mentality in covering the candidates.

"What you might think about," Page suggested, "is somebody is designated at all times to stay with a specific candidate."

"Mark up," Eli said, not looking up from his phone.

"What?" Foster asked.

"Cover someone," Eli replied.

"Exactly. Like soccer. Or, basketball. Playing defense in any sport. Cover your man," Page agreed.

Tim Johnson, the last of the group, walked from the

corridor into the lobby to join the others.

"I'm here. Where have you guys been?" he said. What he didn't realize was that his after shave announced his arrival two seconds before he entered the lobby.

They got up and headed for the bar.

Shipp was screaming at his campaign aides, who informed him that the video was all over the internet.

"Make them remove it," he said. "Right now."

"I'm afraid it doesn't work that way, sir," said Bob Horner, the only staff assistant who could muster the nerve to try to reason with the senator.

"Public place, she's a private citizen. You're a public official. As long as the reporter cleared it with her when he got the video, nothing we can do," Horner said.

"I'm not even certain he needed her permission to post it," he added. "But it will run its course in a couple days."

"Oh, I'm sure," Shipp said, voice louder than his staff needed at the moment. "And all the other candidates will pat me on the back and say, 'Don't worry about it, Tad.'" His eyes were bulging more than anyone could remember. One aide thought Shipp might have a heart attack.

Shipp glared at all of them. Each person in the room tried to avoid eye contact.

"Bob, you and I will discuss this and what we're going

to do," Shipp said. He looked around at the others.

"Anyone else that has," he held up two fingers on each hand, "suggestions", he held the hands in place, "please be sure that you let us know." No one responded.

"6:30 sharp in the morning. Right here. Be on time." He waived them out of his room.

Thirty Three

What Virginia Jackson learned about Charles Reilly's days at the Vermont Law School was that he was one of the smartest students in his class.

According to the unofficial information Virginia got from a faculty member, Reilly had been in an accelerated JD program beginning in 2009. But after just a month of classes, his attendance and behavior became erratic. According to the professor who was sharing his recollections of Reilly, it was not certain that he would actually graduate.

But something happened that snapped Reilly back into line and, according to the prof, the final semester saw him with perfect attendance, full participation in independent study groups and forums, and he aced his exams. He went on to pass first the Vermont Bar Exam and later the New Hampshire exam.

After a short stint working with an environmental advocacy organization for just over a year, he suddenly left Vermont without notice and relocated to central New Hampshire. And yes, it was common knowledge among those who knew him, that Reilly had been working with a firm in Meredith for the past two years.

Virginia told me all this when she called at 8:30 on Wednesday evening. She said there were likely others who might add to the story, but she thought this was probably a reasonably accurate account. Her source was highly regarded at the school, she said, and had been around for a long time. Besides, she added, I think he might've had a thing for Reilly.

"You mean a romantic 'thing'?" I said.

"Yeah. Everyone knows this professor is gay. In fact, he's been regularly involved in different LGBT activities for a few years now."

"Well, if Reilly was gay, it's doubtful the police will let that shape the story they release. Unless, of course, there's some salacious angle that surfaces when the story's been out for a while." She came right back at me.

"Really hard to predict. You watch most television news for a week and you can pretty much count on it. Somewhere, at some point during the news cycle, you're likely to see a story about some crime that has a sexual hook."

I knew she had a point. Some of the news shows, in my judgement, had rapidly moved into exploiting stories for perceived juiciness rather than the facts of the actual events.

"Thank you for getting this information. I'm not going to chase the story, though," I said.

"What about all those presidential wannabe's running

around? You said you might spend some time working on the primary." I'd forgotten that was part of our discussion when I helped her stacking wood earlier in the week.

"Maybe. I'm teaming-up with an old friend tomorrow to spend a couple days over on the coast. Then we're coming back here for the candidate's forum Saturday night at Dartmouth."

"I read about that in The Valley News," she said. "It sounds like the plan is for an informal round-table with candidates questioning each other and a lot of audience participation."

"That's the way I read it. I'm not sure they can pull it off. The idea came from one of the student organizations and somebody high-up agreed to give it a try."

"The story I read said that not all of the candidates are going along with it," she said.

"Right. I think, so far, of the 10 candidates out there travelling the state this week, only 7 have agreed to be involved Saturday night."

"Still going to be a hot ticket. I bet they get a crowd."

"Count on it. I think the interesting thing to watch for is what kind of crowd. Will it be an older group, many already settled on who they will vote for? Or the younger, mostly student crowd and so-called undecideds?" I heard her snicker.

"You're not one of those who refers to older people as Q-tips, are you?" she said.

"Never. Look at my hair. It'll be white before I'm 60."

"Good. Age, like beauty, is really in the eye of the beholder, don't you think?"

"Of course."

"And now that I've done all this snooping for you, and the fact that I have a couple years on you, when are we going to have dinner?"

There it was. If earlier I was uncertain that she might be hinting at a date, this was pretty obvious. And my gut said that it would be OK. Depending on how I finessed my relationship issues with Bonnie Mackin.

"How about Sunday?" I answered.

"Works for me. You can give me a report on why you are going to vote for Donald Trump."

"Nope. I'm still a Bernie guy. But, I will have a thorough, unabridged account of what I see and hear Saturday night."

"I can hardly wait. Call me on Sunday."

When we hung-up, I sat and thought about all we discussed, then about Virginia. And Bonnie.

For sure, like one of those old farmer jokes, you could bet your sweet ass one thing: when my sister next calls to inquire of my 'love life', I'm not sharing any details.

Lapierre convinced himself that he could hold his own in a second interview with the state police.

Now, as he sat in a small conference room with Sgt.

Condon and the same trooper who had been to his home, he wasn't so sure. He stole a glance at the other trooper's name tag; Sgt. W. Costello.

"I know this is not easy for you," Condon began. "It was clear to me when we spoke two days ago that you and Mr. Reilly were very close."

Lapierre felt a lump in his throat. He would not break down in front of the police. He held his breath for a second and nodded in acknowledgement of the statement.

"I would like to start from the time Mr. Reilly arrived at your home last Saturday afternoon. Some of my questions will be the same as those you have already answered, but bear with us." Lapierre nodded again.

Condon looked at Costello, who joined the conversation for the first time.

"And we have some information on Mr. Reilly's recent work for Wehner & Garlow. We'll get to that later on," Costello said. Then it was back to Condon.

"We need you to think about others who Mr. Reilly may have recently had contact with. Anyone, especially anyone who knows the lake and the islands around here."

Thirty Four

Dervil and Walker were arguing about the money. It was not the first time.

"Don't add up right," Walker argued. He was shaking his head, but not looking at Dervil. Eddie Walker never looked directly at anyone.

In the short time he'd known Walker, John Dervil thought the man's behavior often reminded him of a dog that was frightened all the time. Cowering and avoiding any contact with humans.

"Let me say it again," Dervil stated. "The money he gave us for grabbing the trailer, that was a one-time deal." He watched Walker to be sure this part registered. No sign that it did.

"Two grand. Not bad for one night. You saw me give Nate the Nerd two-hundred bucks to use his truck," Dervil said, waiting for acknowledgement. Nothing.

"You got $900 and I got the same, right?" This time, Walker nodded, but continued looking at the floor.

"And we both got some good stuff, yes? That was a bonus. For the drive a week ago up at the lake."

Walker looked-up for all of three seconds, eyes wide

and aimed like search lights at Dervil's face.

"That's what don't add up," Walker repeated. "He gave you a wad of bills. We each got a grand. You said it was gonna' be more."

Dervil watched him for a few seconds, turned away and slowly shook his head.

"Do you understand what a retainer is?" he said.

Walker didn't respond, eyes again looking downward.

"The extra money – it was another grand – that is for expenses for any work we have comin' up." Dervil was now leaning toward Walker and had his hands out like he was holding an invisible log. Or a body.

"I mean we are goddamn lucky that he wants to use us and not some other guys, don't'cha think?" Shrugged shoulders, head down, back to the switch-is-off posture with Walker.

Dervil kept going, shifting to a conspiratorial whisper in order that the others in the bar would not hear.

"You see these other assholes. And how many bars and clubs do you think there are around here. You think that he couldn't recruit about 50 other helpers if he wanted?"

Dervil placed his right hand on Walker's shoulder in a gesture of reassurance. He didn't speak, just let the hand rest there for a few seconds. Finally, Walker gave him a quick glance, then put his head down again.

"This stuff is sorta' new to you, I know. You got a lot a

reason not to trust anybody, I get that," Dervil said. "But, Eddie. You have to trust me." No response.

"If you can't, he's not gonna be able to use us. Simple as that."

Thirty Five

Branchik took two good snorts of the coke and leaned back in the chair. The rush was instantaneous.

Without the help of rehab or any of the other crutches that many drug users tried in their attempts to break an addiction, Arnie Branchik was effectively controlling, all by himself, the use of all substances these days.

A little smack once in a while was his favorite self-reward for the changes he'd made in his life over the past year. He was on top of it.

From laser tattoo removal of the ink on his neck, the artsy all black long-sleeved shirts, to letting his hair grow out on the sides and wearing the $300 herringbone stretch-cotton flat cap, he was a changed person.

And that included his name. For the very few people he felt needed to know a name, he insisted on Arno. But he was real fucking selective in giving even that to anyone.

A new Airstream trailer out here in the woods, more product and more customers than he ever imagined, what was not to like?

It made him wonder why he'd spent so much time with dickheads up north chasing idiots who were unreliable in their purchasing habits, often had little or no money, and almost as often relied on petty theft to support their habit.

After five minutes reclining in the chair, he got up and thought about his stops for the evening. He went to the closet, retrieved the six-inch knife in its case and strapped it to his right calf. He checked the clip on the Sig P220, placed it behind his back in the waistband of his black pants.

Looking around the inside of the Airstream, he was extremely pleased with himself that he'd watched it for nearly a month and then arranged to have it removed to this location. Real comfort. He especially liked the round sink in the galley area and the leather sofa. And they would never find it.

Before leaving, Arno put on a black leather jacket and had a last glance in the mirror. Even to himself he had the appearance of a 1960s beatnik.

So fucking what?

Thirty Six

It was Friday morning at 9:05 when I headed out for the Manchester airport. I was to pick-up Bruce Lyndon after he dropped his rental car. We would drive to Durham.

Two hours later we were going east on 101. The drive would take less than an hour, just 40 miles away. It would give us plenty of time to discuss the itinerary for the next two days and for me to think about the timing and best routes to take.

"We're going to meet this guy at a place called Spanos," Bruce said. "It's not far from the campus."

"Bring it up on your phone. Oughta' be easy to find," I replied.

"I told him we'd be there by 12:30."

As I drove, Bruce was laying out the plan for the next stop, including a 'meet and greet' scheduled for 7 PM in the Granite State Room at the Memorial Union Building on the UNH campus,

"I think I'll skip the rodeo this evening," he said.

"What a heartbreak."

"You really are a lot more cynical than I remember," he said.

"Not always. I guess after cramming on this campaign stuff the past few days, some of it is just so predictable. And when they have real debates, don't you think there ought to be a meter that scores the platitudes when they roll out so freely?"

"Maybe like scoring contestants on a reality show."

"Any system. You never see a moderator or any of the panel call them on it. 'Senator, that may play well back home, but surely you don't expect American voters to accept something quite that simplistic," I replied.

"I read an article by some former speechwriter a few weeks back. A big part of what he had to say was about just how good most mainstream politicians have become at speaking in the abstract. And how it turns off voters." I knew it didn't take a lot to get Bruce warmed-up and I let him keep going.

"The guy went on to suggest that it was the main reason for Trump's popularity, as long as it lasts. Trump speaks in short, declarative statements that a lot of voters like. Even when you think he might be a little shaky on some facts, his comments are perceived as a lot more refreshing." He was now moving his hands around as he talked. I kept my eyes on the road.

"He never adjusts his remarks or answers for different crowds. And he usually throws in a couple words at the end of his answers that have some bite."

"Wouldn't you just love to see a no-holds-barred, 90 minute debate with only Trump and Bernie?" I said.

"Give him a call. You can do it, Hanlon. He's your senator."

"Right."

We were coming into Durham. My dashboard clock showed 11:58AM – 46ºF. It seemed as though it had been overcast for about a month now.

Bruce was looking at his phone. He tapped the screen, then put the phone down.

"Should be up here on the left. Watch for Madbury Road, across from the post office."

"I'm not gonna stick around to have lunch with you," I said. Ahead was a plain white sign that read Spanos – Food and Drink.

"Why not? You'll like this guy. Very witty, thoughtful. You can take off after we eat. I won't get into any serious questions until after lunch, anyway."

"Tell me about him again," I said.

"Career foreign service officer. Might have been CIA at some point. You can't really tell with some of them. He retired here 6 or 7 years ago. My editor set me up with him before the 2012 primary."

I pulled into a parking area behind the restaurant, shut off the engine and looked at my watch. 12:02. Bruce was reaching behind him to get the bag that held his notebook and recorder.

"OK. I'll order some soup and a salad and split as soon as I finish eating," I said.

"Good."

We went inside and got a table.

The restaurant was understated in décor, soft lighting and a few contemporary oil paintings on the walls. I counted only eight tables, all with white linen tablecloths, that could seat up to four people each. There was another room off to the side that probably had additional seating. Our server brought a carafe of water with ice. Bruce told him that we were expecting another person to join us.

Looking around, I saw a well-dressed, elderly couple on the opposite side of the room and two younger women seated at a table in the front where we entered. The other tables were empty.

Five minutes later, while we were looking over the 'above my pay grade' menu, a man entered the restaurant and was warmly greeted by the hostess. They obviously knew one another.

The man looked to be in his 70s, good health and like the couple across the room, had not held back in spending on his wardrobe. Tailor-fitted gray tweed jacket, burgundy cashmere sweater, navy slacks and expensive looking shoes. The hostess was bringing him to our table. Bruce stood and extended his right hand. The man had an easy smile. They shook hands.

"Mr. Millar. Thank you for making time for me," Bruce said, at the same time turning to introduce me. I was now standing as well.

Thirty Seven

Since the obituary had been posted online two days earlier, Margaret Atwood Reilly had been hearing about people leaving their remembrances of Charles and condolences. The director at the funeral home said that he would print all that had been posted so far and would later put together a book with all the messages.

There would be no calling hours and a very private family service at The Woodlands cemetery on Saturday morning. Outside of Blair Watson and his wife Cecile, Margaret did not want others to attend. She'd made that clear to the funeral director, instructing him to turn away any queries about the service and only to provide her postal address for further contact from those expressing sympathy. A time of family grief was a time for family grieving, as far as Margaret was concerned. She had no patience for listening to strangers or people she might not have seen in years.

Not beyond her notice, Margaret was moving into the anger stage of her own grief.

Following two mostly sleepless nights in a row, Warren Lapierre was right on the edge of a total melt down.

The extensive, second interview with the state police which he barely managed to survive without breaking; the haranguing phone calls with the bitch running the phony LLC pumping money into radio and TV ads. He didn't need this.

Then there was the loneliness and the sadness, neither of which he'd anticipated just a week earlier.

Creeping above these concerns and straining his genuine feeling of fatigue was fear and anticipation. The phone call. When would it come?

Since the story was now being carried by both print and broadcast media, it was only a matter of time before he received the call.

Actually he feared the probability of two calls, one from the state police. But they were more likely to just come to his home this time.

It was the phone call from Arno that would influence everything he did from this moment forward.

Thirty Eight

The retired foreign service officer was about the most charming, funny and insightful person I'd been around in a long, long time. Maybe ever.

David Millar - I could only imagine his career resume and genealogy chart - was soft spoken, quick in thought, careful in reply and spontaneously funny.

Less than 30 minutes in Millar's company at lunch, Bruce and I had heard more amusing nicknames for and observations about the current presidential candidates than you might expect from a month of late night TV talk show hosts.

Holding to my previous comment to Bruce, I excused myself to 'do some errands' in order that he might get on with his interview with Millar.

"Don't count Mr. Sanders out," Millar said, standing to shake my hand before I left. "When my father was a young man, they weren't expecting the likes of Calvin Coolidge, either." He gave me the diplomat's smile.

I told Bruce that I would come back for him around 3:30 or for him to text me if they finished sooner.

Leaving the restaurant, I thought about contrasts

between Calvin Coolidge and Bernie Sanders, primarily the taciturn Cal and the often very direct Senator Sanders. Back at the car, I sent a text to Louie. 'In Durham thru Sat am. How's your schedule?'

Then I drove to the main UNH campus to take a look at the venue for tonight's rally, or whatever they were calling it. Walking from the car to the Memorial Union Building, I made a quick check of my National Radio Broadcasters Association photo ID hoping that it was still current. It was good for another 55 days until the end of the year, which did not guarantee that it would pass muster with campus security.

The room was locked up tight but there were posters all around the lobby promoting the event; *Meet The Next President – Share Your Views* in large red and blue block letters on white poster board with stars and stripes screened behind the words. No security or other staff around. I peeked through the glass on the door and saw the room was arranged auditorium style with perhaps 10 or 12 chairs and two mic stands in the center of the room.

My phone gave me a little blip that a message had arrived. It was from Ragsdale.

'Free after 5:30. Need to shower. Where?'

I wasn't sure how Louie would take to Bruce Lyndon, but I knew that Bruce would likely find a way to draw out Louie's social and political views. All I would have to do was a little provocateur work to get things started.

I sent a reply. 'You call it. Can meet anywhere. 7

o'clock good for you?'

With time to kill, I walked to the school's Dimond Library and spent nearly two hours looking at an exhibit on *The Popular Press in New Hampshire* from the mid 18th century. One of the things I learned was that Durham had the state's first printing press in 1756.

For almost 90 minutes, Bruce Lyndon simply had to listen and throw in an occasional two or three word prompt to keep Millar going.

The small digital recorder on the table was getting it all. They were the last two customers in the restaurant and Lyndon made lots of notes. There was plenty of material for the columns he planned to write. Now it was time to wrap it up.

"I just want to come back to your comments about Senator Shipp. Do you think he has a chance here in New Hampshire?" Millar took a sip of cold coffee from the cup in front of him before responding.

"He's not the first, and unfortunately, will not be the last of the type of politician seen in every generation. In many ways, Shipp is reminiscent of Joseph McCarthy, who conducted himself in a similar fashion back when I was a teenager and just beginning to pay attention world affairs.

People like this regularly lace their speeches with

apocalyptic references and bombast. They speak as though they will use executive powers that no former president has had available to them. And, fortunately, are not granted to them by our constitution." Millar shifted in his chair before concluding.

"Shipp is relatively young, mid-40s, I believe. So he is likely to be on the scene for a few years. Like others, he will always have a base, be able to raise some money and get the occasional headline. But ever become President? Very difficult to imagine, even in my worst case scenarios of failed leadership and an imploding democracy. I will be greatly surprised if he breaks out of the single digits here."

Not more than a ten minute walk from the restaurant where Lyndon concluded his interview with Millar, the candidates were arriving in town. The three buses were parked and would remain idle until the next morning.

Staff assistants, along with campaign volunteers, would scramble at various tasks over the next three hours preparing for the evening. The candidates themselves would work the phones and possibly grab a few minutes' rest before heading out for the last event of a very long day, with the primary still nearly three months off.

Someone who would not attend the rally was Warren Lapierre. Just 60 miles away from this particular event, he would explore the likelihood that his campaign events might be over for the foreseeable future.

Thirty Nine

Bruce was able to reserve two rooms at a B & B a few minutes from the campus. It was an old homestead and carriage house near the Oyster River with parking in the rear.

The woman who checked us in gave each of us a key to the front door and to our rooms, provided a quick tour of the main floor living area, then showed us the second floor bedrooms and the shared bathroom.

At 6:30 my phone vibrated and lit up. The caller ID showed that it was Louie.

"Brother Ragsdale," I answered.

"You know, some of my African American friends would not let you get away with that brother shit."

"Nice to hear from you, too. Do we have a plan?"

"Maybe. I'm a little tweaky about going out anywhere in public around here. You wanna' pick up some food and bring it to where I'm staying?"

"We can do that. Any preferences? Pizza, maybe?"

"There's a place that has great Chinese and Japanese food. Mei Wei. It's on the Mill Road close to campus," he said. "Really good, no MSG. I can order, you pick it up."

"Louie, I think they all say 'no MSG.'"

"Yeah, but this place has real Chinese."

"Good. Phone it in. I'll find it. Maybe half-an-hour? But I need directions to find you," I said.

"I'll text after I order the food. I'm about 10 minutes south of town, off 108. Heading toward Newmarket."

"OK."

"You probably should get some beer, too."

"Anything else?"

"If you're still eating a lot of desserts, better get some cookies. Or maybe a frozen Key Lime pie."

"Check."

"Watch for the directions."

"Tweaky?" I said. He was gone.

It was after seven when we found Mei Wei, picked up the food Louie ordered, stopped at a convenience store and got a six pack of Smuttynose beer, three large oatmeal raisin cookies and then were on our way.

The directions were right on; south on 108, a mile past Mill Pond take a left onto Lutze Road, second drive way on the left. A gray Ford Taurus with NH plates parked out front.

As soon as we pulled in, Ragsdale came walking from behind the house. I was getting the food from the back seat and heard Louie introduce himself to Bruce.

"Nice car," I said, shaking his hand. The Ford really looked questionable and well used.

"Suits my role. Gets it done." He gestured toward the

rear of the house. "Come on in."

It was dark, but the house appeared to be a barn red with white trim. One level ranch style with a small deck on the front. We walked past Louie's car, went up two steps to another larger deck, entering through the back door.

I placed the two bags of Chinese food on a butcher block table in the center of a kitchen. Louie took the beer and put it the refrigerator. He looked into the plastic bag that held the cookies and pulled one out.

"Hanlon, you ever hear of chocolate chip? Maybe even a brownie with some nuts?" Louie said.

"Not good for you."

"You eat enough oatmeal for an entire family," was his reply. He put the cookie back in the bag. Bruce might be in for Ragsdale at his best.

"How long you been here?" I asked, looking around the kitchen and into dining area and living room.

"Since the first of October. I and two other guys rotate through." He retrieved three beers, opened them, handing one to Bruce, then one to me.

"You want a glass," he said to Bruce.

"Bottle's fine."

"I 'd like a glass," I said.

"Of course you would." He pointed to a cabinet above the sink. I got a glass and poured some beer.

From another cabinet Louie pulled out dinner plates, put them on the table next to the food, then went to a drawer where he got some flatware which he also placed on the table.

There were three cartons of food, two containers of rice, three fortune cookies, some small packages of sauce, napkins and packages of plastic utensils. Louie opened the cartons of food and the rice.

"So, whatta' we have here?" I said, picking up a large spoon and looking at the first carton.

"Stir-fried pork strips with ginger," Louie said, moving one of the cartons to the side. "Pepper and onion beef." He opened the last carton. "And spicy chicken."

"These all authentic Chinese?" I said. No reply.

Forty

Someone drawing cartoon characters might create a pair like John Dervil and Eddie Walker.

Dervil, barely 5'6' and weighing possibly 200 pounds, had the personality of a jolly individual, except that he was more devious than jolly.

Walker, a little over six feet, was thin and frail looking and anything but jolly. Always wearing jeans, some biker t-shirt and well-worn faux suede jacket, he looked as though he might be on his way to the emergency room for help.

In their time together as partners in 'what's next', Dervil had run the playbook. Now, with some extra cash and, at least according to Dervil, the promise of more money and a supply of 'good stuff', a little tension was bubbling up. Dervil didn't know what to make of it.

"Eddie, what's going on? You're acting a little strange. I do something to piss you off? Now you're not trusting me?" Dervil rattled off.

Walker didn't look right at him, but made the quick glance, averted his eyes and then rubbed the side of his face with his left hand.

"That dude scares the shit out of me," he finally said.

Dervil let the silence hang before responding.

"He's the kinda guy scares everyone. Just gotta get used to it," Dervil said with more than a dose of false bravado. Forced to admit it, he was also a little intimated by their new friend.

What neither of them really knew was that Arnie Branchik had made a real effort to improve his personality. Nearly a year away from New England – in Florida and Louisiana – with a change in his physical appearance and the cryptic new name, Arno was much less belligerent and almost monk-like in his demeanor.

It was wasted on Eddie Walker. He was still frightened of the man. Had he known some of Arno's real past, he might have fallen to the floor and curled into a fetal position.

But for the moment, Dervil had to convince Walker to deal with it. They had a meeting with the man in an hour. Helping with the nasty work in New Hampshire a week earlier, then heisting a practically brand new Airstream travel trailer and delivering it as instructed, Dervil was hoping for regular, lucrative employment. But more than that, he was hoping they might find a couple of party women sooner rather than later.

After tonight's meeting. He knew where. A place across the city open all night. He'd seen single women and women in pairs there before. Hear what Arno has on his mind, then go.

He wasn't sure of the impression Walker would make.

Carefully pulling the camouflage screen down to the ground to conceal the front end of the trailer, Arno slipped behind the wheel of his Pontiac.

Driving with parking lights only, he traveled the grassy road out of the woods for nearly 200 yards until it reached the blacktop. From there, headlights on and another 3 miles to the main highway at the Mass/NH border.

This trip would have him on the road for two days, three at the most. Quick stop in Lowell, then double back for a run up to Portland, ME and an afternoon stop in Portsmouth before coming back here.

One of the biggest changes Arno was adjusting to was more daytime activities. At first he thought it was bullshit. But the man he always thought of as Mr. Smooth – real name Robert Lazelle - had suggested that he could learn more by simply observing people and learning their daily routines.

"Watch. Listen. Think," is what Smooth told him. So, on all occasions now, everywhere he went, Arno worked on that advice. For the most part, it seemed to work. He was absorbing things he might have missed before.

But, there still was an occasional nighttime encounter. This would be one of them.

Forty One

A crowd of more than 300 students, faculty and citizens of the Durham area mingled with politicians, volunteers and political junkies.

Now the candidates were settling into chairs at the center of the room where they would informally take questions and offer brief observations of this week long tour of the Granite State.

There were two microphones on stands at opposite ends of the area where the candidates were seated. Members from the audience were to use these. There were two hand-held mics to be shared by the candidates. At the center was a podium with a mic clipped to it, where a middle-aged woman stood waiting for the crowd to get settled.

"Good evening," the woman said. "Thank you for coming out to meet our guests." She held both arms out acknowledging the candidates on either side of where she was standing. The audience applauded.

"My name is Katherine Hollandsworth. And I would like to take just a minute to explain how the rest of the evening will work. Or, at least how we hope it will work." A few laughs from the audience.

"If you have a question – and we hope that it will be a question, not just a statement of your views – please come to one of the microphones and wait to be recognized before you ask the question." She paused to let this sink in. Some people were not yet in their seats.

"We'll devote approximately an hour for questions from the audience. Then, each candidate will have two minutes at the end to offer comments." The woman looked in both directions at the candidates.

"I think we know all of these people," she said, again gesturing to the candidates. "But, I will give a very brief introduction and then we can start." Two people were already lining up at the microphone on her left.

At the back of the room, in addition to the 300+ audience, were probably two-dozen reporters and camera people. There were another half-dozen photographers moving around the room.

As Hollandsworh finished introducing the seven candidates in attendance, along with brief bios for each, she removed her reading glasses and looked back at the audience. Now there were people in line behind both microphones.

"Let's start over here," she said, pointing to her right. "I believe you were up first," she added, looking at a young man at the front of the line.

"Please introduce yourself," she added.

The man was tall, over six feet. He adjusted the stand

so he could speak into the mic.

"Yes. My name's Nicholas Ridder. I'm a senior at UNH and I have a question for Senator Shipp."

Shipp smiled and tapped the lavalier mic clipped to the lapel of his jacket. He nodded at the student.

"Senator, I suspect by now that you have seen, or heard about the YouTube video, of the woman you met yesterday up north."

Shipp was holding his smile, but he shifted in his chair. The man went on.

"One of the things she said was, that you are a 'false prophet' – referring to Congressman Boehner's term – and she also called you a 'demagogue of the worst kind'."

Shipp's smile now took on the strained expression of a grimace. The student asked his question.

"What's your response to her statements?"

Shipp twisted his neck like his collar might be too tight, tilted his face to the audience and lifted his chin slightly.

"She is entitled to her opinion, as well all know. But she's wrong on both charges against me," Shipp said.

The student, the moderator, and the audience waited for more. Shipp did not offer another word.

Forty Two

A veteran lawyer who'd seen his share of people who struggled with various forms of addiction, Chuck Wehner was not surprised by a phone call from a local minister.

The woman, pastor for a small Unitarian Universalist congregation in Laconia, was an active counselor with one of the 12-step recovery programs in the region. Her name was Agnes Walsh. And she was distraught over the death of Charles Reilly.

"He was such a refreshing voice for all of us," she said. "Every person in the group really responded to the example Charles was offering. I just can't believe that he's gone," she said. Wehner listened.

"The first time he came to one of our meetings, he was quiet and aloof. Almost arrogant. Not nervous, or reluctant to talk. He just seemed bemused by it all," she went on.

"Then, maybe a month ago, he was a different person. It was clear that he'd stopped drinking. I can usually tell. And the genuine warmth and kindness – and support – that he was showing to others, they responded."

"When you say that he was a 'refreshing voice', what do you mean by that?" Wehner asked, trying not to sound as though he was interrogating the minister.

"He just opened up. To everyone. Not in a 'here's my story, I'm a victim' sort of way. And certainly not in any preachy manner." Walsh paused, took a breath, then continued. "What occurred to me a couple weeks ago, watching Charles in the group, then later speaking with him alone, is that he was able to convey that he accepted things as they came and was prepared to move forward. You always hear someone saying, 'it is what it is.' That seems to be a buzz phrase these days. But Charles communicated that without saying the words. And he also made others feel that he was ready to help, if they were ready to act in their own behalf."

"You said that you spoke to him alone," Wehner said. "Do you recall anything about that conversation that," Wehner was searching for his next words, "anything give you an impression that he might be concerned for his own safety? Like he might be in a difficult situation?"

Now Walsh hesitated before answering the question. Then she laughed.

"No, nothing that made me think that. But he did say something that I just remembered. I thanked him for being so supportive of others in the group, especially when someone new attended. I told him that it really made a difference in their lives.

He looked at me and didn't say anything for a minute. Then, with just a hint of a smile, he said, 'I wish that were always true. Just one more life to change.' I waited, but he didn't say any more."

"And that was when?" Wehner asked.

"I think about three weeks ago. After foliage season was ending. A lot of part-time residents and tourists were gone. Our sessions had fewer people," she said.

"I'm not sure what you call it, but as I suspect you know, we refer to it as 'client privilege.' And I wouldn't ask you to identify to me who some of the others are in the group you've referred to," Wehner said. "But, if you're willing to speak with the state police, there's a chance that you might help them with their investigation."

Walsh didn't reply. So, as though he needed to score a point with a jury, Wehner added another comment.

"Just knowing that Charles participated with your group might give them a lead. I didn't know that he was going to meetings."

"Perhaps," Walsh said, not sounding convinced.

"There's a chance that they would eventually discover that Charles attended your meetings. Maybe from his mother, or, some close friend. But talking to you now could save time and might speed things along, if you're willing." He waited for a response.

"I'm sure you're right. How do I go about contacting them," Walsh said.

Warren Lapierre desperately hoped to stay out of jail.
After his second interview with the police, this one at state police headquarters a few miles from his home, the

probabilities were not promising.

Lapierre had offered names of people he knew who also knew Charles. He knew a couple of names of former lovers that Charles had disclosed to him. And he knew the name of a friend and fellow law school student whom Charles had said was just a close friend, not a lover.

One piece of information that he had not shared with the police was Charles being part of a 12-step program and going to meetings two or three times a week. The truth was that Lapierre was in denial about this. He was uncomfortable with the stigma, one that he attached to people who needed that kind of artificial support.

More recently, Lapierre suspected that much of Charles' behavior and attitude was directly fueled by being involved with a bunch of 'self-helpers'.

His real fear and what he had absolutely no way of verifying, was that Charles might have spouted off at those meetings about the same things he was demanding at home. Had he talked openly about 'disgusting and unethical behavior', or, 'sleazy politicians'? And who in the group knew about their relationship?

After all the years being around political campaigns, one of the lessons Lapierre always considered in deciding to help or not help particular candidates, was how well he thought a candidate understood timing.

Did they have self-discipline and patience, or, did they just react to whatever happened, perhaps grab on to the inexperienced advice of a loyal, enthusiastic – and often wrong - staffer? When to move on something, when to lie back.

The question of his own timing, Lapierre believed, had just moved a minute closer to either a complete reset or a very loud alarm.

Forty Three

"So, both of you guys being from Vermont," Bruce Lyndon said, "give me your honest opinion of how far Bernie Sanders is likely to get with this campaign. Where's it going to lead?"

Ragsdale looked at me, gave his trademark smirk, but waived his hand for me to respond. I wasn't going to give him the satisfaction.

"Nope. You're up, Louie." He waited, gave me a nod, then waded right in.

"First, neither of us are 'from Vermont.' I grew-up in Massachusetts, been here for 25 years now. And Radio Rick," he pointed at me, "is from the Commonwealth of Pennsylvania. Where is it, Slippery Rock, Rolling Rock?"

"Punxsutawney," I lied.

"But both of us have been here long enough to know a lot about Bernie. The first year I lived here he finally got elected to congress, 1990. What, he's been in the senate now since 2006?" he asked, looking at me.

"Yes. When Jim Jeffords retired. Bernie is now the longest-serving independent member of congress in history. Won re-election three years ago with more than 70% of the vote."

"You have Feel The Bern bumper stickers in your car?" Louie asked, again with the smirk. "But a couple things you should know," he went on, "One, he's not the same type of candidate as Howard Dean. No matter what happens in the primaries, I'm pretty sure that you will see Bernie giving a speech at the Democratic Convention in Philadelphia next July. And two, both Hanlon and I are likely to vote for him."

"That'll probably put him over the top," Bruce cracked. "What, you have a couple-hundred thousand votes in the general election?"

Calibrating first my surprise at Louie's comments, my response was auto pilot.

"Probably more than 300,000 next year and possibly a record turn-out because of Bernie. I think 2012 had a total around 290,000. Obama had more than two-thirds of that," I answered, then looked at Louie.

"You're really going to vote for him, without knowing whom the Republican nominee is going to be?" I said.

He nodded. "That doesn't mean I think he can win. Even if he gets the nomination, the system is rigged. Too many special interests scattered all around the country, both Democrats and Republicans. They'll do as much as they can to stop Bernie from becoming the next president. Way too much money in play." Now Louie was looking at Lyndon to see a response.

"You're probably right. Everything I've seen shows that

we're in for record campaign spending across the board. I mean we know that Sanders is raising more than people expected right now. But after the conventions, the really big bucks start to flow," Bruce said.

"What is the definition of obscene?" Louie asked. It didn't sound like a rhetorical question. He looked at me, then at Bruce, anticipating that one of us would go for it.

"Disgusting. Morally unacceptable," I offered.

"Offensive. Repugnant," was Bruce's answer.

"Well, my mother said the money in politics was 'obscene' 30 years ago. If she were alive today, she'd probably lie right down in front of one of those campaign buses."

Bruce shook his head, but the appearance was that he agreed with the observation.

"This is the mother who introduced you to good music?" I said.

"One in the same. It's still rock and roll to me."

"Billy Joel?"

"May, 1980. His first # 1."

Lyndon gave us a look of puzzlement. Maybe he was not a pop music guy.

For nearly two hours we'd been yakking politics, reporting and just a snippet of anti-drug efforts in New England – Ragsdale, not surprisingly, was not eager to offer much – and it was time to head back. Bruce wanted to be in Hanover by 8:30 in the morning for his session with the old Dartmouth prof.

"So, you said you get some time off this weekend. When do you head back home?" I said to Louie.

"Probably not getting out of here much before 3 or 3:30 tomorrow."

"A few of us from the old days are getting together at for a pint late tomorrow. Before some of them hustle over to Dartmouth for the evening. You should stop by on your way through," I said.

"Yeah. There's one guy who's been covering New Hampshire primaries for nearly 50 years," Bruce added. "We're gonna' give him a toast. I think you would find his observations of Senator Sanders," Bruce paused, looked at me, then finished "enlightening."

"Eliot is nothing if not enlightening," I agreed.

Forty Four

Arno considered keeping a chart. Aside from who was good for what, how frequently they made a buy, which customers led to more customers, what he really wanted to do was to get a grasp of who was the dumbest.

Driving into Lowell, he thought that maybe he could figure out a point system that would allow him to rank average dumb, really dumb, truly and unbelievably dumb, and this fucking person should be shot.

That was the thing he missed, just fucking shooting some stupid loser. Random murder.

Arno still had in his wallet a photo and description of himself from the FBI Most Wanted website. A year earlier, after a very bloody week in Maine and northern New Hampshire, he was featured on the website as the 'Case of The Week'. For months later he remained on the 10 Most Wanted List, along with terrorists and child molesters.

The printout, given to him by Mr. Smooth, featured his old prison photo over the name of Arnost Waclaw Branchik. Shaved head, the neck tattoo and a steely "fuck you" gaze directly at the camera.

That was then, this is now. He had changed.

As far as these two assholes in Lowell, so far they proved to be handy for a couple things, most recently heisting the trailer and getting it to the isolated spot in the woods just across the NH border.

But he was doubtful the pair would prove to be a good connection to others who needed product. That was Arno's primary reason for returning to New England in the first place. Rake in the cash. Someday soon, Mexico. Maybe one of those islands people talk about. Smooth had to know somebody, somewhere. Make it happen.

He got off the highway, took a longer route on a familiar back street that brought him around to the block where the bar was located. He parked about 150 feet from the entrance, looked at his watch and got out of the car.

Walking to the bar he was pretty clear on what he needed to do with his newest associates. Like any other job, boys. You come through or you don't stay.

Arno would give them a week. Maybe.

Forty Five

The "Meet the Next President" gathering at UNH was, on any reasonable scale, a pretty tame event.

After the opening question to Senator Shipp, most of the questions covered issues or topics already addressed by the candidates at previous forums or campaign rallies. There was one amusing point toward the end of the formal question period when an elderly woman came to the microphone. The moderator asked her to state her name and ask her question.

"Jane Pitkin from River Woods. My question is for you, Miss Hollandsworth," the woman said.

Slightly stooped in posture, white hair, understated tweed jacket, corduroy slacks, she could have been 70 or 90, hard to tell by her face. She was spry and quick to her question. Before the moderator could acknowledge her, the woman was already into it.

"What I would really like to know is... are there more scoundrels running for president these days, or is just that many of them are here tonight?"

The crowd gave her a mixed reaction of laughs, some applause and a few boos. The moderator had the good sense to let it play out before adjourning the public comment portion of the evening.

After 20 minutes or so of mingling with the crowd, all of the candidates and their handlers exited the hall. The schedule for the next day would have them on the buses at 8:30 with several stops between Durham and Hanover.

It was either too late in the week or too early in the morning for Bob Horner, senior staff member and interim campaign chief for Senator Tad Shipp.

Shipp's original campaign manager had bolted after just two months on the job. That was back in the summer and Horner was doing double-duty which simply added more stress. He was ready to bolt.   Not a quitter, and despite the pleadings of his wife, Horner kept telling himself that he could stick it out through the New Hampshire Primary. That was another 95 days.

Regardless of the outcome, he secretly believed Shipp would be extremely fortunate to place third. Horner was determined that he would resign the morning after the vote. He could not tolerate the five months between New Hampshire and the party convention in Cleveland in the middle of July.   For the moment, he would suck it up and get on the bus. He was relieved that Shipp would be riding with others in a private vehicle for the first leg of the trip.

Coming through the traffic circle in Epsom, then into the parking lot of a small strip mall, the three buses were greeted by not very many supporters.

The second Saturday of November, most people were headed to high school football games, crafts fairs, or other outdoor activities that allowed them to enjoy the last of the fall weather. Even with gray skies, it was still way too early to raise the white flag for the winter ahead.

Size of the crowd didn't matter. The candidates, the volunteers, the reporters all dutifully got off the buses, immediately tripling the number of people walking around. And the retailers were happy to see shoppers, period. They didn't care which candidates you liked or didn't like.

It took less than 10 minutes for it to become clear that this stop would be brief, as in "back on the bus" ASAP. On to Concord, two quick stops in Franklin and New London, with a scheduled arrival in Hanover at 4 o'clock. Everyone would get a short break before the evening event at Dartmouth.

When the buses arrived in Concord, they were greeted by a somewhat larger and more enthusiastic crowd. After all, this is the state capitol, and there were more than a few people in town who knew how to get out the voters. In addition to the three buses, several SUVs and other cars carrying both candidates and some elected state officials, arrived in time to goose the numbers and take advantage of any photo ops. The bonus, as far as Bob Horner was concerned, was that the temperature was above 40 and the sun had actually peeked through the clouds.

"Thank you, Lord," he mumbled to himself getting off the bus.

Forty Six

Lapierre packed two large rolling duffels. With the seat folded down, both would fit in the rear of his Buick Encore.

Two large plastic bags of shredded paper sat near the door of his office. They would go in the front and he would take them to recycling on his way through town. The laptop was already in a case on the front seat of the car. One last look around. Nothing that caused him real concern. After all, there was a chance that he would be back here. Maybe two weeks, maybe a month.

He'd spent much of his time thinking of his story while he shredded files. It was plausible.

If he had further contact with the state police, and he was certain that he would, he would simply explain that he was going to try to pay a visit to Charles Reilly's mother in Philadelphia. They'd never met and he wanted to share with her how important Charles had been in his life and what a horrible tragedy that he'd been a victim to some senseless murder.

Lapierre had also worked out in his mind that regardless of what police found in interviewing former acquaintances, including partners or lovers that Charles had in his previous life, that he would convey to Mrs. Reilly his suspicion that someone from the past might be involved in all this.

Of course, Lapierre didn't kid himself that he would actually meet Margaret Reilly. Just in case, he would polish his story. It was a seven hour drive if he took the New Jersey Turnpike route. Weekend traffic could slow that down. In any event, he would have plenty of time to work through his lines. And his emotions, real and fake.

NH Attorney General Kelly Alexakis looked at the three men gathered in her office. It was an unusual Saturday morning meeting.

Each of the men was at least 10 years her senior, each had lengthy service records in law enforcement. And she was pretty certain that each had their own level of skepticism about her appointment to this office.

Representing the state police were Sergeant Robert Condon and his boss, Colonel Richard L. Quincy. As both the state's chief legal officer and law enforcement officer, Alexakis was their boss. The other man in attendance was Meredith Police Chief Ken Storrow.

Quincy was the real veteran in the group. He'd been around for more than 35 years and had been the head of the state police for the past 10. Short notice meetings with the AG were not new to him. He was not a stranger to the mix of outside influences with standard operating procedure when it came to the investigation of major crimes in the state.

"Colonel, bring me up to date with the Reilly case," Alexakis began.

Quincy looked at Condon before answering. Storrow also had his eyes on Condon.

"Sgt. Condon will fill in what we're doing here. But we're also working with state police in Pennsylvania, where, as you know, the victim had family and friends. Also in Vermont, where he was in law school before moving to Meredith."

"Any reports back from them yet?" Alexakis said.

"Pennsylvania's talked with the mother. We just learned the names of some acquaintances there and have passed them along. I expect something as soon as they make contact with those individuals."

"And Vermont?"

"The same. We have more names and the contact, as far as we can tell, is more recent. We have reason to believe that Mr. Reilly made occasional trips back to central Vermont over the past year."

Alexakis turned her attention to Condon.

"Sergeant. New developments here?" she said.

"Not developments, per se. But new information," Condon said. "We've learned that Mr. Reilly was a regular participant in meetings of a 12-step program in Laconia."

No response from the AG, so Condon went on.

"The main counselor for the group is a bit reluctant to share details, but she understands the gravity of the investigation. Apparently she had a high regard for Mr. Reilly. She made the initial contact with Reilly's boss when she learned of his death. He persuaded her to call us."

"I think that we might be able to get us some assistance there," Quincy offered.

Forty Seven

Shortly after dropping Bruce at his hotel in Hanover, I made the short drive back home to Quechee, stopping at the post office on the way though the village.

The clouds were breaking up and there was enough sun to offer hope for the weekend. The views of the hills behind my house gave a different view than just a week ago. Then we had still had remnants of leaves mixed with the evergreens. The wind and rain had dealt with that tableau. Now it was splotches of yellow tamaracks, mixed evergreens in some spots and an awful lot of brown.

At the top of my list was a phone call to Bonnie. I'd avoided it for a few days and did not expect hoots and cheers when we connected. The little road trip and all the conversations focused on politics and other matters allowed me to delay what might be inevitable.

The call went to her voicemail. I gave it my best, most concise offering.

"Bonnie Althea Mackin. This is Michael Perry Casey Hanlon. Hope that you are well. Happy to be back. Please let me hear from you."

While it amused me, I was pretty sure that at best, I

would get a some grief about the message. And the 'not so best' would be no return call. Life is like a pinball machine. Nothing more than ricocheting off circumstances. Who gave me that piece of wisdom?

And while I had avoided calling Bonnie for several days, I had not forgotten my conversation with Virginia Jackson and our talk about having dinner on Sunday night.

Of course, Virginia had made an effort to round up some information on the guy who drowned now that we thought suspicious and not an accident. Even though this was interesting news, it was news that I had not shared with Bonnie. She was there on Saturday night.

Nice guy, Hanlon. Maybe you should call your former wife and see how she feels about you these days. It was getting to a point that when I had these self-exploration thoughts and heard the voices, I could pretty much nail Ragsdale's inflection and blame it on him.

Spooky. My phone buzzed with a text from Louie.

"Forgot that Becky, sister and some other women hunkered down big quilt show. Where is the keg party?"

Before he began his current gig as an undercover whiz, Louie worked with a couple of different municipal police departments and knew something about real keg parties. Old reporters having a pint or two would simply reinforce his view of knee-jerk liberals in the media.

'Jasper Murdock Ale House. See if you can find it,' was the message I sent back.

I put my phone down on the counter and began

scanning through three days of newspapers. Not 10 minutes later, my phone buzzed again.

'The Norwich Inn. Exit 13 off I-91. What time?'

Jesus. The guy simply doesn't miss a trick.

'5:30. Do I need to alert anyone?'

'Only for your own safety, hotshot. I will be there.'

Bruce Lyndon waited for the arrival of the last person he planned to interview on this trip, a retired Dartmouth College Classics Professor.

It was during the previous election cycle that Lyndon first met the man. Long time scholar, popular teacher and well-versed in academic minutia, the man was surprisingly new to the world of politics. This seemed even more peculiar to Lyndon when he considered that the man had spent his entire teaching career in a town that was a required stop for all serious presidential aspirants.

One thing that appealed to Lyndon the most about the prof was how widely read the man was. Not a surprise for an academic, for sure. But the eclectic nature of what he read in relation to world affairs and, in particular, politics in the United States, seemed unusual. At least for a classics professor.

On the other hand, Lyndon never heard the man once mention television.

Forty Eight

Dervil wasn't sure why he was there alone. All he knew was that when Arno left them at the bar last night, he very emphatically told Dervil that this was a solo assignment.

"Get there early, before noon. Leave your car by the road. Stay behind the trailer. You can leave at dark." That was it.

Saying that he needed a little help, Arno told him that he wanted to be sure that nobody was poking around, or that no hikers stumbled across his little hideaway.

On top of that, he was fucking certain that he was not about to let anyone else know where the trailer was.

"Since you made the delivery, Devil Man, you get the honor," he told him.

This was not the first time someone played with his name. First grade, he thought. Walking along the leafy, narrow road – barely wide enough for a vehicle to get through – he remembered the little girl.

"Are you the devil, Johnny?" she chided him.

Couldn't remember her name. Thought he could still see her face. Verna? Valerie? Vauda? What was her name?

Robert Lazelle was borderline sadistic in the way he manipulated Branchik.

When they first met a year ago, Lazelle assumed the role of a guy looking for a regular supply of drugs, any drugs. He claimed that he could help with distribution.

It was a fishing expedition and it worked. A week later, Branchik was seated across from Lazelle in his spacious condominium in downtown Portland. That was the beginning of pulling the strings.

After Branchik had done some really nasty things up north, he managed to elude police all the way through western Maine and New Hampshire, then wound up hastily seeking work with Lazelle and his partner, Richard Marco. As they had been looking for the right person to run their illicit operation in northern New England, it came as no surprise that Branchik was at least smart enough to figure that out and come back to them.

Of course, within hours of Branchik wreaking havoc in the wilderness, Lazelle knew exactly whom the feds and state police were chasing. Once Branchik contacted him for another meeting, it was simply a matter of which string to pull first.

Now, here they were on a sunny Saturday afternoon, in the same condo almost exactly a year later, and Lazelle was listening to Branchik talk about the operation. The two-hundred-grand that Branchik brought along made the conversation move right along.

"And you're OK with the two new recruits down in

Lowell?" Lazelle asked.

"For now. One of them is pretty quick. He's a slob, but smart enough. Not so sure about his buddy." Lazelle raised his eyebrows at this.

"I don't think they're a risk with the cops. Just have the feeling the partner might've not had a lot growing up. Seems fucking petrified every time I see him." Branchik continued. "You know. Like someone's gonna steal his lunch." Branchik laughed at his own observation.

Lazelle nodded and gave the judge's smile. "How about you? Everything working the way we planned, no problems that we need to know about?" Lazelle asked.

Branchik was not about to let on that, yes, for the time being, everything is working as 'we discussed.' But, in six months, fellas, I'm outa here.

"Right on the mark," Branchik said, then added, "You can fucking tell the economy's is better. Some people have upped their weekly buy."

"That's good. Richard will be happy to know things are looking up," Lazelle replied. And what Lazelle did not say was that he and Richard Marco had concluded that their original concern was also on the mark; Branchik was stealing from them.

Back to the age old question. Which comes first, greed or stupidity?

Forty Nine

The three bus Candidates Caravan - nearly bumper to bumper at 60 MPH, was lined up like a fleet of tour buses having just dropped all passengers. They rolled off the interstate in Lebanon and turned north toward Hanover.

Right on schedule, the buses would deliver the candidates, staff and campaign volunteers, and a pack of reporters to the Dartmouth College campus.

"Not soon enough," might have been the reply in unison from the drivers. But nobody asked.

It would be dark in just over an hour and it was still three hours until the evening finale, to be held in the college's Hopkins Center. The event was free and all tickets had been taken two weeks in advance. On the streets in front and behind the hall were five satellite trucks ready to stream a broadcast to all parts of the country. It might not get the audience numbers of college football, but it was sure to please political junkies unable to be there.

A long touchdown pass away, or a two minute brisk walk to Dartmouth's recently renovated Memorial Field, the Big Green football team was beating Yale 35- 3. Back in

Durham, UNH beat Central Connecticut State 57-14.

A blocked punt away, inside the hotel, Senator Tad Shipp was right on the verge of losing it completely. In what made other candidates and campaign professionals shake their heads in disbelief, Shipp publicly humiliated a staff aide for forgetting to have a camera ready to take a photo with a supporter. Never mind that there were possibly 20 smart phones around with cameras. Shipp yelled at the young woman nonetheless. She was in tears.

"Pay attention," he shouted. "That's your job. Take the photos and upload them to the website. That's how we get donations."

Annie Gray, a 20 year-old college student, had taken a semester off to work with Shipp's team. She was not particularly excited about Shipp's candidacy, but wanted to have the experience of working on a campaign. That she came from a prominent, active political family in Texas was another factor in her enthusiasm.

The supporter, a man wearing both a Shipp for US hat and sweat shirt, wasn't sure what to make of the incident. His wife got a photo anyway.

Across the street from the buses a mixed crowd of supporters and protestors waved signs and shouted. The different media camera people were capturing images very similar to most campaign stops. The major difference being that this stop included several competing candidates in the same location at the same time.

After a week travelling around the state in this first ever group campaign adventure, some candidates were giving the impression they thought it was a success, while at least three candidates, most notably Tad Shipp, gave off the vibe that they were not comfortable with the shared spotlight.

There would be approximately 1,000 people inside the auditorium in a couple hours. It was uncertain that the evening ahead would change the views of candidates about "let's be sure to do this again next time."

Of course, for some of the candidates, after New Hampshire, it was unlikely there would be a 'next time' running for President. But it was a real possibility that a couple in this crowd would run again numerous times in the future. Going back to 1952, in 16 previous Presidential primaries in the Granite State, the election was perceived as a first real test of a candidate's ability to garner votes and move to 1600 Pennsylvania Avenue a year later.

For more than 60 years, millions and millions and millions of dollars have been spent on lengthy campaigns. Whether that is good or bad for democracy is debatable. The chances of it being openly discussed by any of the candidates? Perhaps someone in the media pool will chase down that question before the next primary in four years.

Fifty

Margaret Reilly and Blair Watson sat alone in her study. Outside it was cold, dreary and starting to get dark. A slow, steady drizzle had started before the service for Charles. Now, three hours later, the rain only underscored the bleakness of the day. Margaret asked her maid to bring a pot of tea. "We should go out for something to eat," Watson said softly. Sitting on the edge of a 250 year-old, Louis XV upholstered chair, he rubbed his hands nervously back and forth over his knees.

She shook her head and gave a weak smile. "I can't eat, Blair. Not right now. But Leona can fix something for you, if you like."

"I'm not all that hungry myself. Just might be better if we went out." He looked around at the bookshelves, the antique lamps, the art and the photos in the room. "You will have plenty of time to sit here in the days ahead," he added. As soon as the words left his mouth he regretted the obviousness of his statement.

"No. Let's just visit for a spell. Do you mind?"

Dervil was ready to pack it in. Arno had told him, "you can leave before dark."

Nearly five hours schlepping around up here in the woods and trying not to freeze his ass off, he'd been here long enough. He started back to his car parked nearly 200 yards away from the trailer.

Keeping his eyes to the ground as he walked and thinking that the Airstream was actually pretty cool, he was startled to see the headlights of a car moving slowly in his direction. He froze. Dervil saw that the front of the car was black and mounted with a push bumper. The white roof had a light bar across it. The synapse and the neurons worked properly. Dervil instinctively turned to run back to the woods and the camouflaged trailer.

He heard car doors opening.

"Stop. Police. Put your hands in the air," the male voice shouted. "Do not take another step."

Dervil only thought about another step. But now the neurons were flooding his brain with signals to do exactly what the voice told him to do. Simultaneously, perhaps on an adjacent synapse, a flash of news stories about people being shot by local police played out in living color.

He stopped and raised his hands.

"Keep your hands in the air. Turn around very slowly."

Dervil did as instructed. What he saw was, in fact, a man in a police uniform with a gun aimed at him. From the driver's side of the car, a second policeman was aiming a gun at him.

Standing with his hands raised, watching the policeman on his left approaching, Dervil could see into the back seat of the of the squad car. There was another passenger, the silhouette of a smaller person.

Fifty One

By the time I arrived at The Norwich Inn, the pub was nearly full. All but one table was occupied and there were no empty seats at the bar.

Ragsdale was one of the people at the bar. He had a pint of beer in front of him and was looking up at the TV behind the bar. I stepped behind him and tapped his right shoulder. He turned around more slowly than one might expect. I decided that it was a professional tactic.

"That your group in the corner?" he asked, tilting his head to the left. I looked at a noisy group of several guys at the far end of the room.

"Nope. I think we might be in the library," I said.

"One of those guys is wearing the full Orvis. I figured he was friend of yours."

I looked again at the group in the corner. One guy – wearing a brown tweed vest over a Donegal sweater and corduroy slacks with leather trim – just might be the best dressed man in the place.

"Nah. I imagine they're Tuck School alums."

The bartender looked at me and gestured with his hand. I turned to study the list of microbrews on the chalk board behind the bar.

"Whistling Pig," I said.

"Pint?" the bartender asked.

"Yes, please."

It was really pretty noisy. But it was a football weekend and a good crowd here, both in the pub and the main dining room.

"Let me see if Bruce and the others are out front." I walked through the lobby and sure enough, the room the Inn called it's library was crowded with several people I recognized, including Bruce Lyndon, and others I didn't know.

When I walked in, the senior reporter they were toasting was telling a story about meeting Jimmy Carter outside a shoe store in Keene 40 years earlier. Bruce spotted me, waived and started in my direction.

"They're about to head to Hanover," he said, nodding back at the crowd behind him.

I looked at my watch; twenty of six.

"D'you get an early start?" I said.

"No, I just arrived a few minutes ago. But those who have seats in the auditorium need to be inside an hour before it starts."

"Aren't you going?"

"I decided to give my seat to a young AP reporter down from Montpelier. I've seen enough of these. We can watch the closed circuit feed in the press room. That all right with you?"

"Fine. Let me get Louie. He's back in the bar," I said.

"You think he wants to go watch, too?"

"Not a chance. He's pretty careful about where he goes and who he hangs out with."

"Right," Bruce said.

"I'm a little surprised he's even going to have a drink with us."

Bruce pointed at some empty chairs and a sofa in the living room across from the library. I nodded and went off to get Ragsdale.

I paid for the beer and we went to join Bruce. There were a few others in the living room, including two or three who might also be reporters. They were not part of the group in the library toasting Eliot Page.

Louie put his beer down and sat in one of the chairs. I sat in the other. Bruce settled into the sofa. Music from the overhead speakers was more noticeable in this room. I chalked it up to the TV and all the talk in the bar.

"How was your visit with the Dartmouth professor?" Louie asked Bruce. "Any prediction on who he thinks will win in February?"

"Interesting guy. Far as I can tell, he's one of those progressives you were grumbling about."

"Really?" Louie said. "Hard to imagine."

"Seems to have more of a global perspective than you might hear from, uh, a run of the mill liberal."

"Did you get the sense that he was a Bernie supporter?" I asked. "Hard to find a candidate more progressive then he is. At least the ones getting any regular media attention." Louie gave me his smirk.

"Hanlon. Bernie's a socialist. If he gets very far, you can bet they'll hammer the hell out of that label in the advertising against him. A progressive will seem like Newt Gingrich," Louie said.

"But to your question," Bruce said, "No, the professor didn't offer a prediction on who would win in New Hampshire."

"How about Shipp? He's blasting the airwaves with commercials. Is anybody picking him?" I said.

"You're kidding, right?" Lyndon said. "After the New Hampshire Primary, that guy doesn't have a prayer." He took another drink of beer.

"Eh-h-h, I wouldn't be so fast on that," I replied. "A lot of people out there are really pissed off."

"Sure. But will they vote? *That's* the question."

He held his bottle out to me for a toast, then added, "Don't count on it. I've already seen this movie a couple times."

We clinked his bottle and my glass. I watched the three reporters across the room, all in a trance with their laptops.

"Shipp may not get the votes, but that doesn't mean he will fade away, " Louie observed.

"Oh, he's pretty effective at getting attention. He'll stick around," Bruce agreed.

The music on the speakers was distracting me. I often

have a problem being drawn to background music that's too loud. And ever since I met Ragsdale, if it was anything recorded in the last 50 years, I felt he would quiz me.

I pointed at the speaker. Louie nodded.

"That was a big hit. Who is it?," I said. He gave me the smirk and tapped his right temple.

"Five bucks or another pint," he replied. I listened for maybe 10 seconds, then shrugged.

"Let's make it easy. I'll give you a hint," Louie said. "Sting co-wrote this song and is a back-up vocalist. It was their biggest hit. Summer of '85."

I wracked my brain. Where in the hell was I the summer of 1985? It came to me. It took a minute to run some songs through my head. Guitar riff on the speakers.

Ragsdale was smiling, Bruce was watching our little game without comment.

"British group, yes?" I said.

"Duh," Louie replied. I held my right hand out to him.

"Give me the money," I said.

"Give me the answer," he retorted.

The song was *Money For Nothing*. I was pretty sure I had it.

"Dire Straits," I offered.

Louie gave me a look of mock surprise.

Fifty Two

Warren Lapierre was heading south on I-93. There was more traffic than he'd anticipated.

Crossing the Merrimack River and approaching I-495, he decided to take the longer route southwest around all the suburban communities that circled Boston. He would pick-up the Mass Pike and head west to New York, then south again toward Pennsylvania.

Lapierre had absolutely no intention of contacting Charles Reilly's family. He knew about the mother but was uncertain of other relatives and really didn't care. He would simply use this trip away from New Hampshire as a cover until he knew where the investigation was headed.

He couldn't see himself staying away for an extended period. Over the years, he'd travelled some, had attended a couple of national conventions, went to Europe once for a month. He was always eager to get back home.

One thing even more certain; he couldn't see himself in prison. That frightened him as much as anything.

The traffic was moving along. His dashboard clock showed 5:50PM. He calculated three hours to the New York border, Albany, then pick up I-87.

There was now a NH state police car at the scene with two troopers, along with two patrolmen from the Pelham Police Department, the same two who had frisked John Dervil, checked his ID and hauled him in for questioning.

The story coming together was that the local cops, acting on the tip of a 13-year-old boy, had driven out to the remote spot off a back road and discovered the Airstream trailer.

The teenager found the trailer earlier when he was out bow hunting for deer. He told the cops that he'd noticed the flash of metal through the brush and thought it might be the old wreckage from an airplane.

When they had gone to the site with the kid as their guide, Dervil had been coming out of the woods from the trailer. His own car had been parked at the road.

The state police would also be interested in having a little talk with Dervil, now in custody back at the Pelham station. There were no plates on the trailer, but there was a manufacturer's identification number that would help police track it. The trailer looked brand new.

One of the Pelham patrolmen, an Army veteran who had served in Iraq, walked around the site where the trailer was backed into the woods. He was impressed with how much effort had gone into hiding the trailer, particularly the eight foot wide camouflage screen complete with leaves, twigs and grass. The screen was mounted on two trees and rolled down like a large window shade.

Branchik, Arno – what's in a name? Lazelle didn't say this to the thug, but it was something that amused both him and Richard Marco.

After getting Branchik into place a few months earlier, Marco was the one who had inspired him to find a different name. Even if he were successful at ducking the FBI and the police, dealing with those he used to distribute the smaller quantities of drugs would require a new name.

What amused Lazelle and Marco was that Arno took on a persona with the new name. That surprised them.

They had no doubt that he was still a cold, ruthless and vicious psychopath. But he wore the name as much as he wore the change in wardrobe, the change in physical appearance, the superficial change in manner and speech.

"Arno, bad guy being cool," Lazelle once quipped to Marco. "If it works for him, who are we to judge?" And so far, it seemed to be working pretty well.

Arno left Portland and Lazelle behind. He would do what he needed to do, more effectively and profitably than anyone else could and he would not think twice about asking for help.

The new name was also a boost to his self-confidence.

Arno liked what he was doing. He very clearly saw himself not working for others.

Six months, new game.

Fifty Three

Sergeant Condon decided it was time to put some surveillance on Warren Lapierre. He had only just arrived at this decision with a little nudge from his boss.

"There's something else going on here," Colonel Richard Quincy had told him. "Focus on Lapierre. You said yourself that he didn't sound solid."

"No discrepancies in his story, just something about the way he tells it," Condon replied. "Like he's trying to convince himself."

"Keep me informed. Anything you learn, any new names, I want to know as soon as you know," Quincy said.

"Colonel, the 'something else'. You're not referring to the gay partner relationship," Condon said.

"No. The AG is leaning on this one. She's not playing the publicity angle, although that's a little bit harder to determine these days."

Condon didn't reply with his thought and assumption that all politicians, appointed or elected, weave a little public relations into everything they say or do. It was just the new norm. He did it, most of his seasoned officers did it. School teachers and healthcare professionals did it. Use words and information that are more palatable for those on the receiving end.

"I agree," Condon said. "A year in the job, she's completely professional."

"Which doesn't necessarily preclude that she has, let's call it, 'higher aspirations," Quincy replied.

"I'll get it started. A trooper will go out first," Condon added, "I may have to coordinate with Moultonborough PD and some deputy sheriffs."

"Watch him for a few days. Everywhere he goes, who he sees. And let me know anything coming back from the Vermont State police or the guys in Philly."

The average citizen almost anywhere in the US is used to seeing the state police or highway patrolmen in uniform.

Someone knocks on your door wearing a suede jacket over a shirt, tie and casual slacks, and then shows you a badge and informs you that he is a state police detective, the average citizen may have – in a rural state, anyway – a brief delay in processing the information.

That was the case when Detective Sgt. Jim Logan stood at the front door of Joseph Gessler in Tunbridge, Vermont. "I would like to ask you a few questions about a former student," Logan said.

Gessler got it immediately. He'd heard the news of Charles Reilly's death a few days earlier and instantly connected it with the policeman in front of him.

"Come in," Gessler said, standing aside to allow entrance to the hall way of his carefully restored 19th century farm house.

Just as quickly, Gessler connected the probability that the police had some inkling of his close friendship with Reilly when he had lived in Vermont.

375 miles south in Pennsylvania, a detective with the Philadelphia Police Department was getting little traction with calls to people who knew Charles Reilly.

Considering the caseload just in the 19th district, Lieutenant John Hinkle didn't have a lot of spare time to chase out of state queries. Three actual phone interviews and two voicemail messages was all that he could justify for the moment. There might be more time available on Monday.

Fifty Four

After two-and-a-half hours watching and listening to the presidential candidates interact with the audience, Bruce Lyndon looked at his notes.

Mostly quotations with a candidate's initials noted next to them, the seven pages of scribbling that would be difficult for others to read represented the last chunk of information Lyndon needed to write his essay on New Hampshire 2016. Unlike most of his younger colleagues, Lyndon still used a note pad in combination with his laptop. It was easier to do in a setting like this where he could type a draft narrative while listening and occasionally looking at the big screen monitor.

When he heard something he thought was interesting or potentially useful to his theme, he made note of it. But the backbone and structure of the story would remain the views expressed by non-politicians.

With still nearly three months until the first primary and a year until the election, he knew other events could change it all. But he was sticking with his working title for the piece, *Is The System Really Broken?*

I left Bruce in the media room set up inside The Hopkins Center. One hour watching and my interest was fading.

Ragsdale said that he would stick around, so via text messages we agreed to have dinner. I suggested a small café in Hanover but wasn't sure that we could get it in. Big crowd in town and it was twenty of nine. Maybe.

A two minute walk from the auditorium, Tapas Candela Lounge, as expected, was crowded. But a couple was vacating counter seats near a window and the host said he could seat me there. I said my friend would be arriving in just a few minutes.

When Louie came in, it struck me that he could play a number of roles, undercover or not. His ponytail was just long enough to be cool, but not down his back like a 1990s country singer. European style black leather jacket, charcoal tee shirt under a navy v-neck sweater, gray slacks and casual black shoes, this guy could fool a lot of people. And if he dyed his hair black and really went for the artsy look, who knew?

Chinos and hiking boots were making me feel like a bumpkin. Everyone in the place was better dressed than I. Possibly the only piece of my attire that could be considered fashionable was the burgundy linen shirt.

"This one of your regular spots?" Louie asked, rolling his eyes and giving the smirk.

"Yeah, I try to come here at least once a week," I lied.

He did the not-so-obvious, slow glance around, trying

to take in the crowd, probably 40 patrons in all.

"I've only been once before," I said. "Good selection of wine they serve in flights. And I had a great short rib with pineapple risotto."

"The Scooter," Louie said. "Old broadcaster. And he was a great Yankees shortstop."

"Rizzuto. Did he make it to the Hall of Fame?"

"Yes," he said, while looking at the menu card. A young woman in a white shirt and black slacks, and a small gold ring in her left nostril, came to take our order. She introduced herself as Megan.

Louie actually smiled at her and cocked his head toward me.

"He says that your wines are good," and looking back at the card he asked her, "Would you have white or red?".

"Are you going to have some food?" she said.

"Yes," I said before he could respond. She smiled and looked at me.

"Let me tell you our specials for this evening, then you can decide on the wine."

Megan proceeded to list the specials. Louie went for Churrasco with plantains and I ordered Sweet Potato Gnocchi with Vermont sausage. And we ordered both a flight of 3 small glasses of the red and 3 of the white.

When the wine came, we sniffed and sipped and I pretended I knew the difference. After tasting the second red, a Tempranilla, Louie asked Megan for a regular glass of that wine with his dinner.

"Anything exciting at the candidates forum?" Louie said, turning back to me. "One of those bright and shining stars look good enough to be the next president?"

"Hard to say. I sort of like the former governor from Ohio."

"Be sure you call me when you actually cast a vote for a Republican," Louie responded. "But was there anything you heard that would get you off the fence and go back to reporting?" He waited for my reply. I shook my head.

"That's it? Doesn't seem very convincing."

"Nah. It's all changing. What Bruce is doing, and he's a print guy, is actually spending some time trying to piece together a really informative story. You can't do that in radio anymore," I said. "Maybe on public radio, or some FM alternative station in a big city. Podcasts? I don't know."

"Why do the stories have to be informative? Especially about politicians. You think people will listen?"

I wasn't sure which of his the questions was serious and how much of it was predictable smartass.

"I think you're generalizing again," I said.

"Right. And being completely unfair to the 'elected class."

"Your comment last night when we were talking with Bruce. You really do believe the entire political system is rigged?"

He stared at me before responding. "Yes, at the national level. Let me spell it out for you." He proceeded to slowly spell and enunciate each letter:

"S-U-P-E-R. P-A-C-S."

"There was an article in the New York Times that claimed 158 families are donating more than half of the early money in this election cycle," I said. "It had this graphic showing a pyramid of Monopoly pieces with just a few red ones on top."

"R-I-G-G-E-D. Thank you Citizens United." He shook his head.

We drank some more wine, scoped out the others in the café and waited for our dinner. I wasn't sure if Louie could take much more of the political talk, so I laid off.

Megan arrived with our food. Maybe I could get him going on 'best places to eat' from his undercover tour?

Bonnie Mackin knew the relationship was in trouble. She had not returned his phone call, had not felt any urge to be with him this weekend, and was not at all sure where things were heading.

If anything, she was now more uncertain than only a few days earlier when she set the January 1st deadline to evaluate what the future held with Michael Hanlon. Aside from the overall casualness of his attitude toward their relationship and his ambivalence about having children, there was a new development; an old boyfriend had returned and rekindled her interest in him.

Billy Carlock was a year older. He'd been in her sister's class in high school and Bonnie had gone out with him numerous times during college and shortly after she came back to Vermont. Then he had left for California for a couple of years, but was now back for the winter, he said.

They had had some beers and some laughs. He looked great. Coming from a large family, Billy had a brother and four sisters, they all got along great. Bonnie surmised that Billy was OK with having children, if it ever got that far.

She would not just ignore Michael. There had to be a way to resolve this without being thoughtless. She was not a selfish person.

Fifty Five

The Pelham Police were skeptical of Dervil's story that he was out for a walk in the woods and returning to his car when they came across him.

His weak explanation for running was that he was nearly finished with a two year parole and panicked when he saw the squad car. They were checking that story.

"And you didn't notice that shiny travel trailer back there in the woods?" asked Officer Brian Collins.

Dervil looked down at the floor avoiding eye contact. His right hand gave a slight movement as he rubbed his fingers over the thumb.

"Not 'til the kid showed it to you," Dervil said. "Your headlights were aimed right at it. That's when I saw it."

"How long were you out there?" Collins asked.

"Half an hour. Maybe longer," Dervil said. Fleeting eye contact.

"You do that very often? Take walks?"

Dervil didn't answer. He sensed they were going to stay after it until he tripped up with his story. The questions were the same questions asked back at the scene before they brought him to the station.

"The number you are trying to reach has a voice mail box that has not been set up yet," the woman's voice said.

The phone was on the floor, under the driver' seat of John Dervil's car. Eddie Walker didn't know that. It was his sixth attempt to reach Dervil in the last three hours. Now he was calling every 15 minutes, getting the same result.

Walker put his phone back on the bar in front of him. Not one time since early August had Dervil failed to show. After meeting at a couple other joints, they'd settled on Willy's Tavern as their preferred hangout. It was the first time Walker was on his own since they had teamed up. He was anxious about Dervil's unexplained absence.

Arno's curiosity about the new drop guy in Portland was not so strong that he would risk being seen anywhere in the city.

Once he left the meeting with Mr. Smooth, back to Massachusetts and his new network. Four months now working this area and he was getting in a groove. Only one fuck-up back in August and that guy was no longer a problem. His replacement was considerably more reliable.

He tapped the speed-dial on his phone to call John Dervil.

"Double the radio and TV for the next two weeks," said Tad Shipp.

Bob Horner knew the campaign had the funds. The requirement by broadcast outlets that all political buys be paid in advance was not a concern.

What was a concern was the mix of commercials they had available. He knew every spot better than Shipp did. He had worked with the ad agency in developing the scheduling and rotation. And none of the commercials on hand was likely to improve the image of his boss.

"Senator, we may have to get some new footage," Horner said. Shipp turned back to look at him, eyes showing surprise.

"Am I mistaken in the belief that we have recorded every speech, almost every minute of this campaign for the last three months?" Shipp asked.

Horner quickly nodded in agreement. "We have done that, Senator. But I think what we could use right now," he paused and looked at his note pad. "It would help if we could show you with your family. Your wife and daughter. A broader appeal than just politics."

Shipp seemed ready to explode, but turned his back to Horner for a full five seconds before replying.

"Just politics?" Shipp said. Horner braced himself for a verbal assault. Shipp took two steps toward him.

"Just politics. It is all politics. Here in New Hampshire, out in Iowa, South Carolina, Florida. Everywhere, now and for the next 12 months, it is only politics." Shipp's voice was restrained, but Horner knew the signs. He could go off any second.

"We have the family stuff on the website. Plenty of photos. You want me to go buy a dog, too?" Shipp said.

"Senator," Horner began cautiously, "you are correct. We have some really good photos and video on the website. But there are a lot of people, especially older voters, they're just not going to see the website.   After the woman confronted you and the reporter put the video on the internet, we need something that will offset that."

"These people, especially the older voters as you say, if they won't see our website, why would they see the YouTube video?" Shipp demanded.

"They probably won't. But it's getting some play on the cable shows. They've even shown clips of the woman."

Horner had his attention. The reference to the cable shows was almost like quoting scripture. And he knew, much like choosing only certain passages from the Bible, an awful lot of cable viewers adhered only to the network that reaffirmed their existing societal and political opinions.

Fifty Six

Louie followed me home. The drive from Hanover to Quechee took 20 minutes.

When his wife reminded him that she had her sister and two other women visiting for the weekend, and the quilt show, Ragsdale made a quick decision to spend only a half-day at home and then hit the road back to my neck of the woods. He would spend the night here before going back to the coast on Sunday.

He took his bag to my guest room and came back to the living room.

"You're a lucky guy, Hanlon. I'm envious," he said.

I knew the tone and fed him the response, expecting something glib.

"And why am I a lucky guy? This time."

"The little routine you did earlier, asking me about my favorite restaurants? Being politically incorrect, by the way, about our choices in the Northeast Kingdom." I nodded.

"My apologies. I'm sure there are a few great places."

"That's it. Only a few. Down here, it's like an oasis. That town has to have more restaurants per capita than any place I can think of. At least up here in the woods of the north country," he said. "You expect that in Boston, or Providence. But don't you think it's a little unusual for a small college town?"

"Small college town, yes. But seriously changing demographics in the last 10 years. The medical center, a bunch of little tech companies, and some small businesses tucked away all over the place. The mix is not the same as it was first time you passed through here 20 years ago."

"You want anything to drink? Brandy, port?" I added. He held both hands up and shook his head.

"I'm good, thanks."

"I mean, I think Hanover has been a cultural oasis, to use your term, for a long time. Certainly all the years I've been around here."

"Yeah, it's what I miss the most where we live. I keep trying to get the guys at the fire department to consider sponsoring ballet. Maybe some opera classes."

"Hey. I'll come do woodchuck tai chi. I have a green belt. Like those fitness commercials on TV. We could tie it in to 'Chukkin' with the Oldies.'

"Anything new in the intimacy department?" Louie said, changing the subject.

"My sister give you that line? I'm glad you're not as crude as one of my other friends."

"Getting laid sounds like you're installing tile. And even back in my Army days, a lot of the terms that got thrown around for sex are pretty juvenile," he said.

"I agree. But movies and a lot of stuff on TV are not

making it any better. You'd think there would be more unfavorable attention to some of the language."

"What about the lyrics in the hip hop? You listen to any of that?" he said.

"You know I do, all the time. Sorry, Captain. I wouldn't know a hip hop artist from a hip replacement specialist."

"Back to your friend Bonnie. Or, is it someone else already?" He gave me the combo, smirk and judgmental snicker.

"Eh-h-h," I waggled my left hand sideways. "A little tense at the moment."

"What's the problem?"

"Well, Dr. Phil. Now that you ask. You see, she's 16 years younger, or maybe you hadn't noticed. She wants to have kids, or didn't I tell you. And..."

He held up his hands and shook his head. "Hey, I know. Try to see it my way. We've all heard it. Good luck."

"We could throw in 'Ask Mr. Sensitivity' as part of the oldies and the tai chi," I said.

"No, I get it. She's young, you're not so young. You really can't blame her."

"I don't. We had a great time just last weekend over at Winnepesaukee. But when we get to that discussion, it's like we're in a roundabout and not taking the next turn."

"So what else do you hear about the guy they found?" Louie said in his second attempt to take the conversation to left field.

"I'm surprised nothing's been in the paper. John

O'Neil, the old guy on the island, told me that any minute word would be out that it was now classified as a 'suspicious death.' I haven't seen anything."

"What's the guy's name who drowned?" he asked.

"Reilly. Charles Reilly." Might have been the beer and wine working on my head, but I couldn't remember if I'd discussed with Louie the snoop work Virginia Jackson did and the information on Reilly's days as a law student. "The guy graduated from Vermont Law School a few years back," I started.

Again, Louie holding his hands up. "Tell me tomorrow," he said, getting up from the chair and staring for the guest room. "I'll be up early," he added.

"Yeah, I know. I'll set-up the coffeemaker. Just flip the on button." I got up, started for the kitchen, then turned around.

"Try to see it my way. Beatles, yes?"

"*We Can Work It Out*, Winter, 1965," he said. "The year I was born."

Scooping coffee into the basket, I wondered if Louie's mother had left him her collection of 45s.

Fifty Seven

Sunday morning and no sighting of a white Buick Encore with NH plates, Warren Lapierre's vehicle. It was not in the garage of his home in Moultonborough.

When the state police failed to locate the man after late evening and overnight surveillance, Condon put the BOLO onto the northeast system for all state and municipal law enforcement agencies.

Condon reported this to Colonel Richard Quincy , who reported it to AG Kelly Alexakis.

It took Alexakis just two minutes to decide that it was time to go public. She told Quincy they would hold an early afternoon briefing for the media that should get the story on the Sunday evening news.

"Are we prepared to release Lapierre's name?" Quincy asked.

"You said no response at the door, no answer to the phone calls. He is a person of interest who may have information that will aid in an ongoing investigation," she said. "Yes, we will use his name."

"Thoughts on entering the house?" Quincy asked.

"We'll have the warrant before the briefing. Send your people out while we're talking to reporters. They're going to be on it and running over there as soon as we say his name."

"One o'clock for the briefing?" Quincy said.

"Pretty short notice. Better make it two. I'll try to get over there before 1:30."

There was no discussion about where, Quincy knew the media briefing would be at the Department of Public Safety State Police Headquarters in the Hayes Building, only five minutes from Alexakis's downtown Concord office near the State House Complex.

Quincy's Public Information Officer would be on the phone in minutes getting the word out to reporters.

After the conversation with Quincy, the Attorney General placed a call to Blair Watson, uncle of the victim. Listening to the connection through the line and getting a voice mail prompt, she left a brief message asking for Watson to call her back. If he had a cellphone, he had failed to give her the number.

Without sufficient evidence or reason to detain John Dervil, Pelham Police released him. They were able to confirm his story about a soon to end parole period for imprisonment in Massachusetts where he had several previous arrests, two of the most recent related to drug possession charges.

He was taken back to his car parked well off the main road near the mysterious, camouflaged Airstream trailer in the woods. Being a weekend, the police had no information on the owner of the trailer. There was no license plate and a call to the Airstream Company in Ohio to check the vehicle manufacture number would not produce results before Monday morning at the earliest.

Candidates, staffers, some volunteers and one bus

now assigned for reporters only, were about to leave for the 60 mile trip to Concord.

With just an outdoor state house rally remaining on the schedule at noon Sunday, some of the press corps bailed out Saturday night. No doubt in the weeks and months ahead, or at least through the first primary, various people would examine and speculate on the merits of future Candidate Caravans. It was way too early to make the case that it had been a hit.

Now it was back to individual campaigns, zig zag trips all over the country through the end of the year, then, for those who had the campaign treasury to support it, one last four week push in the Granite State in January and early February.

At the moment, it appeared that there would be at least 20 candidates still in the chase in NH. Some might drop out of active campaigning and allow their names to remain on the ballot, but short of write-ins, there would be no additional names placed before voters.

Bruce Lyndon took a public shuttle van for the trip to the Manchester-Boston Regional Airport. There was a chance that he would return in two months, dependent on future candidate debates and polling.

A couple of days at home would be real treat. Probably not enough to get the rest he really needed, but a welcome breather before taking on a similar trip across the snow covered corn and soybean fields of Iowa.

Laptop open as he worked on the draft for his essay, now titled *Three NH Primary Voters Take Another Look*, Lyndon inserted numerous place holders with blanks in the article. His understanding with the interviewees was that they would spend some time on the phone a month before the election, just in case there were new developments, issues or events not adequately covered.

His deadline to submit the 10,000 words essay was January 15th. Rarely did his editor suggest major changes and the piece was slated to run on Sunday, January 24th, the weekend after the Martin Luther King holiday and more than two weeks before the NH primary.

Leaving church services in Berlin, Linda Snider was surprised when a man came up to her and told her that she was an embarrassment to the congregation after saying what she said to Senator Tad Shipp.

Walking in front of her and holding their son's hand, her husband, Kevin, did not hear the man's comment.

At first she didn't recognize the man. She'd been speaking to a friend and was momentarily startled.

"Mrs. Snider, what you told that reporter was atrocious. You are an embarrassment to all of us," the man gestured to others leaving the church in front of them.

Before she could think of a response, the man had turned and was walking away from her. She looked at her friend, Rhonda Wilson, someone she'd known since moving back to town shortly after she and Kevin were married.

"He's an old crank," Rhonda said. "Don't worry about it. It's a free country."

The incident was not the first time Linda thought about how different life could be in a small community compared to her experiences while living away from New Hampshire in a suburb of Cleveland, Ohio.

In his office in Tulsa, Oklahoma, lawyer Bobby Williams watched the YouTube video several times.

The part he liked best was, "I can't imagine how you possibly fooled enough people in your state to actually get elected." And he really liked when the woman added, "He is a demagogue of the worst kind."

Bobby was pretty certain that Tad Shipp would not be president. A Democrat in a red state, he was also pretty certain that he could beat Shipp in the next election for the Senate seat in four years. The guy was a complete phony.

Fifty Eight

Ragsdale was headed east back to the NH coast a little after ten o'clock Sunday morning.

There was a light, misty rain but the temperature was above 40 and the drive would be OK. Boring, but OK. The drabness of the landscape and the overcast clouds did not make for a cheery frame of mind heading back to work.

On the other hand, Louie thought, not a whole lot about my line of work is particularly uplifting. And that thought led him to recall a conversation with his wife at the end the summer when he had had some time off.

They'd talked a lot about why Louie continued working undercover, was he getting too old for it and could he deal with a reassignment that might tie him to an office and some administrative job?

Nah. He was really good at what he did and believed that apprehending scumbags was important work. Sure, there was no shortage of victims and people who could be helped. There appeared to be some attitude changes both with the public and those in the judiciary regarding better ways to deal with addicts. That was probably good.

But not for two seconds did Louie believe that the truly evil, money crazy, soulless exploiters who lived off the weaknesses of others, deserved one ounce of his compassion. Not gonna happen. Find them, lock them up, get ready for the next group. They would always be there.

While approaching the exit for Route 101 east, Louie decided that besides the gloomy weather, his funk had more to do with a) a little guilt over abandoning his wife and her friends back home, and b) all the talk with Hanlon about politics and a renewed frustration with his own perception that the system was totally corrupt.

The phone mounted on the dash in front of him showed that he had a new text message.

It was almost noon when I called Virgina Jackson to see if we were still on for this evening. Even if Bonnie called, it would be a little awkward to beg off from the dinner date. But Bonnie didn't call back and I wasn't completely surprised. "Michael Hanlon, good morning," she said. I often forgot about caller ID.

"Do you think it's possible to program your phone so that it shows another name when you place a call," I said.

"NSA's probably already figured a way."

"Like changing the greeting on your voicemail. Maybe you could have several different names to use. I mean, I know the carriers have your actual number registered. Just program in options to change the caller ID."

"Why not?" she said. "And like domain names when you create a website, the caller ID names could be used only by you."

"Think of the revenue stream. The phone companies could tie in some theme specific to your interests. Soccer Man. Amazing Woman. Or maybe some connection to your alma mater, with colors, like the shirts and hats you can buy."

"What a thrill. Pick up your phone and the ID says, call from AB Battlers."

"Who?" I said.

"AB. Alderson-Broaddus. The school nickname is 'The Battlers."

"Is that really a college?"

"Yes. My husband went there. Played football. He's been dead three years and I still get alumni donation requests."

The reference to her late husband gave me pause. I wasn't sure where to go with the conversation. Virginia noticed my hesitation. "You're calling to tell me where you would like to go for dinner, yes?"

"I'm flexible. It's my treat, but your choice," I said.

"Let me think about it. What time are we considering?"

"Sunday night. There shouldn't be any problem with a reservation. Seven o'clock OK?"

"Seven is good."

"When you decide where we're going," I said, "let me know if you think I need to wear a jacket."

"I'll call you later this afternoon."

"Sounds good."

"Michael," she said.

"Yes?"

"Thank you for waiting until noon to call. I like to read the papers on Sunday morning."

"Here's a thought. If the caller ID option idea works, you know some minister somewhere is going to get GOD." She groaned at this suggestion.

"You're sitting around in your warm pajamas Sunday morning reading the paper. Phone rings. Look at that caller ID."

"I will call you later, Michael."

"I'm here."

Fifty Nine

Dervil's phone showed three missed calls from Arno and seven from Eddie Walker's number.

Eddie could wait. He was probably hunkered down in his apartment with all the shades drawn anyway. But he had to call Arno immediately.

As soon as he got him on the phone and began his story about the kid and the cops finding the trailer, and that he had been held overnight, Dervil could almost feel the chill through the phone. Arno went silent.

"Hey. I was doing exactly what you told me to do. I stayed in the woods behind the trailer for nearly five hours. By the time I was coming out, it would be dark in another 10 minutes." Still no response from Arno.

"Whaddya want me to do? I told the screws that I was out for a walk. Didn't see the trailer until they took me back there."

Now Arno replied. "While the police were keeping you overnight, do you think they might have checked your background?"

"I told 'em about the parole. They checked that. That's why I ran."

"You ran?" Arno said.

"Yeah. When I first saw it was a police car."

"You ran. That is just fucking great, Devil Man."

"I was scared." He could hear Arno let out a breath.

"Oh, I'm sure you were." Again the silence. Finally, Dervil started in again.

"Well at least I got to you before you went back there."

"Indeed. At least you did that." Arno's appreciation would not extend to letting this dickhead function much longer.

"I'm going back to Lowell. I haven't talked to Eddie…"

Arno cut him off. "I will be in touch," he said, before ending the call.

Warren Lapierre was really not sure why he actually stopped in Philadelphia.

When he had left New Hampshire less than 24 hours ago, his thinking had been that he would drive probably to South Carolina. He knew another political operator down there, very much like himself, a get-the-cash, keep your-mouth-shut kind of guy. Lapierre had last seen the man at an under the radar gathering shortly after the US Supreme Court ruling in favor of Super PACs.

But now, he was walking across the lobby of a hotel where he'd taken a room at $459 a night. Having finished breakfast, he walked straight to the registration desk. He needed information that he wasn't sure would be found in a phone directory or online.

"May I help?" said the young man behind the desk.

Lapierre sized the man up. Thirty. Good haircut. Nice hands. Soft brown eyes. Was he gay?

"Yes, please," he replied to the question.

The young man waited.

"There are some people here that I am trying to locate. I'm positive they are not listed in the phone directory. Very private family."

The young man gave a nod. He placed his fingertips together and silently tapped them a couple times.

"A friend of mine used to live down here. I know his mother's name. And I think that I know the section of the city where she lives. But I've never spent any time here."

"Our concierge," the young man was pointing across the lobby, "Daniel. He may be able to help."

Lapierre pivoted and saw a middle-aged man at the concierge desk. He turned back and thanked the desk clerk.

On the first pass through Lapierre's house, police found nothing particularly interesting.

There was a section of one file cabinet drawer that might have had some files removed. The desk in the office had a printer and fax machine, but no computer. A space on the desk where a computer might have been located was now empty.

It was difficult to tell if clothes were missing from the closet in the master bedroom. Food in the refrigerator was all relatively fresh, nothing spoiled.

Downstairs in the garage, both bays were vacant. In the storage area above where the cars would be parked, there were four tires covered with white plastic, some boxes of books and a medium sized suitcase. Next to the suitcase was an empty spot of approximately 10 square feet. The dust outline indicated that something had been stored there.

When Sergeant Condon got the report on all this, he was just as perplexed as he'd been 48 hours earlier after the second interview with Lapierre. He didn't completely believe the man's story, but Condon could not point to any specific act or suspected omission. It just seemed off.

The press briefing was scheduled for two o'ccock. That left enough time to give Quincy an update. Condon picked up the phone.

And in addition to the preliminary 'nothing here' report on Lapierre's home, there was still the hope that some lead will emanate from information related to several individuals who had attended the 12-step recovery program that Reilly attended. But that was also incomplete and would likely take a few more days.

After listening to Condon for two minutes, Quincy urged a refocus.

"Go back to all of the phone records. Land line and

cellphone. Every call for the past six months," Quincy said.

"That's already underway, sir. It'll take a day or two."

"Well then, Sergeant. We have what we have. See you in an hour."

Condon knew that Quincy and the AG would have one more session together before the meeting with reporters.

Sixty

Ragsdale was now back at the house shared with two other undercover drug cops.

Actually, one of the other guys was a drop-in, as he worked out of a local police department two towns away. It was this cop who had sent a text to Louie two hours earlier.

Now they were sitting in the kitchen where the cop was giving Louie a rundown on an incident involving a guy picked up by two patrolmen and a new Airstream trailer parked in the woods under camouflage.

"What's a guy from Lowell doing up here walking around in the woods? In street shoes, no less. And," he emphasized, "he just happens to be on parole for his second drug conviction in five years."

The cop telling Louie this was an eager, 29-year-old by the name of Frankie Sullivan. Only recently assigned to undercover work, Sullivan was as enthusiastic as a boy scout going for his first merit badge. And Louie was his role model.

"Okay," Ragsdale said. "Get to the part about the trailer. Camouflaged. Really?"

"Yeah." Sullivan had a big smile and his eyes went

wide. "Brownie, one of the Pelham cops, says it was like the stuff the Army uses in the desert."

"Camo netting," Louie said.

"I guess. Said it had leaves and branches stuck in it. You would never see it from the air."

"Sully, when you were at the academy, didn't they show you some of this stuff?"

"Of course. And I musta seen a hundred videos. But you don't think you're gonna see it up here ten minutes outa town."

"Maybe the guy's a hardcore hunter who just wants a little comfort."

"Oh, sure. What's he huntin over there, ducks?"

"What was the kid hunting for?"

"Brownie said he had a bow. You ask me, the kid's not gettin good information. I don't think there are any deer around there."

Ragsdale and Frankie Sullivan went at it like this for several minutes before Louie held his hand up.

"You're giving me a headache. So now we know about this trailer. They're going to find out who owns it, where it came from and why it's there." Ragsdale paused to be sure this was sinking in. "When we know something more, we take another look at the situation."

Sullivan almost went into a pout.

"What about the yellow Nissan SUV?" he said.

"You ever seen it?" Louie responded.

"No. But, the guy who told me to watch for it, he saw

it. He says they're dealing."

Ragsdale held both hands out. "And tell me again who this guy is who told you about the Nissan."

"Guy is pissed off at his son. Kid was a hell of a basketball player until last winter. Then shitty grades at school, everything started falling apart. His ol' man says that the boy is now doing drugs."

"And the Nissan?" Louie exaggerated.

"Belongs to one of the kid's asshole buddies from Massachusetts."

"Please. Don't start again with the Massholes routine. Ever occur to you they might hold a similar view of you?"

"Whatever," Sullivan said.

"Did the old man, or anyone, report this to police down there?" Ragsdale said.

"You know those guys. They're runnin their own undercover. They got their hands full all the time."

"But Franklin, we do communicate, yes? They didn't explain to you that you pick up the phone when this kind of shit is going on in your backyard?"

"Yeah, yeah. That's how I got here. My chief goes to one of your task force meetings down in Mass, next thing I'm on loan to you."

"You're not happy, I'm sure we can arrange for you to go back," Ragsdale said.

"C'mon, Louie. Cut me a little slack here. I'm just giving you everything I hear."

Ragsdale backed off. For the moment.

But Louie knew that with some of the younger cops – it seemed especially true with Frankie Sullivan – if you didn't stay right on top of them, their eagerness could get them way out in front of where things really were on any given day.

"Stay in touch with your pal Brownie. Ask him to keep us up with what they learn about the trailer. And get the guy's name they let go," Louie said.

Sullivan gave a thumbs-up gesture and stood from his chair.

A hair under six feet, slim build and rosy cheeks, he looked really young. So far, Sullivan was not permitted to have contact with suspected dealers. Louie thought if it wasn't for the work pants and construction jacket he wore as part of his cover, the kid would look more like 16 than 29. But he was eager.

As Frankie was going to the door, Louie spoke up again.

"Sully. Get the location of the trailer. Maybe we'll take a run by before they haul it in."

Sixty One

Virginia made a reservation at a place called Country Fare, a small restaurant across the Connecticut River in Plainfield, New Hampshire.

I left the TV on mute for the end of the Patriots-Washington Redskins game while I showered. When Virginia had called earlier, she had said that she'd never been to Country Fare and that it had been recommended by a friend. She also suggested a jacket might be appropriate. You never knew these days who would let you get away with a jacket and jeans, or no jeans allowed. So I went for a pair of navy wool slacks, a tattersall button down shirt with no tie and a charcoal herringbone sport coat. The hiking boots wouldn't cut it, so I wore brown leather casual shoes.

Thinking of Ragsdale's observation in the bar about the guy wearing a 'full Orvis', I imagined he would call this outfit a 'full granddad.'

At 6:55, I pulled into Virginia's driveway and she came out the front door. It was the first time since her mother's funeral that I'd seen her not wearing slacks or jeans. I couldn't tell what she was wearing under her wool coat, but it wasn't slacks.

"I thought it would be colder," she said, getting into the car. The temperature on my dashboard showed 38ºF.

"Didn't look at the weather. Maybe we're getting a second round like the spell two weeks ago," I replied.

People in this part of New England had long grown accustomed to Indian Summer at the end of October, but any mild weather in November was a bonus.

Leaving her driveway I hit the button for my four-way flashers before backing up. As soon as I turned, she asked about the flashers.

"Why do you do that?"

"What, the emergency flashers?"

"Yes."

"It makes me think about backing up. I don't have a camera, I want to signal anybody behind me." She looked behind us.

"We're on unpaved road, nobody around. That's your house over there. Nobody coming out of that driveway."

"Habit."

"Maybe you could get one of those construction or heavy duty truck back-up signals."

"This place is across the Windsor covered bridge?"

"Yes. Turn left toward Saint Gaudens and it's another two miles. On the left. There should be a sign."

Bonnie Mackin decided to go see Hanlon rather than call him. Sunday evening, he's home watching football.

But he wasn't.

250

She went back to her car and sat for two minutes before deciding what she needed to do. The hidden key was inside a ceramic planter on the deck. Michael had made a point of showing her last spring. She'd used it before to gain entry when he was not at home.

Inside, she walked around the kitchen and the living room. The house had that smell of indoor plants freshly watered. He had plants in each room.

Bonnie had been there six months earlier when Michael had been recovering from a gunshot wound. She'd purchased a spray can of lemon scented air freshener and it took him all of 10 seconds to let her know that he didn't like that stuff and much preferred the smell of his plants.

She walked into his office and sat at his desk for a minute. Then it came to her. She went downstairs to his media room, chock full of books, videos, CDs and DVDs.

Kneeling to a lower shelf that held a long row of CDs, she found a boxed collection Motown hits. She pulled it out, studied the list on the box and removed one of the discs. She took it back upstairs to the office and again sat at the desk.

With a plain sheet of paper from the printer, she began writing a note. The Motown CD was on the desk next to her.

Sixty Two

The Sunday evening news on WMUR 9 showed the New Hampshire Attorney General along with the head of the State Police standing together at a podium.

Colonel Richard Quincy was speaking into a microphone, but what viewers heard was a female reporter explaining that the state's two top law enforcement officials had spoken just a few hours earlier at a press conference.

"Quincy, accompanied by Attorney General Kelly Alexakis," said the off camera voice, "told reporters that a drowning last week in Lake Winnepesaukee was now classified as a 'suspicious death'. The head of the state police went on to say that a Moultonborough man, previously questioned by police, was now a 'person of interest' in connection with the death of Charles Reilly of Meredith."

The audio went from the reporter's voice to that of Quincy at the mic.

"We believe that Warren Lapierre, a friend of the deceased, may have information that will assist in the identity of persons who may have wished to do harm to Mr. Reilly. Following earlier questioning by New Hampshire State Police, Mr. Lapierre is now missing from his home in

Moultonborough."

The sound cut away from Quincy and back to the woman reporter.

"Authorities say that Lapierre is believed to be driving a white Buick Encore with NH registration." As the reporter continued by asking viewers to contact state police with any information, a two-line trailer appeared at the bottom of the screen. The top line in bright blue showed the vehicle license plate number – GL 4391. Directly below in red letters was the phone number for the state police.

Unsuccessful and somewhat relieved that he did not find an address for Margaret Reilly, Lapierre decided that he would spend a second night in Philadelphia.

One of his roller-coaster memories of Charles' stories about his mother was a joke Charles liked to tell about three mothers bragging to each other about their sons.

Each of the mothers claimed great accomplishments by their respective offspring and heaped praise on the thoughtful gestures and kindness the sons extended to them.

The punch line of the joke was that the last mother to speak boasted that her son had a special doctor that he went to see every week and that they talked just about her.

Even with the rather mercurial nature in regards to his

mother, Charles had never actually said anything mean or hateful about her, at least not within hearing of Warren. And while Lapierre never spoke of his own mother, he'd convinced himself at an early age that he despised her and had never missed her since her death 30 years earlier.

Warren decided that he would find a gay bar and see what was happening in the City of Brotherly Love on a quiet Sunday evening.

Sixty Three

It was all that Arno could do to restrain himself from just driving back to Lowell, yanking Dervil out of the fucking bar and shooting him between the eyes.

After more than two weeks of repeated trips past the driveway where the Airstream trailer had been parked, Arno concluded that no one was at home. That's when he had also concluded that he could arrange for it to be parked elsewhere. The window shades inside the trailer were closed and the tires covered in white vinyl to protect the rubber from sunlight. It had been obvious that it was going to be there for a while. That's when Arno had hatched the plan for Dervil and Walker to do a second job in less than week.

Now the fucking cops had it. Only two nights inside the trailer, Arno had not fully settled himself there. He was still working out of a second floor apartment in nearby Lawrence, but planned to make the hideout in the woods his base of operation until he was ready to head south.

Nothing left behind in the trailer. Except fingerprints. Once they had the prints, it would take about two hours for the cops to realize that Arnost Waclaw Branchik was back in New England. After that, about two minutes for the full blown manhunt to start all over.

Arno turned off 495 at Exit 35C, looped right and headed for downtown. Almost no traffic so it would take only five minutes to get there.

The first time Arno had visited Lowell, he had been told that with a sizeable immigrant influx in recent years, the population was made up of nearly 40% of people not born in the US and that there were seven active languages in the city. His contacts and activity made him believe that was probably accurate.

Smarter, more cautious and with a determination to survive that he had not possessed only two years earlier, Arno still had a language that had never failed him and that everyone could understand.

John Dervil sat at the bar waiting for Eddie Walker. The phone call earlier in the day might have gotten Walker back on board. Or maybe not.

Walker was really spooked. He'd been a reluctant participant from the beginning of his friendship with Dervil. Motivated more by money, which he rarely spent, and less by the availability of cheap and easy drugs, Walker had slowly allowed himself to become an accomplice.

The first trip to New Hampshire a week ago had been a little strange but no real effort. All they had had to do was meet Arno at a public boat dock late at night and drive him 30 minutes back to his car on the other side of Lake

Winnepesaukee. They each got $200 and some pills to sell for their effort.

The trailer heist was only a little more work. Get their hands on a pick-up truck for a few hours, meet Arno, hook up the trailer and tow it to a remote location. That got them $1,000 each.

Now, after going missing for more than 24 hours, Dervil was back with a story about being detained by cops in a New Hampshire border town and the news that the cops were on to the trailer.

Eddie didn't like any of this. He also didn't like the thought that Dervil was skimming the proceeds they got for aiding in the distribution of illegal substances.

Walker sat in his apartment and thought about all this. Unlike previous meetings, nearly every day for months, he was not so quick to go spend time with John Dervil. Let him wonder where I am for a change.

Sixty Four

"So tell me, Michael Hanlon. Old fogies or all college students," Virginia said. It took me a beat to get the reference to her question.

We were seated at a table in Country Fare, a quiet, nice little restaurant on the banks of the Connecticut River in west central New Hampshire.

"Last night? Yeah. It looked like a pretty good mix. I wasn't in the auditorium, but from what I saw on the monitor, I'd say more students than not."

"Big crowd?" she said.

"Probably close to a thousand people. Bruce said the auditorium holds over 900. There were others watching on big screens in another part of the building."

"Any of the candidates look better than others?"

"I think Rubio. He's a little more polished and more articulate than he was a couple years ago."

"What about Trump?"

"Pretty consistent. Blunt, direct, sometimes funny."

"Sometimes simplistic, don't you think," she said.

"Yes, most of the time. But he appears to have more appeal this time around."

"You saw that Webb dropped out."

"Yeah. When I was doing my homework before going

with Bruce over to the coast last week, I watched some stuff online. C-SPAN had Webb's press conference. But clearly not out of it, just going to thumb is nose at the Democrats." Surprisingly, Virginia was showing some interest in the presidential race. Having oysters and some cauliflower with blue cheese for appetizers, we had a bottle of house chardonnay on the table in front of us. I poured the wine and she kept at me with the questions.

"My husband really liked Webb. We sent donations when he ran for the senate in 2006. He squeaked through. Surprised a lot of people."

In previous conversations, when Virginia mentioned her late husband, I wasn't sure how to respond.

"He is really an interesting guy. Besides the military service and politics, he has a law degree and he's written several books. One really good one about Scots-Irish influence in building America."

"Did you see the Democratic Debate last month?" I asked. She had her mouth full, but nodded affirmatively.

"I got the clear impression that he and Bernie Sanders have a mutual respect and maybe a friendship."

Virginia wiped her mouth with her napkin and took a sip of wine.

"That was my feeling, too" she said.

"There's a thought. If Hillary gets the nomination, Webb and Bernie could team up as independents," I said.

"There's already speculation. I read an article this

morning that alluded to just that scenario."

The server arrived with our dinner. We'd ordered the special for the evening, home-style roasted chicken for two with sides of asparagus and pureed sweet potatoes.

As soon as the waiter left, a young man in his mid-20s, I picked up the conversation with a question about Virginia's view of the likelihood of the US electing its first woman president.

"I remember eight years ago, a lot of people were saying the US was not ready for either a woman president or an African American. You think Hillary has a chance of being elected?"

"I remember all that, too. Not all the pundits are on TV or write syndicated columns. Everyone has an opinion and with the so-called 'social media', more people are quick to express their opinions."

She put her fork down before continuing and looked directly at me. Could have been my imagination, but Virginia appeared to be just getting warmed-up.

"They were wrong about a black man being elected, weren't they? And the 'not ready for a woman' hogwash' probably dates back to Margaret Chase Smith in my mother's youth. Yes, I think Hillary has a very real chance of being elected."

While we ate, Virginia talked about living in New York and Hillary Clinton's time in the senate, about other women in politics during her lifetime, including the former governor of Vermont, Madeline Kunin, and the women presently serving in the senate and in the governor's office here in New Hampshire.

Eventually we talked about our meal. The chicken was spectacular. We tried to guess what seasonings had been used in roasting it. The asparagus had been sautéed in garlic and the sweet potatoes had a hint of maple syrup. For desert, a blackberry apple crisp and decaf coffee.

Outside the restaurant, the clouds had opened up and there was a waxing crescent moon that made for some shadows as we walked back to the car.

"I never met your husband. Your mom talked about the two of you. Do you mind telling me about him?" I said.

"Richard. He was a really sweet man. You wouldn't have necessarily thought that looking at him. But when he was not in uniform - thoughtful, considerate. Just an ordinary guy."

Millie Robinson, Virginia's recently deceased mother, had been devastated when she'd told me about her son-in-law's death in Afghanistan three years ago. I recalled that she also talked about him being a genuinely sweet man. And that he had just turned 50 a month before being killed.

"He was a marine?"

"A lifer. Right out of college. I didn't meet him until a few years later."

For the rest of our drive home, I heard about how they met, married after dating only two months and some of their life together and apart, Richard on tour somewhere, Virginia back in New York working her way through the chairs of corporate law. Mentioning his death, she did it almost in passing.

"Then in May three years ago, he was gone. A land mine near Kandahar," she added, then went quiet.

When we arrived at her house, she reached over and patted my hand before getting out of the car.

"Thank you for dinner. Next time, on me," she said.

"Thanks for doing the spade work on the Reilly guy."

"Any more on that? Have they found anyone?" She was standing outside the car with the door open.

"Not that I've heard."

"You think you can get away from those horrible things living in the country. Not true anymore," she said.

"I'll call John O'Neil over on Bear Island tomorrow. See what he's heard."

"Good night," she said, and made the motion of blowing me a kiss when she closed the door.

Sixty Five

Ragsdale changed into his work clothes. He really thought of it as putting on a work uniform, much like baseball players.

Depending on where he might be assigned, the variation was normally a pair of jeans, some crew neck shirt or a pullover on top of another shirt, and either running shoes or hiking boots. He'd explained to his wife, Becky, that sometimes it was the home team uniform, sometimes the road uniform.

Tonight, it was definitely the road team: black jeans, burgundy velour sweatshirt, leather jacket and the boots. He combed his hair and put a new black rubber band on his pony tail.

At 9:15, he left the house and headed for a bar in Portsmouth, one he hadn't been in yet. He would spend an hour or two checking out the patrons, then head back before midnight. Frankie Sullivan would be back at the house when he returned.

At least that was the plan at the beginning of a new week.

"**Fuck Eddie Walker. We don't need him for this,**" Arno said. He was holding Devil's right arm in a very tight grip with no sign of letting go.

"Where we going?" Dervil aksed.

"Back to the trailer," Arno replied, as they exited the bar.

Dervil stopped and the motion forced Arno to stop. Arno turned and jerked on the arm.

"Why are we going back there? If the fucking cops haven't pulled it out of the woods, they're probably parked right there next to it."

Arno pulled Dervil's arm to get him moving again. The car was a half-block away.

"I don't give a shit about the trailer now. There's another way in," Arno said. "I have some personal belongings that need to be collected."

"Inside?" Dervil exclaimed.

"Not inside. Buried. Farther back in the woods." Dervil's right arm was starting to hurt where Arno squeezed the tendons at his elbow.

Two minutes later they were in the car and headed north. Arno stared straight ahead as he drove and didn't speak.

John Dervil could feel the perspiration under his arms, at the collar of his shirt and in his underwear.

He thought about Eddie Walker and wished that he was along for the ride.

And he recalled Eddie's comment about Arno.

"That dude scares the shit out of me."

Looking at the dimly lighted dashboard, Dervil saw the speed was right at 70 MPH. Stealing a glance at Arno behind the wheel, he saw that the man's eyes were locked on the road, mouth shut.

When Walker arrived, there were five other people in the tavern. Dervil was not one of them.

Eddie took a seat at the bar where he and Dervil would normally sit.

"Beer?" Walt the bartender asked. An older guy with thinning hair and a gray mustache, Walt knew that Walker usually had one bottle of inexpensive beer which he would then nurse it longer than most people might. Eddie nodded.

"Missed your friend," Walt said, placing the beer in front of Walker. "Left about 20 minutes ago."

Eddie looked around as though he expected Dervil to come walking back in. "He say anything?" Eddie asked.

Walt shook his head. "Nope. He was talking with

another guy for a few minutes, then they left."

"Guy with a beard?" Eddie said, moving his right hand like he was stroking an invisible goatee.

Walt shook his head. "Yeah. Wearing a cap," Walt added, patting the top of his head.

Eddie felt a flutter in his intestines and his left knee gave an involuntary jerk. He took a gulp of his beer and looked around again.

Sixty Six

The New Hampshire State Police got a hit on the license plate for Lapierre's car. It was spotted by two Philadelphia policemen on a routine evening patrol in the center of the city.

The car was parked on the street and, according to one of the Philly cops, appeared to have been there for a while. The hood was cold.

The cop went on to tell the NH dispatcher that the neighborhood, Washington Square West, had a lot of bars, restaurants and clubs and that it might be a while before the driver returned.

This information was relayed to Sergeant Rob Condon who got on the phone with a follow-up call and without much effort was able to convince the Philly PD to assign a patrolmen to keep an eye on the vehicle.

Back in Laconia, New Hampshire, some 390 miles northeast of Center City Philadelphia, 14 people were getting up to leave a Sunday evening group session of an addiction recovery program that met in a church basement.

Agnes Walsh, the minister, shook hands with a young woman who appeared to be in her early 40s. The woman was new to the group.

"That didn't take long," the woman said quietly with the slightest smile. She was taller than Walsh, possibly 5'9" or so, with long brown hair and dressed in biker jeans and leather jacket with a fleece vest underneath. Walsh held the woman's hand in both of hers and didn't reply.

"I really am a recovering alcoholic," the woman said. She was also a plant by the state police, something she hoped the others wouldn't pick-up too quickly, although she was sure that Walsh knew.

"It's nice to have you with us," Walsh finally said, releasing the woman's hand. "Thank you for coming."

When all those attending introduced themselves at the opening of the meeting, the woman had said her name was Carolyn and that she'd been sober for five months.

"Was this the normal turn-out for a Sunday evening," Carolyn asked. Walsh nodded.

"Better than normal. Usually we have 9 or 10 people for this meeting. Counting you, we were up by four tonight." It was Carolyn's turn to nod.

"You know about Charles, the man we lost a week ago," Reverend Walsh said.

"Yes." Carolyn took a sip of black coffee from a paper cup. "Do you know if any of those here this evening, were any of them a friend of his?"

"Not that I am aware of. I don't always know who may be acquainted, or who may see each other outside of these meetings." Again a nod from Carolyn.

Avoiding a prolonged silence, the next question made it clear to Carolyn that Agnes Walsh had made a determination about her presence from the start.

"Did anyone here tonight pique your interest?"

Carolyn hesitated, made and held eye contact with the counselor. Again the brief smile before she spoke.

"I have probably attended more than 200 of these meetings. The part about being sober for four months was a lie. I have been clean of drugs and alcohol for over five years."

"That is wonderful," Walsh said.

"I suspect that you know this better than many, but only about 10% of the people who get into most step programs can stay clean. They really do benefit from the support." She took another sip of the coffee before continuing.

"We all come from different places, different circumstances, but very similar stories. So everyone in this group interests me. I sponsor three friends in other groups." Carolyn then shook her head and added, "My first reaction is that no one I saw this evening stirred any suspicions."

"That's good to hear," Walsh said.

"I do think that I will come back. Maybe your Wednesday meeting."

"You're welcome anytime."

Sixty Seven

I sat at my desk and booted up the computer to check email before getting ready for bed.

More SPAM than the average person is entitled to, the town's daily listserv with items for sale, lost animals and a variety of opinions on town affairs, a humorous story from the woman barber I see every three weeks, and a lengthy email from Bruce Lyndon.

Bruce went on in his message about some of the things we had talked about during his week in New Hampshire, attached a draft of the piece he'd written after the interview with Dartmouth prof, and ended by saying that we should consider creating a Presidential pool like the March Madness college basketball pool that we participate in each spring.

'You have a lot of time, Michael. Set it up. I'll send my money,' was his close.

I typed a quick reply. 'Sure, will get right on it. But it will focus on the real election a year from now,

NOT February in NH!' I had no intention of spending time organizing a pool that might attract a bunch of smartass reporters, several of whom would be late getting their money in before the deadline. But I did tell Bruce that whether or not he returned over the winter, we could connect by phone and pick apart the results of the NH Primary.

Getting up from the desk, my eye caught an envelope and a CD in a plastic case lying on top of my printer.

I recognized the CD. It was one from my Motown collection. The envelope had my full name written on it in blue ink, Michael Perry Casey Hanlon. It was Bonnie's handwriting.

Before entering the bar on Daniel Street in Portsmouth, Ragsdale called his wife.

When she'd finished giving him more half-hearted grief for avoiding her sister and the other women at their home for the past three days, she settled into an enthusiastic description of the two days of quilt shows and the amazing talent of some of the quilt makers. Louie had long ago learned to show some interest without being a wise guy.

After just a couple more minutes of chit chat, Louie told her that he loved her and was really looking forward to the week off at Thanksgiving.

In another bar an hour south of Portsmouth, Eddie Walker ordered a second beer. The bartender obliged without comment.

Eddie's imagination was in overdrive. While he had only 40 bucks in his pocket, the rest of his cash from the past month, along with a handgun, a folding hunting knife in a nylon case and a slim collection of clothing, were all back at his apartment.

What Eddie concluded was that the best plan for him at this moment was to wait for one more hour for either a phone call from Dervil or his return to the bar, preferably the latter. And without Arno.

Until yesterday, Eddie spent much of the last week becoming more and more pissed at Dervil. When he had gotten the story about Dervil being picked up by cops in New Hampshire and held overnight, his annoyance had begun to subside. It had been replaced with a mix of concern and fear.

Sitting in this tavern alone, where the only person he might trust was the guy behind the bar, Eddie no longer felt concern from Dervil's story.

All that Eddie felt now was fear.

At 10:15, Warren Lapierre left the nightclub on 13th Street in Philadelphia. He passed a couple of other spots that looked promising, but his interest in meeting someone new simply wasn't there. He was too old for this.

Approaching his car, he clicked the electronic key, the lights flashed and the driver's door unlocked. Getting behind the wheel and preparing to close the door was when two uniformed policemen appeared, one on either side of the car.

"Mr. La Pear," the cop closest to him said. He pronounced it like the fruit.

Warren held the car door open, but didn't respond.

"Is this your car, sir?" The cop said.

Warren nodded. "Yes. Is there a problem."

"Could we see your license and registration, please." The other cop, now standing directly opposite Warren next to the front passenger door, was shining a flash light into the back seat.

Opening the glove box to retrieve the registration card, Lapierre turned and handed it to the cop.

"My license is in my wallet," he said, patting his left breast to indicate a pocket inside his jacket.

"Please step out of the car and remove your wallet slowly."

"What's this all about," Lapierre asked, doing as instructed, pushing off the seat and stepping onto the pavement. Even with several ounces of alcohol in his system, the alarms in his brain were loud and clear on what this was all about.

Sixty Eight

Arno and Dervil sat in the car, lights off, engine idling. Both men had stood outside the car taking a leak in the cold night air when they had arrived 20 minutes earlier.

"OK, let's do it," Arno said, opening the driver's door. Dervil reflexively opened his door and he got out.

On the drive up from Mass, Arno told Dervil as little as he wanted him to know about going to retrieve something buried in the woods nor far from where the trailer was parked, assuming the trailer was still there.

But whether the trailer was there or not didn't matter. Arno was confident that his 18 x 24 inch aluminum box, double-wrapped in contractor plastic bags, buried two feet in the earth and covered with fallen trees, would still be there. He'd chosen the spot far enough back in the woods not to attract attention.

The Sig in his coat pocket, knife strapped to his leg, Arno popped the trunk and a light came on. He reached in and got a camper's battery powered lantern and a shovel.

"Take this," he said, handing the shovel to Dervil.

Unlike his earlier physical treatment when he had squeezed Dervil's arm and hustled him from the tavern to the car, Arno had dialed back his tone and unfriendly behavior a few minutes into the drive.

Now it was all business. He'd said nothing once they arrived, other than "let's have a piss." Then he had sat in the car, smoking and scanning the radio dial as though he were listening for something in particular.

Arno turned the lantern on and closed the trunk. He held the lantern up between them and patted his right pocket so Dervil could see the bulge of the gun.

"The path's up ahead. Don't be stupid, Devil Man."

Nothing running through John Dervil's mind involved doing something stupid.

They were possibly a half-mile from the grassy road that led to the spot where the trailer had been parked. Arno was able to pull his car into the woods here, also off the road, and a hard-to-find trailhead was somewhere ahead of them.

Dervil moved in the direction in front and away from the car with Arno and the lantern right behind him. After less than a minute, Arno tapped him in the back with the lantern.

"Hold up," Arno said. He raised the lantern above his shoulder and swung it to his left.

"Right there. See it?" Dervil didn't respond.

"Next to the tree with the fungus all over it," Arno said.

Dervil saw the dead tree and moved in that direction.

Condon was about ready to get into bed when his phone buzzed. It was his contact at the Philadelphia Police Department, Lieutenant John Hinkle.

"We have your guy. He was brought to our 9th District station about 30 minutes ago. I just got the call," Hinkle said. "Says he had no idea that anyone in New Hampshire was looking for him."

"Hold him overnight. I'll have someone on the first flight out of Manchester in the morning."

"Let me know who's coming down and what flight they're on. We can meet 'em at the airport," Hinkle said.

"Thank you. And please tell Mr. Lapierre, if he starts to give you any real static, that we have more questions on a matter that he is quite familiar with. He'll get it."

Condon made the call to Colonel Richard Quincy to apprise him that Warren Lapierre was now in custody in Pennsylvania. Concluding a very brief conversation, Quincy simply said, "You go.

Lapierre had been told that his vehicle would be brought to the 19th district station and would be there when he was released. He'd also been told that after a check with New Hampshire State Police, who requested his detention, there was a possibility that he would be free to go within a couple hours.

Now they were telling him that, in fact, it would be tomorrow and that someone from New Hampshire was coming to question him.

The Philly police made it clear that he was not under arrest at this time and was free to make phone calls. They even let him keep his mobile phone in the room where he was being detained. They also offered coffee, which he declined.

Lapierre sat on a thinly padded, fabric covered chair, alone, in a stripped-down room with only a table and one other chair. There was a wall-mounted phone and the standard issue mirror on the wall, high and to his right. He knew the mirror had a room on the other side and that the glass allowed anyone in that room to observe him.

He took out his phone and placed on the table in front of him. The screen came to life when he put the phone down, face-up. He needed to think about whom he would call.

Placing both hands on his thighs, leaning forward and moving the hands slowly back and forth on the creases of his slacks, he watched the phone as if it might ring at any second. It did not.

Eddie put seven dollars on the bar and got up. He knew from previous visits that his brand of beer was $2.75 a bottle. A buck-fifty was plenty for a tip.

The clock above the bar showed that it was five after eleven. Without a word to the bartender, Eddie went out to the street, exactly one hour after he had started his second beer.

The walk to his apartment was only 10 minutes. It was cold, he walked fast. Taking the phone out of his coat pocket, he tapped the phone icon and looked at recent calls. The last call from Dervil had been four hours ago. All the time he'd been sitting at the bar in Willy's, the phone hadn't made a beep.

While this guy Arno hadn't done or said anything specific in front of Eddie that would justify the fear he now felt, it was his eyes. Menacing look didn't cover it. Lots of tough guys and some who pretended to be tough could make themselves look menacing. Eddie had seen it plenty of times.

What Eddie had seen only a few times in his 37 years was a person with eyes that were totally and completely without life. And one of those times it had actually been a guy who'd just been killed in a car crash. A teenager, Eddie and a friend were the first to arrive at the crash minutes after it happened. He had never forgotten the open but lifeless eyes.

The first time he had really noticed Arno's eyes was the night they picked him up at the boat dock to take him back to his car.

Arno had gotten in the backseat of Dervil's car. The dome light had been on when Eddie turned to look at him. Arno had held his gaze until Eddie quickly turned away.

Now walking at a pace just short of a trot, Eddie watched for cars behind him and in front.

Sixty Nine

The 7 o'clock flight Monday morning from Manchester would get Condon to Philadelphia at 8:47.

Depending on morning traffic, the 10 mile ride to the downtown 9th district police station should be under 20 minutes. Having a city squad car as your limo should make the trip pretty damn quick.

Before the plane left the gate, Condon opened the Lapierre folder to review notes from two previous interviews, as well as a copy of phone records for both a land line phone at the Moultonborough home and a cell phone. A previous look at the phone records had not raised any red flags.

When questioned about some of the numbers in the second interview three days ago, Lapierre had been able to identify private citizens contacted in his work as a political consultant. The State Police were in the process of following up on the names provided. Events of the past 48 hours now made a top priority.

Condon focused on the statement and information from the first interview a week ago, the day after Reilly's body had been pulled from the lake.

He could still see the calmness that Lapierre had

displayed in describing events of the two days preceding Reilly's departure from the Moultonborough house. Lapierre had claimed that his partner had shown no signs of distress or concern about anything going on in his life.

It was two days after that interview that police changed the classification from drowning to suspicious death. Then the Friday evening second interview at the station in Tamworth.

Condon had not yet spoken with Carolyn Wilson, a paralegal dispatched by Colonel Quincy and the AG's office to assist with the investigation. He would call Wilson before questioning Lapierre, hoping that she might have information from a substance abuse counseling session she had attended last night in Laconia.

Sergeant Will Costello, back in New Hampshire, was attempting to pull together information to verify Lapierre's income, which he claimed to be in the bracket of $150,000 to 300,000. If and when he was placed under arrest, that number would be easier to confirm.

Flipping the page of the typed notes in front of him, Condon shifted his mind to the second interview. He clearly recalled Lapierre's discomfort in acknowledging that Charles Reilly had become adamant in his attendance at meetings of the 12-step recovery program.

Then there were the names of friends and possibly a former lover in Vermont. Condon made a note to call the Vermont State Police investigator to see what he might have discovered with his work over the weekend.

Unless some significant new information surfaced in the next few hours, Condon would try to persuade Lapierre to return as a cooperating witness in the investigation. He knew from the phone conversation last night with Quincy that the alternative was to place Lapierre under arrest and force his extradition from Pennsylvania.

No sleep, no food, no caffeine, no phone calls. All self-induced by Warren Lapierre.

The man slouched partially reclined on the chair, legs extended, hands open palms up and resting on his crotch. In the assessment of Lieutenant John Hinkle, the man was as close to a zombie as he was ever likely to see. Hinkle was struck by Lapierre's resemblance to one of the characters he'd seen in a bad movie.

With each question Hinkle asked – coffee, use the bathroom, have a stretch – Lapierre moved his head only enough to nod in the affirmative or give a slight sideways twist in the negative, like a baseball pitcher taking signs from a catcher. He gave absolutely no verbal response.

Hinkle studied the man for a minute. The breathing seemed to be normal, no signs of physical stress. If it was shock, it was unlike anything Hinkle had ever seen. Still, he went back to ask another officer to come take a look.

Seventy

Frankie Sullivan got his breathing under control. An early morning runner, Sullivan had just returned home when he got the call from Officer Bill Brown of the Pelham Police Department.

Returning a phone call from the night before, Brown informed Sullivan that the body of John Dervil had been discovered in the woods not far from the Airstream trailer. Dervil was still in the clothes and street shoes he had worn when released by police Sunday morning.

"One shot in at the base of the skull and another in the right temple," Brownie said.

Sullivan's call to Brown the previous night had been at the instigation of Louie Ragsdale. Ragsdale had been curious about the trailer and thought that he and Sully would "take a run by before they haul it in."

He showered, dressed and was out the door 12 minutes after the call with Brown. The drive to the task force house and Ragsdale was only six miles.

Frankie was pumped.

Eddie Walker tried two more calls Monday morning to John Dervil. No answer.

Walker gathered his clothes, money, gun and hunting knife and shoved everything into a cheap duffel. He put the cash in the bottom with the gun and the knife. Gallagher Station was within walking distance and Eddie could take a bus or train to get out of Lowell. His first thought was take the T into Boston, then decide where he would go. No other ideas came to him so that's what he decided to do.

One more quick call to Dervil before he left the apartment. No answer.

Arno sat in his car outside Willy's Tavern. The place wasn't open yet. It was an oversight he now regretted. When he had first connected with the pair back in the summer, he had learned where Dervil lived but never had bothered to learn the exact location of Walker's apartment. Now he would try to get that information from one of the bartenders, or wait it out until Walker showed-up.

Shooting the Devil Man was the first time Arno had killed with a gun in nearly a year and his second murder in two weeks. The sensation was still the same and he liked it. But part of the new persona was that he would exercise restraint. After last night, that might be more of a challenge than he was prepared to accept.

Seventy One

The dream was about my sister. We were sitting on our grandmother's porch in Bellefonte. I was 12 and Laura was 15. In the dream, I could see the red and white potted geraniums along the bannister.

"You're going to meet lots of girls, Michael. Don't be so upset that Jeannie has another boyfriend," she was consoling me.

The conversation had actually occurred in that very location many years ago. It was after my first adolescent heartache over a lovely girl who lived in my grandmother's hometown a hundred miles from where we lived. I was there on vacation and Laura had just arrived a day after my lovesickness was beginning to bloom.

Besides the roasted chicken, asparagus, pureed sweet potatoes and apple blackberry crisp, what had stimulated my dream was the letter Bonnie left the night before.

Sitting at the kitchen table drinking coffee, I reread the three page letter. What a novel way to say, "I'm sorry, but this isn't working." Part of me wanted to laugh, but I knew that when Bonnie wrote the letter, there nothing was funny to her.

Well, almost nothing.

The mischievous component of her personality must

have kicked in when she composed the letter in my office while I was out of the house. Having dinner with another woman.

'Michael – I am sorry that we couldn't talk about this in person. I've given it a lot of thought for weeks now. Our relationship is not working.'

She went on to talk about how much fun we'd had, the hiking, the popular music we frequently debated, working in the garden, the baseball games we'd gone to, playing with her golden retriever, joking with Ragsdale about me being too old for someone like her and so on.

But the clincher (she didn't use that term but it was easy enough to conclude) was our different views on starting a family. She wanted kids and I was ambivalent, at best. There it was. Aside from a brief mention of an old boyfriend who had recently moved back to the area and whom she wanted to spend some time with, she said she hoped we could remain friends and that we could quickly overcome any awkward situations.

The last part was clearly a reference to the inevitable future contact we would have, as she was employed by one of my best clients, Frank Montagliani at Green Mountain Builders. I would likely see Bonnie every time I went there.

The absolute best part of her letter, though, was at the very end. She asked me to play tracks 16 and 17 from the Motown CD that she'd left with the letter. I played them last night and, finishing my coffee and reading the letter now for a third time, I played them again.

Back-to-back Smokey Robinson and The Miracles: *The Tracks of My Tears* and *The Tears of A Clown*.

It had been two months ago when we had sat in my downstairs media room drinking beer and laughing with Louie and his wife Becky. Ragsdale had gone into his Oldies DJ mode and had been rattling off music trivia. A little later in the evening, after Louie and Becky had left, Bonnie had put this CD in again for an encore.

I refolded the letter, put it back in the envelope, removed the CD and placed it back in its case, then headed for the shower.

Seventy Two

Lieutenant John Hinkle led Sergeant Rob Condon to the room where Lapierre had been for more than 10 hours.

"He used the bathroom once. No coffee. Hasn't used his phone. Now he's just totally shut down," Hinkle said.

Condon walked down the short corridor behind the Philadelphia detective and stopped in front of a black metal door. Hinkle turned, nodded at Condon. Condon nodded back and they entered the room.

Lapierre's eyes came up but his head didn't move. He looked at Condon, then dropped his eyes again.

"Mr. Lapierre. How are you doing?" Condon said. No response. Condon looked at Hinkle, who gave him the universal 'what gives' gesture with both hands and a shrug.

Condon pulled out the chair opposite Lapierre and sat. He crossed his arms and rested both elbows on the table.

"Were you able to visit with Mrs. Reilly?" Condon said.

Again, Lapierre's eyes shifted up, brief contact, then away looking at the far wall.

"I hope to speak to her while I'm here," Condon added as he looked at Hinkle. "We had someone attend one of the meetings in Laconia last night," Condon said. "Could be something that'll we'll learn there."

The truth was that when Condon had spoken with Carolyn Wilson not an hour ago, the chances that any useful information might come from others in that support group had appeared to be very unlikely.

Condon unfolded his arms, laid both palms flat on the table and leaned away into the straight back chair. He held that position for a few seconds, then leaned forward. If he stretched just a little, he could place both of his hands on Lapierre's chest and push him over backward.

"You're a smart man, Mr. Lapierre," said Condon, trying not to sound patronizing. "I'm sure that you know this. Right now, you are the best source of information we have. We want to find who did this. Who killed your friend Charles Reilly?"

Lapierre raised his eyes again and there was a slight twitch of his mouth. He wetted his upper lip with his tongue, clamped it down onto his lower lip, then took a small gulp as if he was swallowing something.

Condon waited, hands still on the table between them, eyes fixed on Lapierre. After what seemed like a long time, but in reality was less than 15 seconds, Lapierre pulled himself up straight in the chair and placed his arms on the table, wrists up. His knuckles almost made contact with Condon's hands. He looked directly at Condon.

"I know who killed him," Lapierre said. "I'm ready to go back." He raised his hands from the table, held his wrists close together and pushed them toward Condon.

Condon looked over his shoulder at Hinkle, then turned back to Lapierre.

"Why don't we talk about this for a few minutes? Tell us what you know."

A little before noon, AG Kelly Alexakis got the call

from Colonel Richard Quincy. Condon was bringing Lapierre back to New Hampshire and should be here by 6 PM.

She picked up the phone to call Blair Watson with the new information and to relay her belief that police would soon know who killed his cousin.

"I am personally grateful for your consideration," Watson responded when he got this news. "No doubt, your office has many other things to be concerned with," he added.

"We have an outstanding state police force, one of the best in the country," she replied. "I know that all those assigned to the case will not rest until we apprehend the person who committed this crime."

"Nothing will bring Charles back. But his mother may find solace when we learn why this happened," he said.

Quincy and Alexakis agreed they would let the press know that Lapierre had spoken with New Hampshire police and was returning to the state voluntarily.

They also agreed that there would be no live media

briefing until after a thorough interrogation of Lapierre upon his return.

Alexakis expected phone calls from reporters and anticipated that someone might stakeout the airport. But there are four major airlines serving Manchester and she doubted that Condon's return with Lapierre would be spotted.

She would tell all reporters the same thing: Colonel Quincy will alert you to a briefing just as soon as it is scheduled and there is new information to be released.

Meredith Chief Ken Storrow learned that Lapierre was on his way back to the state but didn't know details of what Condon had learned in his interview with the man.

Storrow also got the back channel word on the woman who had attended a support group meeting the night before and that it was unlikely there would be productive information from anyone in that group.

Approximately 80 miles south of Meredith and Lake Winnepesaukee, another police chief, Joseph Stark in Pelham, was learning that the Airstream trailer found in his town by two of his officers, had been traced to the manufacturer to an RV dealer in Wheeling, West Virginia. Contact with the dealer further revealed that the trailer had been purchased the previous summer by a retired coal miner 85 miles to the southeast from the town of Arnettsville and that efforts to reach the man were underway.

Stark's small department was now working with the state police regarding the body of a man found near the trailer just this morning. All the information related to one John Dervil, his brief detention by Pelham Police and the previous arrests and prison record, could help to expedite this new case.

Eddie Walker went into the men's room at Gallagher Station, stepped into a stall and took some cash from the bottom of the duffel.

Shoving five $20s into his pocket, he went to ticket machine, purchased a card that would cover more than a trip to Boston's North Station. Waiting for the train, Eddie pulled out his phone. No incoming calls. One more try to reach Dervil. Nothing.

There were more than a dozen other passengers boarding in front of him. The trip would be 47 minutes. He studied the schedule and lines from the map he picked up at the transfer kiosk. It looked as though he would have to make two changes to reach South Station and expand his travel options.

He put the map away and looked over the other passengers. Eddie could almost believe that Arno was somewhere on the train with him.

Seventy Three

What Ragsdale learned upon arrival at the trailer

in the woods was that the state police were on it.

A full forensics team had been dispatched first to cover the site where the body had been found, then to do a thorough sweep of the trailer.

After a brief discussion with one of the local cops, Ragsdale put his ID lanyard around his neck. He instructed Frankie Sullivan to do the same. They walked a short distance through the woods to where the techs were.

Inside the taped-off area where the team was now working, there was a spot on the ground where it appeared there had been recent digging. A small mound of dirt was to one side of the hole which looked to be about two feet square. The hole was possibly two feet deep.

Louie could tell that Frankie had all systems on alert. He might try to get right on top of the techs if left to his own initiative. But he didn't. Instead, Frankie tapped Ragsdale's right arm and pointed at the hole in the ground.

"You think the shooter was gonna bury the guy and panicked?" Frankie asked. Ragsdale shook his head.

The body was gone, but small plastic yellow flags in the ground indicated where the body had been discovered.

"Something was in the ground," Louie said, pointing

at the hole.

After watching for another minute, Ragsdale and Sullivan went back toward the trailer. The Pelham cop who was guarding the trailer seemed to know Sullivan. He'd only met Louie a few minutes earlier when the two had arrived.

"Sully says the guy had a drug conviction record and did some time," Ragsdale said.

"It's what I heard. You'll have to talk with the chief." The Pelham cop appeared to be in his late 30s. Certainly younger than Louie and older than Sullivan. The name on the plastic tag on his chest was Morrison. He was maybe 5'8", solid build, nothing remarkable about his face.

"You expecting the chief to show up?" Louie asked.

"Here and gone. Came out first thing when we found the body," Morrison said.

Ragsdale looked at him. "You found the body?"

The cop shook his head. "Hatch and Ingalls. They were doing a preliminary sweep before the state guys came in to see the trailer."

Looking at Sullivan, Ragsdale jerked his head to indicate their visit was over.

They walked back to Sullivan's truck and climbed in. Before Frankie could start the ignition, Louie held his hand out to stop him.

"Your guy was right about the trailer. Whoever did the

camo was damn sure nobody was going to find it."

Ragsdale was looking back at the trailer.

After my shower I sent a text to Ragsdale that he was stinking up my house and that I'd bet marines didn't do that. Monday was the day I normally spent at least 15 minutes cleaning the house and doing laundry. Under one of the twin beds in the guest room/office where Louie had slept Saturday night, I found a pair of dirty socks.

At the end of the text I asked, 'Didn't you guys get demerits or have to run 5 miles for that kind of shit?'

No reply.

Our daily paper, The Valley News, had a brief AP story about New Hampshire State Police looking for Warren Lapierre as one 'person of interest' for the ongoing investigation into the death of Charles Reilly.

I decided to call John O'Neil over on Bear Island to see what scuttlebutt he'd picked up in the past few days.

"John. It's Michael Hanlon in Vermont."

There was a hesitation at his end. You never knew with some older people if they remembered your name.

"Yes, Michael," he said. "How is that beautiful young friend Bonnie?"

"She's fine. I just had a letter from her." Where was I going with this? Too much, too personal to explain to a relative stranger.

"Has she gone back to school?"

That threw me off. Why would he think she was in school? The letter.

"No. She's busy at work. We're just catching up on a few things," I lied.

"Well, give her my regard. We enjoyed her company."

"I will do that. John, the newspaper over here has a story about a guy the state police are looking for."

"Think they've found him," he said. "Kenny says he's on his way back to New Hampshire."

Score one for Hanlon. I knew that John would know something not in the news. Score two for John. And I wondered if he had called Chief Ken Storrow, his former student, or if it had been the other way around?

"This was an AP story. Over the weekend," I said.

"The man lives on Moultonborough Bay. Has a big place. Word is they were partners. He and Reilly."

"At the law firm?" I said.

"Not business partners. What's that new term they use? Significant other. Domestic partners."

"Huh. That's going to goose things a little. If they think he did it, crime of passion and all that."

"Hard to say. Not sure they've placed him under arrest yet," John said.

We talked for a couple of minutes about the never ending political coverage and how happy we would be after the primary was over. I told him that I would give him a call next week. Fortunately, no other reference to Bonnie before he got off the phone.

Seventy Four

Arno was back in the car with his second cup of coffee. The tavern was still closed, but a man had just unlocked the front door and gone inside.

Watching the door and waiting for all of five minutes, Arno got out of the car and went into the bar. Not all of the lights were on and the man was setting up the cash register.

"Sorry. We don't open for another half-hour," the man said. Arno kept walking toward him. The man abruptly closed the cash register drawer.

"I can't serve you anything until we open," the man said.

"Not a problem," Arno replied. "Just need some information."

"You're a cop?" Arno shook his head and smiled. He pulled a $50 bill from the right pocket of his jacket, which also held the Sig P220.

"Not a chance. Just looking to reconnect with an old friend." He placed the $50 on the bar.

Arno knew when he saw the man unlock the front door that he was not the bartender on duty last night when he came to get Dervil.

"What's your friend's name?"

"Eddie. Comes here a lot with another guy." Arno pointed at the end of the bar farthest from the door.
"They usually park themselves down there at the end," he said. "His pal's name is John. I think he's out of town for a while."

"Right. Eddie is the tall thin one. Quiet. Drinks beer. His buddy has screwdrivers."

"That's him," Arno said.

"They usually don't show up 'til late afternoon. Sometimes in the evening." Arno already knew this.

"Yeah. I'm trying to find where he lives. Got a little work I need help with this afternoon. Like I said, John is away and I need to see if Eddie can help me."

The bartender gave no indication that he bought this. He left the money on the bar in front of him.

"Friend, I really don't know," he said, shrugging his shoulders. "The only time I see 'em is when they come in here. I'm gone by 6:30, so have no idea when or where they go. Wish I could help."

"Not a problem. I'll stop back." Arno turned to leave.

"Hey," the bartender said. Arno stopped and looked back. The bartender was holding the $50 bill.

"Hang on to it," Arno said. "You might be able to help me later."

The story Lapierre gave Condon and the Philadelphia detective was a little disjointed.

He'd repeated that he knew who murdered Charles Reilly, but didn't have a name. And he didn't have a description of this unnamed killer.

Condon's questions, as well as a couple from Hinkle, only led to Lapierre falling back to the non-communication act. But Condon wasn't so sure that it was an act. He thought the man might have been on some medication and was now off.

Lapierre gave no response when asked about prescriptions or other substances. At one point, after he'd repeated "I know who killed Charles," Lapierre locked eyes with Condon for few seconds, then he repeated the gesture of holding his arms out, hands close together and wrists up, as though he expected Condon to place him in cuffs.

Finally, shaking his head when asked if he wanted to speak with an attorney or anyone else, Lapierre nodded yes, he would return to New Hampshire. It was all a little strange, Condon thought.

Now they were on a plane headed to Manchester.

At 4:20 Monday afternoon, the hit on finger prints found inside the Airstream trailer set off alarms and triggered a rash of phone calls.

The FBI, state police in both New Hampshire and Massachusetts, as well as sheriff departments in five counties and all local police departments within 100 miles of Pelham, now knew they were looking for a man wanted for multiple murders and drug trafficking activities.

When the confirmation came in that the prints belonged to Arnost Waclaw Branchik, it was as if like all those privy to this new information had just knocked back about a quart of some high octane caffeine drink in unison.

The only law enforcement person not to react this way was Louie Ragsdale.

Louie's reaction was to look up from his phone, glance across the room at Frankie Sullivan working on his tablet computer, and to flash back to some very unpleasant scenes from a year earlier. A lot of blood, a log yard in Maine, running through the snow, a lot of shots fired.

Ragsdale slipped his phone back into its case and stood. He looked at his watch.

"Sully, what time are you leaving?" Louie asked.

Sullivan lived with his wife two towns away, a 20 minute drive from the house the drug task force was using for this assignment. Only Ragsdale and another veteran undercover cop alternated in staying overnight.

Sullivan looked up, hunched his shoulders and spread his hands apart. He flipped his left arm over to look at his watch.

"I don't know. Maybe another half-an-hour. Five or so. Whadda'ya need?"

Ragsdale rubbed both his temples very slowly and

methodically. He pursed his lips and with a thumb and two fingers, scratched the space between his nose and upper lip. He let out a breath.

"Think the wife will let you have a night out?" Louie said.

Sullivan looked at him and took his hands away from the tablet.

"What's up?"

Seventy Five

Everything Colonel Richard Quincy had thought about for several hours went on hold.

A talk with Condon when he returned, meet with the Attorney General, speak to reporters. All that would wait. The focus at this very minute was launching a full-blown manhunt for a vicious murderer.

Of all the crimes attributed to Arnost Waclaw Branchik – kidnapping, murder, drug trafficking, auto theft – two of the most brutal were believed to have occurred in New Hampshire. Quincy knew that before all this was over, the list of charges would be longer.

Three state police cars, with two troopers in each vehicle, had immediately been dispatched to Pelham. There would be more. And agents from the Boston office of the FBI were on their way to New Hampshire.

The only photos available of Branchik were older mug shots when he was arrested and convicted as being part of an auto parts theft ring working in northern New England and Quebec. They were the same photos used for the FBI posters and online . Shaved head, tattoo on left side of neck, a once broken nose and cold, mean eyes.

Quincy gave a last look before leaving his office.

I stared at the text message and felt a chill. The text was from Louie and predictably cryptic.

'Branchik has surfaced. Not far from here.'

After a minute replaying the events of a year ago in Maine and northern New Hampshire, I typed a response to Ragsdale.

'Somebody spotted him? Where?' No reply.

It was going on five o'clock. I knew that if anything about Branchik was out to the public, it would not show up on the TV news before six.

Walking into my office, I went to the computer and logged on to the New Hampshire Public Radio streaming audio. If they had it, it would be on one of the local news break away segments during *All Things Considered*.

I went back to my phone. Still no reply from Louie.

Frankie Sullivan called his wife to tell her that he needed to help with something and would be late, maybe a couple of hours.

As soon as he finished the call, Frankie put his phone down and turned back to Ragsdale.

"This guy sounds pretty fuckin bad," Frankie said.

A few minutes earlier, Ragsdale had given Sullivan a quick summary of the activities of Arnie Branchik.

"You have no idea."

Louie pulled his coat on and went to the bathroom. When he came out, Sullivan was standing by the door holding his own jacket and hat. Ragsdale slapped him on the shoulder.

"Saddle-up, pardner. We'll take your truck," he said, stepping in front of Sullivan and opening the door.

Seventy Six

The plane pulled up to the gate at 5:43. Condon waited for others to remove their articles from the overhead compartments and move to the front.

Standing, he backed into the aisle to let Lapierre get up from his seat. Ground attendants were already on board removing newspapers, magazines and any litter left by passengers.

Before leaving Philadelphia, arrangements had been made for Lapierre's car to be impounded, to be retrieved later. The hotel would hold his personal belongings subject to further word from police.

Lapierre had declined a snack on the plane and only drank water. Now, he moved forward slowly with Condon behind him. A female attendant stood at the bulkhead in the front of the plane. She gave a nice smile and thanked her last two passengers.

Kelley Alexakis knew about the scramble with multiple police cars coming from different directions.

She was glad that no media briefing had actually been scheduled, and with the help of an assistant was preparing another press release to go out within the hour.

Confirmation that Sergeant Rob Condon was back with

Warren Lapierre in tow had reached her office five minutes ago. The AG now shifted her thinking to the possibility that a dangerous killer was on the loose in New Hampshire.

All the most recent horrific crimes committed by the killer, that police knew about, had occurred just before she was appointed Attorney General. Now there appeared to be a real chance that he would be apprehended and face additional charges during her watch.

In the Boston office, FBI Special Agent Alex Porter was new to the region. A recent transfer from the Milwaukee field office, Porter had spent the early part of his career working the upper mid-west and with Canadian law enforcement agencies in Ontario.

Porter quickly reviewed the case summary of a kidnapping, murders and related events from a year earlier. His predecessor who worked the case, Special Agent Gary Guidi, was now in the Miramar, Florida office. Guidi and his FBI associates had compiled an extensive file on Arnost Branchik. It was the 'go to source' for all bureau activity in pursuit of this particular criminal.

When it involved an ongoing investigation, it was customary to assign agents steeped in local bureau caseload history and geography. Porter knew that as well as anyone. He also knew that he would make his best effort to be part of imminent activity just up the road in New Hampshire.

At 7:30, the Pelham Police Station gave the appearance of hosting a seminar on what to look for in purchasing a new or used law enforcement vehicle.

Located between two traffic rotaries, the back parking lot had a total of 19 visiting cruisers, patrol cars and unmarked vehicles. These were in addition to six of the 11 marked units from the Pelham Police motor pool.

Inside, Chief Joseph Stark was about to give a recap of events of the past two days that had led to the discovery of the body in the woods and the finding of Branchik's prints inside the hidden trailer.

Sitting in the back of the room, Louie Ragsdale kept an eye on Frankie Sullivan like a father watching his five-year-old on the first day of trout season.

Stark took a drink of water from a plastic bottle and shuffled some papers on the table in front of him.

"Good evening," he said, looking around at the men and women assembled in the conference room. "I know there will be a lot of questions before we finish. Let me get started. And then Colonel Quincy has some things to tell us."

Seventy Seven

Willy's Tavern had nine customers on a cold Monday evening. One was Arno. None of the others was either Eddie Walker or John Dervil.

Arno knew where Dervil was. In the woods in New Hampshire covered with some dead tree branches. What he really wanted to know was where Dervil's sidekick had disappeared to.

The bartender Arno had spoken with earlier in the day was now off duty and gone. Before he left, he had volunteered that he would be happy to get in touch if Walker turned up tomorrow, or the next day.

"You want, leave your phone number with Walt," the guy said. "One of us can call you."

"Thanks," Arno replied. "I might do that."

No bartender was about to get his phone number.

Now, a half an hour later and still no sign of Walker. Arno went to the bar and asked if he could get another cup of coffee. As bad as the coffee was, it would be his fifth mug since he had arrived more than two hours ago.

Arno decided he would give it another 30 minutes. He had other things to do, other people to see, other plans to make.

His brief encounters with Walker had given him the impression the man was both a chicken shit and a base sticker. If absolutely necessary, this could wait for another time and another place. But not for very long.

Warren Lapierre had dozed on and off from the minute he sat down. The warmer inside temperature at state police headquarters in Concord, in contrast with the cold at the airport, had had a quick effect on him.

The fact that he'd had no sleep in more than 36 hours simply put him over the top. So he was a little slow in responding when Condon came back into the room.

"You're sure that we can't get you some food," Condon said.

Lapierre blinked his eyes twice, took in a breath and slowly shook his head.

"Think you're up to talking some more? I'd like to record our conversation and have an officer take some notes."

Upon his return, Condon had checked again by phone with both Quincy and Alexakis. They were in agreement that Lapierre should not be placed under arrest at this time. Subject to new information, or a change of heart about cooperating, an arrest could be made later.

Absent the Miranda warning, Condon frequently offered to let Lapierre call a lawyer or family member. He continued to decline with only a slow shake of the head.

Opening the door to the interview room, Condon

leaned out and made a motion with his arm. A young woman in a police uniform entered. She carried a pad and two pens. Condon gestured for the officer to take one of two seats opposite Lapierre. He took the other chair.

"What I would like to do," Condon began, "is go back to some of what we talked about at your home last week. Then we can come back to your statement that you know who killed Mr. Reilly."

No response from Lapierre. Condon braced himself for another stretch of conversing with an automaton.

Seventy Eight

Nothing on NHPR about state police apprehending a man in connection with the investigation on the drowning now suspicious death at Lake Winnepsauke a week ago.

Then again, John O'Neil, my unofficial source, said himself that he wasn't sure that police had 'arrested' the man known as Warren Lapierre.

But the WMUR 9 news at 6:30 included a brief mention that the state police were interviewing a man who returned to the state and might have information on the Reilly death. The anchor woman used Lapierre's name in her report, but offered nothing specific.

No mention at all regarding anything having to do with Branchik. And Louie had gone silent, which made me a little concerned.

At 7:45, I picked up my phone and dialed Louie's number. Enough with the texts.

Four rings and straight to voicemail.

"Sometimes I'm here, sometimes I'm not. You know the drill."

"Brother Ragsdale. It's your guy lost in the Green Mountains. Need some personal advice on advancing my love life. Soon. And, should you have any update on previously sent text, by all means, please let us know if we can expect a campaign contribution in the near future. There could be a triple match to any donation you make. But the deadline is looming. Hope you are well."

My sorry attempt at humor was just that. A weak effort to bring a little levity to a potentially bad situation. Louie would know.

Absolutely not one thing at all funny involving Arnie Branchik. I would be anxious until I heard something back from Ragsdale.

Colonel Richard Quincy was briefing the gathering now. He'd been talking for five minutes.

Ragsdale's phone vibrated. He pulled it out, looked at the screen and tapped the voicemail icon. The message was from Hanlon. He put the phone back in its case.

Of all the law enforcement people in the room, more than 25 people, Ragsdale and Sullivan were the only two who appeared to be afterthoughts for an invitation list. Some of the other local cops knew Sullivan and some of the state cops knew Ragsdale. It wasn't just their civilian dress. There were a couple of suits and some plain clothes cops in attendance. Louie and Frankie, together, just cast an odd mix to the scene.

The truth was they had not been invited. It was Ragsdale's call to Quincy an hour earlier that had gotten them in. Even Chief Joseph Stark was somewhat puzzled.

But here they were, along with all the others, listening

to an overview and the beginning of a plan to find Arnost Waclaw Branchik.

The FBI guy from Boston would speak next.

Seventy Nine

Much to Sergeant Rob Condon's amazement, the man had begun to talk in coherent sentences. The digital recorder was getting it all. The female officer with the pen and pad was writing.

Once he slowly responded to Condon's first question about the afternoon of October 31st at Lapierre's home in Moultonborough, the man hadn't stopped.

It had come haltingly at first. With some long pauses. Then, with a steadier, deliberate pace and the recitation of a sequence of events and actions, he had laid out the story, only stopping for sips of water every few minutes.

"Charles and I started arguing. First, at the end of the summer. He would get really drunk. Say outrageous things. In front of friends. Called me names. Instead of pond scum, he would call me 'PAC scum.' Got a lot of laughs. Even I thought it was funny at first. Then he would get really mean."

Lapierre took a drink of water and looked at both Condon and the woman cop.

"Have you ever been around a person who drinks too much and then turns nasty on everyone?" he asked.

Condon nodded.

"That's what was happening with Charles. Every weekend. During the week, we wouldn't talk much at all. I was starting to go crazy. Then at a party Columbus Day weekend, we had some people over, the weather was still nice, it was the last time he drank, I think. He threatened me. Charles said that if I didn't stop 'throwing around sleazy money', he would try to see that 'you and your fellow PAC scums all go to jail.' It was the first time I thought I wanted to kill him."

Lapierre paused, dropped his head forward as if he'd fallen asleep, and after a few seconds, took another sip of water and resumed the story.

"The next day, it was a Monday, the holiday, he didn't come downstairs until early in the afternoon. He was still pretty hung over. I had to leave. Go to a cocktail party in Wolfeboro.

"Charles was walking around in his shorts and a bathrobe. Wouldn't bother getting dressed. And wouldn't talk to me. Didn't respond to anything I said or asked him. Finally, I said that I had to leave and would be back around 7. I told him that I would fix something on the grill and maybe we could talk then.

"Just as I was going out the door, he said that he wasn't kidding about 'some people need to go to jail.' Then he said that he was going to Vermont to see a friend and wasn't sure what time he would be back."

Condon, not for the first time, wondered about the veracity of the information that had been given to the

Vermont State Police detective who had spoken with some of Reilly's friends. Lapierre went on.

"I came home that evening. Around 9:30, Charles was not back. I nibbled on something and watched the end of the football game on TV. I went to bed around midnight. Charles didn't come back until sometime the next day."

Condon cautiously interjected a question.

"What about the house he rented in Meredith. You think he might have stayed there?"

Lapierre gave the slow shake of the head. "He almost never stayed in Meredith after we met. Most of his clothes were here." Lapierre looked around the interview room. "At my house is what I mean."

Condon nodded that he understood.

"The next weekend," he stressed the word next, "Charles told me that he had stopped drinking." Lapierre looked at Condon for a response, then added, "Just like that. Told me that he had 'had his share' and hoped 'never again to have a drop of alcohol.'

"I was relieved, but didn't think it would last. But if he was able to cut down, that would be good.

"Over the next few days, our conversations were better. Superficial for the most part, but civil. Nothing mean like before, when he was drinking.

"Almost every day, I was on the road somewhere. He would stay at his office late, not get home until after I did. Usually around 8:30 or so." He took a sip of water, this time followed by a deep breath.

"On Friday night, we had a late dinner. I thought we would watch a movie. But Charles wanted to talk. For over an hour, he tried to explain how he honestly believed that what I was doing was wrong." Lapierre stopped and looked at Condon.

"Now I know that he was right. It was wrong. It is wrong. How we get money, how it gets spent.

"But then, listening to him, I was terrified. I've been doing this for a very long time. I know a lot of people and a lot of people know me. If something happened that my work became part of some state investigation into political fundraising, it was likely that I could go to jail.

"Charles knew that. Even though he'd stopped drinking and wasn't belligerent anymore, it was the one thing that he wouldn't let go.

"He gave me a flat ultimatum. If I wanted him to continue to be a part of my life, stop 'the sleaze', find another way to be involved in politics, or it was over.

"Then he added, 'eventually someone has to pay for all this corruption.' I thought that was a repeat of his threat from earlier. I did not want to go to jail."

There was a silence that lasted possibly a full minute, as though Lapierre and Condon were both absorbing the irony of his last statement. Finally, Condon broke the silence with another question.

"What did he do after that?"

"Nothing. As far as I know. He didn't bring it up again. I think that he was giving me some time. Maybe hoping that I would change things.

"But I was more frightened than I've ever been in my entire life. And I got desperate."

Lapierre cast a glance at Condon, then took another deep breath before going on. The cop taking the notes continued writing, never making eye contact with Lapierre.

Condon thought about taking a short break, but it was obvious the man had more to say.

Eighty

Arno's bunking options had gotten thin when the trailer had gotten hot. Now it was back to small, not particularly appealing motels away from the interstates.

Since returning to New England in the summer, he had made a point of knowing where a lot of down and out, barely operating motels were located. He never stayed in the same motel two nights in row.

Keeping clothes and all his possessions in the trunk and back seat of his car, Arno had not yet settled into the trailer. All that he left behind were some toiletries acquired from the cheap motels. While he didn't think small town cops were going to fool with any DNA testing, he was concerned about his finger prints inside the trailer.

Off state Route 38 just across the border in New Hampshire, there was a small lake. Next to the lake were a few cottages, a motel and a snack bar, all dating back to the 60s. The name of the place was State Line Cabins. A good spot on trips to and from Portland, Arno had scouted it before but this would be his first stay there.

When he pushed the buzzer at the office door and went inside, a young Indian man came from the small office behind the registration desk.

"I'd like to rent one of the cabins," Arno said.

"I am very sorry," the man said in the Indian, sing-song delivery that many stand-up comics imitate. "All of our cottages are now closed for the season. We do have some very nice rooms."

The man produced a map showing an outline of the motel with rooms going in both directions from the office. He placed the tip of a pen on one of the rooms on the map. The single room was available at the off-season rate of $69 a night, which came to 75.21 with tax. Arno gave the man four $20s, took the room key and parked his car behind the motel. Five minutes and three trips to the car later, he was in the motel room with the TV on.

With the days growing shorter and the weather beginning to change, Arno again thought that his timing was off. Having spent seven months of the past year in Florida and the south, now was the time to be headed back there, not screwing around up here in the north.

Inside the aluminum case on the floor next to the bed were two additional handguns, sufficient materials for making an improvised explosive, two fake driver's licenses, a flat 14inch bar with leather wrapped at one end, and over $200,000 in cash.

As soon as he had another $50,000, it would be time to head south and establish his own operation.

Eighty One

More than an hour after he began his story, Warren Lapierre was completely spent. He sat at the table in New Hampshire State Police interview room number three and appeared to be falling back into a catatonic state.

Condon waited to be sure the man wouldn't think of something to add. Lapierre had closed down. Again.

The final words in his lengthy confession were, "I was desperate. This is all on me."

What the digital recording would make clear was that despite repeated offers to have an attorney present, the man had simply wanted to get the story out of his mind. Lapierre had said that both before Reilly's death, going back to the middle of October, and especially from the minute he learned that Charles was actually dead, he could measure by the minute the rushing onset of fear, desperation, hopelessness and now the sense that he was going mad.

Condon summoned another state trooper to join them in the interview room. The new cop helped Lapierre to stand while Condon recited the Miranda warning. He was placed in hand cuffs and led to a holding cell a floor below the interview rooms.

"He gave us a name of a man living in Portland, Maine," Condon said. "I spoke to Colonel Hewitt in Augusta. He'll call as soon they have him," he added.

"What's the name?" Quincy asked.

"Lazelle. Robert Lazelle. Sounds as though Lapierre's known the guy for a long time."

"Did he say Lazelle is the killer?"

"No. Claims that Lazelle is a fixer. Collections, money laundering, unpleasant tasks. Probably drugs. Said the guy is real slick, has contacts all over the Northeast."

Quincy looked at his watch: 9:17.

"I have a few more minutes with Chief Stark, then I'm headed back. We'd really like to get this Branchik guy. If he's still around here," Quincy said.

"Anybody see him? Or you just have the prints?" Condon asked.

"No reported sightings. The feds are convinced that he's changed his appearance. That certainly won't help."

"Listen, Rob. Good work with Lapierre. Let me know what you hear from Maine."

Condon assured him that he would call first thing. Next up was a call to the Attorney General. Quincy told Condon to go ahead and make that phone call.

When Kelly Alexakis got the abbreviated version of Lapierre's confession, she thanked Condon and said that she would wait to speak with Quincy and for any news from the Maine State Police before going to the media.

I was about to turn off the Chargers and the Bears on TV when my phone chirped. Volume on mute, I looked at the phone. Ragsdale.

"Hey," I said.

"The scumbag's out there. Found a guy's body. And Branchik's prints on the inside of a camping trailer," Louie responded.

"Where?"

"Parked out in the woods between Pelham and Nashua, near the Mass border."

"How'd the guy die?"

"Two shots to the head. One at the base of the skull, just like the Canadian car dealer last year."

"Anything else in the trailer?"

"Nada. Looks like he might've spent the night there, but nothing else. Some dry goods and stuff they think were already there," Louie said.

I remembered the inside of a ski chalet in Gorham a year ago where Branchik had spent some time. It was pretty Spartan, too. But the chalet belonged to another slime ball.

"Is this a hunting camp?" I said.

"Nah. Pretty nice Airstream. Local cops think it's only been there for a short time."

"So, the search resumes, eh?"

"Maybe half the New Hampshire State Police Force, bunch of locals. And the feds got here pretty quick."

Louie told me that he and his drug task force guys

were not part of the manhunt yet, but that he wasn't out of it, either. He'd made certain that his previous encounter with Branchik was on the record, as well as his willingness and availability to help now.

I said that if and when it was practical, I'd appreciate hearing what happened. He said that he would send a text message or call.

"Stay smart, stay safe, Louie."

"Always."

I turned off the TV, got the coffeemaker ready for the morning and headed for bed.

Eighty Two

At 11:26 PM, four Maine State Troopers entered the quiet lobby of the East View Condominiums located in downtown Portland.

There was a man seated behind a desk off to the right of the lobby, near some large potted plants. An African American of light complexion, he wore a burgundy blazer over a button down white shirt and navy necktie. His gray hair and gold, wire-rimmed glasses made the man appear to be in his 60s, possibly older. He looked startled at the sight of four state policemen approaching.

"Good evening," one of the troopers said. "We're here to see Mr. Lazelle."

The man behind the desk adjusted his glasses and reached for a phone in front of him.

"That won't be necessary," the trooper said, extending his right arm across the desk to indicate that calling Mr. Lazelle was not what they had in mind.

Putting down the phone the man straightened himself in the chair.

"Fourth floor. There are just two units. Lazelle is 401, on the left."

The man waved an open hand to show that the elevator was around the corner from where he sat.

"Thank you." The trooper nodded to his fellow officers and stepped back.

"Corporal," the lead trooper added, looking at the youngest guy in the group, "stay here at the desk, if you would, please."

Not 30 seconds after the elevator door closed,   the three state troopers were standing in front of condo 401. Even though any imminent threat to their personal safety was unlikely, two of the troopers held H & K 45s at the ready.

When the door opened, one Robert Lazelle, veteran financial guru, entrepreneur, longtime political donor, drug and illegal firearms dealer, knew instantly that his life was about to take a turn that he had not anticipated.

It was Tuesday morning shortly after eight o'clock when FBI Special Agent Alec Porter got on the phone with his predecessor in the Boston office, Special Agent Gary Guidi, now working in Florida and the Southeast.

Porter filled in the background on events of the past 24 hours and the renewed hunt for Arnie Branchik. When he'd finished, Guidi remained silent for a few seconds, then was like a runner out the starting block.

"Look at the notes. One of the things we determined right after they got the girl back, was that Branchik had a pattern of staying at non-descript motels," Guidi said, adding, "No video that we could find, but his description fit with three different clerks we interviewed."

"I saw that," Porter said. "And that was a big part of the effort in the weeks after he disappeared."

"Let the state guys do main street, shopping plazas, bars and clubs and all that. Put your guys on the motels. Gotta be a ton of those rundown places up there."

Louie Ragsdale called his boss early and was happy to get the return call.

"This is the slowest run we've had in two years," Ragsdale said. "One bust on a woman trying to sell in Portsmouth three weeks ago. Weak case. And pretty quiet since that," Louie said.

Marty Evans, a DEA Deputy Director for New England, New York and Pennsylvania, was the chief administrator working with individual states and their drug enforcement teams. Ragsdale was one of only a few 'floaters' in the region and had been with the Northeast Anti-Drug Task Force since its inception in 2006. So he knew Marty pretty well and Marty knew him.

"You looking for time off to go hunting, Louie?" Marty asked.

"Not at all. I'm scheduled for a week at Thanksgiving. But something's happening up here that I'd like to hook up with. I think I can help out."

"What is it?" Marty said.

"You remember the bad ass killer we chased in Maine last year? Guy who kidnapped the two college students?"

"Kind of hard not to remember. What's his name, Brottchik?"

"Branchik. Arnie Branchik. Real piece of shit. Killed at least three people that we know about. Now they think he's back around here."

"In New Hampshire?"

"Yeah. Not far from where I am right now. They found a stolen Airstream trailer in the woods. Branchik's prints in several different spots inside the trailer. And, purely coincidence, a twice convicted dealer from Massachusetts showed up dead a day later. Body nearby in the woods. Two shots to the head."

"So, what're you saying, Louie?"

"Free me up for a few days. Call somebody at the FBI Boston office. See if you can get me on the team."

"You don't really believe they'll do that," Marty responded.

"Don't know if you don't ask. At least set up a phone call. Let me talk to the guy leading the charge."

"I'll see what I can do. Don't hold your breath."

"One other thing," Ragsdale said.

"Yes?"

"We have this young local cop with us. Loaner whose chief probably wanted him out of his hair for a while. He's helping spot and track suspect vehicles, chasing rumors and that. No contact with sellers."

"And?"

"Good kid. Full of piss and vinegar. Just needs a little direction. If we can swing something with the feds, I'd like to take him along."

"Christ, Louie. You want me to get you a couple of tickets to a Patriots game? Anything else?"

"Don't know if you don't ask."

"OK. I'll get back to you." Marty clicked off.

Ragsdale poured another cup of coffee and waited for Frankie Sullivan to arrive at the house.

Eighty Three

There was no reason to go back to Portland. So Arno would not 'reach out' to Mr. Smooth until the end of the week, as discussed.

What a fucking pansy phrase, 'reach out'. But Lazelle used it often in conversations about new recruits, new customers and possibly new opportunities 'unrelated to your activities to date'.

Arno decided his best play was to stay close enough to Lowell that he could double back and hope to find Eddie Walker. So he broke precedent. He decided to spend a second night at State Line Cabins.

The room was comfortable enough if not 'very fine'. There was almost no traffic on this road, as far as he could tell from last night and this morning. Maybe 10 cars total. And it was a half mile out to Route 38.

After a shower, he put on the same black jeans and a fresh one of three black long-sleeved shirts from his bag. He carried the aluminum case to the trunk, drove the car around front to the motel office and went inside. He was prepared with the $80, which he placed on the counter.

"Another night, if that's OK," he said to the same man who had checked him in 14 hours ago.

"It is perfectly fine. We are very happy to have you as our guest," the man said. "The bed is comfortable?"

"It's good," Arno said. "One thing. Is there a wash and dry place around here?"

"A laundry. To wash clothing?"

"Yes. I have some clothes ..."

"We would be very happy for any of your washing," the man replied.

Arno studied him for a few seconds, then smiled. The guy was genuine. Wanted to make it in this country.

"It's just a couple of shirts, a pair of jeans. Some socks and underwear," Arno said.

"That is no problem. Please bring your washing here, to the desk."

Back in his car, he went to get something to eat at the first drive-thru he could find. He always avoided going inside at restaurants or diners during daylight hours. Now that he had decided to keep the room for another night, he also decided that he would not go back to Lowell until late in the day.

Eddie Walker, let's have a talk about your friend the Devil Man.

Eighty Four

Condon was meeting with Colonel Quincy and the AG to coordinate next steps with the Maine State Police.

As fully expected, Robert Lazelle's lawyer responded immediately, arriving in Augusta about the same time the troopers brought him in.

After placing him under arrest for suspicion of aiding in a capital crime, then more than an hour of questioning at 1:30 AM, the lawyer suggested that with some rest and further counsel, Mr. Lazelle could be ready to discuss cooperating with the investigation if they resumed their session this morning. That was scheduled for 11 o'clock with Maine's Attorney General to sit in.

Following a meeting with a court appointed attorney, Warren Lapierre had been placed in a cell. He later would be moved to a federal facility in the northern end of the state to await possible further charges and a trial date. It was anticipated that he would ask to hire his own lawyer.

Quincy agreed that the AG's office should schedule and lead the media briefing on the developments in the Reilly case. He wanted to remain focused on the search underway for Arnost Branchik.

Virginia Jackson called me at lunch time to ask if I'd heard about Vice President Joe Biden's press conference.

"No. Did he announce?" I said.

"Just the opposite. Says he will not be a candidate."

Part of our political discussion at dinner Sunday night had revolved around what Biden's entry into the race might do. She had been of the opinion that he wasn't up to it and would have a hard time challenging Hillary Clinton. I hadn't been so sure.

"OK. It's still eight plus months until their convention and all those primaries coming up next spring. Things get bogged down and no clear leader in the race, I wouldn't count Joe out of it," I said.

"I would. You watch, he's going to be campaigning for Hillary by this time next year."

"Is this some sisterhood thing?" I asked.

"No, it isn't. She's smart, qualified, experienced. She's ready. And she's a grandmother."

"Can't wait to see how the ad folks work that. You're going to see subliminal AARP stuff creeping into her TV spots. Lock down the boomer vote."

"You know, Michael. It's a little hard to figure where you will land with your vote."

"Hey. I told you. I'm Bernie all the way."

I switched her off politics for a couple minutes and told her about the hunt for Branchik. Back in the summer, she'd sat slack jawed when I gave her the story of all the things that had happened in Maine with a kidnapping and murders the previous year.

"You hear these things," she said, "and believe me, I heard some truly nasty stuff all the time I lived in the city, and it makes you wonder. How does someone become a monster like that?"

"Right. How does it happen? Now we have teenagers shooting up schools and churches."

"The modern history of crime in America, back to the time of the pilgrims, has always included some element of random and not so random brutality," she said. "Just ask some First Nations people. And maybe the descendants of some slaves in this country."

"Pardon the pun, but it ain't black and white. Too many threads woven into this tapestry," I offered.

"Then we get to the death penalty."

"Don't go there," I said. "I'll come sit in on one of your classes sometime."

"Criminal law and the US penal code are not my bailiwick," she said. "It can often be interesting and depressing at the same time."

Before we hung up, I filled her in with the little information I'd learned about the man now talking with police on the Reilly case.

"We'll see where it goes. You could have a TV crew and satellite truck on campus before it's over," I said.

"Let's hope not."

Eighty Five

"**This is how it'll work, Louie,**" Marty Evans said. "I really talked you up. There's new guy in Boston who's running this. His name is Alec Porter. I'll text you his number."

"Good," Ragsdale said.

"I told him all about your encounter with Branchik last year. Told him that you know the New Hampshire coast like the back of a striped bass. Then I lied. I told him that you were one of the best agents we have."

"What's this 'were', kemosabe?"

"About the young cop. What's his name?" Marty said.

"Sullivan."

"He travels with you, he's your charge. Got it?"

"No question."

"And, you be damn sure that you square it with his chief first. No hotdog stuff."

Five minutes later, Ragsdale was on the phone with Special Agent Porter. They agreed to meet at 3 o'clock at the Pelham Police Station.

"Sully," Ragsdale said when he got off the phone. "Call your chief. Ask if we can stop by around 2 o'clock. I wanna talk to him about a new assignment."

The case Ragsdale made to include Frankie Sullivan went over better than he had anticipated.

Sullivan's chief acknowledged that it was the kid's energy, eagerness and smarts that had gotten him the temporary assignment to the task force. He went on to say that he expected some 'great things' from Frankie and that an experience like this would only help him in the long run.

All this was exchanged with Ragsdale while Frankie was out back, at the Chief's suggestion, catching up with fellow officers he hadn't spent time with in almost a month. Ragsdale would bring him up to speed before the meeting in Pelham in 30 minutes.

Special Agent Porter travelled with four other agents in three separate vehicles. They would be the first thrust at checking motels, per Special Agent Guidi's suggestion.

After a brief introduction to Pelham Chief Joe Stark, the agents divided into pairs to begin scouting the motels. Stark made a short list before they left the station.

It was agreed that one pair would work their way northwest of the town, in the direction of where the trailer and body were discovered. The other team would start at the Mass border and work to the northeast.

"I would hit Route 38 first. Go south on Bridge Street down to the town line with Dracut, then double back this way," Stark suggested. "There are a couple places on that list," he added.

Robert Lazelle's attorney, Milton Washburn, of the old downtown Portland firm of Christian, Peters and Washburn, was moving toward a deal.

It was possible, Washburn said, that his client might have access to information regarding 'contract individuals' who might be able to assist police in the investigation into the death of Charles Reilly.

Furthermore, Washburn noted that Mr. Lazelle had recently become aware of 'questionable activities' involving the finances of several of his clients. Washburn dressed it up as a rash of 'apparent greed and total disregard for others' following the Great Recession.

And it was possible, Washburn added, that in the process of compiling information to be shared with the state, Mr. Lazelle could, in fact, 'furrow up' still other material that might be of some use to prosecutors, 'here in Maine and in other states'.

The Maine Attorney General, Jane Tarleton Miller, waited for a few seconds to be certain that Washburn was finished. Apparently, he was.

Miller stood from her chair and stared at the two men.

"It all sounds like a load of horseshit to me, Mr. Washburn. But, by all means, put it in writing. We'll have a look. In the meantime, your client's bail hearing is set for 10 o'clock tomorrow morning."

Miller left the room. Washburn closed his brief case. And Robert Lazelle, in hand cuffs, was escorted out by a Maine State Trooper.

Eighty Six

Arno left the motel again at 4:30. A 20 minute drive to Lowell, right down 38 and across the river.

Of all the times he'd been in this city, not once had he been to the office of Richard Marco. Going all the way back to his first gig with Marco five years ago, every meeting had been at some restaurant, diner or bar.

It didn't matter. Mr. Smooth seemed to run the operation, at least anything Arno was connected to. That only became apparent when Arno had had his first sit-down with Lazelle a year ago. A week after that, he had found himself getting one of those 'offers you cannot refuse'.

Driving into the city this time of day was a lot better than driving out. The traffic, especially on 495 and Route 3. Why the fuck do people put up with that every day? A flashback to Florida and the set up Marco and Smooth had arranged there for Arno for a few months. He knew day one, and they must have suspected, that he didn't fit there. The way his head was working then, he coulda been dead in a week.

But as difficult and frustrating as it was not to kill about 10 dickheads, he survived and made it back to the

Northeast. Things here were working better than he'd thought they might back in the summer. And his cut, just like they promised last December, was getting better every month.

Arno turned onto Bridge Street, headed for downtown, passed the canal and took a side street shortcut to Central Street and Willy's Tavern. If Walker wasn't there, or didn't show by 7 o'clock, tough shit.   I can do this almost every day for a month if that's what it takes.

Eddie, we need to have a quick word. I have some information from your friend Dervil.

Arno found a spot and parked at 4:57 PM.

The two FBI agents working south of Pelham, Carl Henderson and George Becker, were both in their late 20s.

Even though Henderson and Becker had been with the bureau for five years, both men had worked out of the Boston office for less than a year. And they had never been part of an active hunt for someone who had made the Most Wanted list.

Starting at a small motel with fewer than 40 rooms right at the Mass/New Hampshire line, they stopped at two more on their drive back toward the center of town. At each stop they showed their IDs, questioned the clerk on duty and were permitted a look at all room registrations for the past two weeks. In one case they were able to see a whole month. They asked for and were given printouts.

Showing and leaving behind a copy of the FBI   poster

at each stop, the agents always pointed out the financial incentive information. **REWARD:** The FBI is offering a reward of up to $100,000 for information leading directly to the arrest of Arnost Waclaw Branchik.

Approximately half-way between the border and the center of town, two miles from the police station where they started, they passed a small sign at a side road.

"Turn around," Henderson said.

Becker slowed, pulled off the pavement, then did a 180 turn to go back to the side road.

The sign read 'State Line Cabins' with the arrow pointing east.

Eighty Seven

Ragsdale was mildly surprised at how laid back the new agent-in-charge appeared to be.

But when he thought about it for a minute, he would have had a hard time pointing at any FBI man or woman in his experience working with the multi-state task force, who fit the old stereotype of 'uptight and always right'.

Porter explained what the four agents were doing in Pelham about checking the motels.

"You know that New Hampshire troopers, along with some of the Pelham PD, are all over Hillsborough County and beyond," Porter said. Louie nodded, Sullivan shifted back and forth like a boxer just in the ring.

"Chief Stark's had the trailer covered since Sunday morning, even before we learned about the prints. Now there are six men out there in different spots."

"He's not coming back there after he shot the guy and left him," Ragsdale said.

"Probably not," Porter said. He studied Ragsdale, then went on.

"Maybe best thing for you two is some help with the motels. It would be dumb to check only the mom and pop places. Chief Stark says there are some of the lower bracket national chains around, too."

"We can do that," Frankie Sullivan blurted. Louie gave

him a look. Sullivan nodded and gestured with his hands and arms at the same time, as if to say 'let's go'.

"You know with this area?" Stark said to Ragsdale.

"Yes."

"Then," Porter added, now he gestured in Sullivan's direction, "Have at it."

When they reached Sullivan's pick-up in the lot and climbed in, Louie pointed at the police radio mounted under the dash.

"That's why we're in your truck. Lock in the frequency and keep the volume up." Frankie did as instructed, then slowly pulled out of the Pelham PD lot.

"Head west. There's a Motel 6 about 10 minutes from here," Louie said, as he placed a handful of FBI posters on the seat next to him.

Kelly Alexakis got the news that Warren Lapierre was under a 'suicide watch' at the prison in Berlin.

Because of staff shortages, the NH Department of Corrections was considering allowing trained inmates to conduct suicide watches, a model used in federal prisons and some other state facilities. The approach had shown at least some success.

Lapierre was taken to the Northern NH Corrections Facility in Berlin, two hours north of the state capitol. With an inmate population of just under 700, Lapierre being the newest arrival, he would be closely watched by guards until his return for court appearances.

Alexakis had also been in touch with her counterpart in Maine when she had learned of the arrest of Robert Lazelle. The reports coming from Colonel Quincy about the manhunt only 40 miles south of Concord were giving the AG a shift in focus from much of the routine white collar criminal activity her office handled.

She had little time to observe or think about presidential wannabes running all over the state.

Eighty Eight

Agent Henderson's call went straight to Alec Porter's cellphone. He was quick to the point.

"Possible live sighting. Two hours ago. We need a team, south on Route 38. There's a road that runs out to a small lake," Henderson ran everything together.

"Wait. Here? In Pelham?" Porter said.

"Yes. A place called State Line Cabins. Some cottages and a small motel. Manager says they had a guy check in last night. This morning he paid for another night, but he's not here."

"Changed his mind and took off?" Porter asked.

"Maybe not. He picked up some laundry they did for him around 4 o'clock. When he paid for the second night he told the manager not to bother with maid service," said Henderson.

"Hold on." Porter held the phone away from his ear and partially covered it. He spoke to Chief Joe Stark.

"Place called State Line Cabins. Couple of miles from here." Stark nodded.

"Yeah. Out by Dutton Pond," Stark replied.

"Can you send somebody to check for prints? Becker and Henderson are there now." Stark turned away to get someone from his town department to meet up with the federal agents.

"Local guy's on the way," Porter said, back on the phone. 'We'll get some others out there."

"Carl," Porter added, "stay alert. If it's Branchik and he didn't take off, that means he's coming back."

When he ended the call, Porter thought about what he'd just told Henderson. He walked to Stark's office to discuss the next step.

Stark and Porter went to the dispatcher on duty, where Stark told the woman to contact two of the town patrol units and send them to State Line Cabins.

Unlike the wanted posters being left at motels, the sheets the agents used included a copy of finger prints on the back. Any similarity with the prints would trigger an immediate response and have additional force on the scene.

Henderson and Becker did a quick look at the motel room where they found an unmade bed and used towel in the bathroom, nothing else.

There were tire imprints in the grass at the back corner of the motel. The manager told them the man had parked his car there, rather than in the paved lot in front of the room.

On the sign-in card at the desk, he'd simply written 'rental' in the space for vehicle information. The manager said the car looked older, he thought it was an American model and that it was a medium green color. He didn't notice the plates and doubted the housekeeping woman had seen them as she did not go to that end of the motel, per request. The only other guests at the motel were an older couple up from Massachusetts. They had checked out just before lunch. The agents had their names and address should it be necessary to contact them.

Navi Patel read the FBI poster again. The only thing about the man's face in the photographs were his eyes. The man's head was shaved and in one photo you could see a tattoo on his neck.

The man who checked in last night had had a mustache and beard, with longer hair bushing out from underneath his hat. The hat was something Navi had once heard called a driving cap. He'd seen some older cricket players wearing them when he was in England.

Registering under the name James Fain, with an address in Portland, Maine.

Navi showed the poster to his wife. **REWARD:** The FBI is offering a reward of up to $100,000 for information leading directly to the arrest of Arnost Waclaw Branchik.

Eighty Nine

With Dervil out of the picture and Walker not making an appearance, Arno was going to have find a new drop man for some leg work. This corner of the city was too profitable to ignore.

Before he had gotten the hard-on for the Airstream trailer and the phone call to handle a task up at Lake Winnepesaukee, Dervil and Walker had been just two more dickheads who could help move some product.

They were users themselves, but didn't appear to be too far out there yet. In less than a month, they'd peddled more than Arno expected. Now, a change in the line-up.

He looked around the sad cases hanging out at Willy's Tavern. No promising prospects. Everyone in this crowd appeared to have quite a fondness for alcohol, but possibly not for anything else. No bleary-eyed, washed-out souls. No jittery, jacked-up firecrackers hoping for a quick score.

And no Eddie Walker. Arno looked at his watch; 7:21 PM. He put money on the bar and left the tavern.

"Looks like a match," Henderson said. "We have a thumb and two fingers on the bathroom door and the door to the room. The Pelham cop with the field kit dusting surfaces in the room used powders and a UV light. She showed

Henderson the results which they compared to the FBI sheet of Branchik's prints.

Porter once again held the phone away from his ear and motioned to Chief Joe Stark in his office.

"We're going to get some other units out there. Set up a perimeter," Porter said into the phone. "If we think he's coming back, Carl, we want this guy."

Less than 60 seconds after the call ended, the second FBI team was redirected to the motel, along with two more Pelham patrol cars and four NH State Police units. It was very likely that still more law enforcement personnel would be involved within a matter of minutes.

Arnost Waclaw Branchik was now closer than he'd ever been, at least as far as Porter knew. Everyone wanted the man behind bars. Again.

Ragsdale tapped up the volume button on the mobile transceiver unit mounted in Frankie Sullivan's truck.

Sullivan began to slow the vehicle as they listened to the Pelham dispatcher.

"Ten-eighteen. 38 south, Currier Brook Road to Dutton Pond. State Line Cabins. All units ten-forty."

Even if Louie wasn't up to speed, Frankie knew the 10-18 urgent code and the 10-40 for no lights, no siren.

Ragsdale made a circling motion with his right hand for Frankie to turn around. Emergency flashers on and slowing almost to a stop for the car behind him to pass, Sullivan maneuvered the truck so they were now heading east back toward Pelham.

Louie calculated that it could take them 10 minutes to get back as they were almost in Hudson when the call came over the radio.

"Keep your 4-ways on 'til we hit Route 38," Ragsdale said. Sullivan let the truck's emergency lights continue and increased his speed to 70 on a 50 MPH secondary road.

It was impossible to know what activity prompted the 10-18 urgent code. The dispatcher might come back on with other information before they got there.

Ragsdale tapped the volume button up another notch. While Frankie concentrated on the road, Louie   brought his focus back to an image of Arnie Branchik.

The voice in Ragsdale's said, "We'll get you, scumbag."

Ninety

Ten years in the US, Navi Patel and his wife Ananda had never imagined what they saw at this moment; police crowding their living quarters talking into hand-held radios.

"Any road, any trail, any parking area," Porter said to the cops in the tiny motel lobby, "cover it." He looked at the faces of every person in the room to be sure they'd absorbed his directive.

Without official jurisdiction over the local and state cops, Porter had to trust they all could function together on short notice and that they would follow the training each one of them had completed to become a law enforcement officer in the first place.

Arno was back in the car heading for the motel. No luck at Willy's. He'd decided to wait and spend the next day scouting other establishments for new blood. Then he would call Mr. Smooth.

Growing up in Chicago and learning to deal with some mean fuckers, coming east and earning his due with a bunch of two-bit auto theft assholes, it didn't take long to see where the real money was.

The prison stint had made him tougher and helped his

rep. No one who really knew Arnie Branchik was going to fuck around. It was this realization that had begun to grow nearly a year earlier and now fed his drive to 'go it alone'.

What he'd become accustomed to and now missed was the gratification from committing acts of brutality and violence. It was better than drugs, although he was pretty gratified with his coke. It was often better than sex, but he liked to combine the two when possible.

Driving in the dark, compulsively checking his thrill list of past accomplishments, Arno wondered if aging actually influenced one's attitude.

He knew from prison that there were a lot of tough guys and some really bad motherfuckers out there. He simply had to put a few of them to work for him now.

Crossing into New Hampshire, he turned into a fast food drive-thru for a burger and some fries. When he got his order, he pulled to the customer parking area to eat.

Killing the engine, he looked at this watch. 8:03 PM.

Warren Lapierre sat on the edge of a bunk in a prison cell. Back in his zombie demeanor, he wasn't sure that he could speak if he tried.

The guards were checking on him every few minutes. They would look in, say something to which he would not reply, then leave, only to come back again.

Following the confession earlier with the state police, Lapierre had no real idea of what was being done with the information he had shared. He spent no time thinking about Robert Lazelle and had no clear thoughts about what might or might not be occurring outside these walls.

Lapierre was exactly in the very location that he most desperately did not want to be back when he had first conceived the idea of having Charles Reilly murdered.

Richard Marco was just a little anxious. The afternoon phone call from Robert Lazelle's lawyer was possibly the first time in more than 25 years when Marco had had a real concern about their partnership.

With Lazelle in police custody, even if only overnight, someone needed to contact Branchik and tell him to go underground. Now.

Marco went to his desk and pulled out the burner phone he used for calls like this. When the phone booted, he scrolled the contacts for Branchik's number.

Ninety One

Three roads connecting with Currier Brook Road were now blocked by police vehicles, as well as two old logging trails and a pull-off area two miles from the main road.

The parking lot in front of State Line Cabins had two unmarked vehicles and three state police cruisers. A state police K-9 unit was on the way.

After Ragsdale and Sullivan got there, they were talking with two NH troopers when a call came over the radio. A cruiser positioned close to Route 38 had engaged with a driver in a dark green Pontiac that had made a quick turn and was now speeding away.

Instantly the two troopers were in their cruiser and moving with Sullivan's truck right behind them.

The chatter on the radio had the Pontiac heading south on a side road, not the highway. When Sullivan heard this he swerved his truck to the left. Louie looked at Frankie as he cut through the corner of a field and came out 50 yards farther on a road going downhill.

"These roads meet down from the lake," Frankie said. "If he's on the road I think he took, we got him."
The state police cruiser was still heading out Currier Brook Road above them. A second cruiser had joined in.

Sullivan's truck came to an intersection at the bottom

of the hill. He stopped, shifted to neutral and waited, nervously tapping the steering wheel with both hands. Ragsdale was watching the road coming from his right.

Twenty seconds later, headlights approached. The driver of the Pontiac didn't look at them as he raced by.

"Game's up, asshole," Frankie said, pulling the truck out to chase the Pontiac.

"Where's this road go?" Ragsdale said.

"Straight to jail, do not pass go. Dead ends in about one minute."

Not a full minute after it passed them, the Pontiac was stopped at a clearing where the road ended. As Sullivan approached, Ragsdale pulled his gun out and shot one of the rear tires on the Pontiac. The right corner of the car sank.

A man got out the driver's door and fired back, hitting the outside mirror on the driver's side of the truck, with a second shot shattering the windshield.

Frankie was flat on the seat and Ragsdale was getting out the passenger side. Neither of them were hit.

The man started for the woods when Ragsdale fired. The shot hit him in the right hip. He went down half-way, turned and fired back, then tried to make it to the woods.

Ragsdale knelt on his right knee, gripped the pistol with both hands and fired again. The man went down.

Sullivan was out of the truck and joined Louie as they walked toward the man on the ground. Both had their guns aimed at him. He showed no sign of shooting again. A cruiser came to a stop next to Sullivan's truck.

Marco got no answer on Branchik's phone, just the message, "Tell me what you need. I'll get back to you."

"What I need is for you to check in. Small problem here," Marco said, not leaving his name or number. Branchik would know.

And Branchik would know. He just wouldn't be calling back anytime soon.

Lazelle had considered various scenarios and none that he could come up with showed much promise for the long haul. Eventually, he was going to jail.

He was reasonably confident that his lawyer could dance and deal for a while, that he could name others who were not going to be pleased, and that he might get a lesser sentence than the judicial guidelines called for. But he would do some time.

It had occurred to him before and he had dismissed the thought. Now he had to act on it. Speak with his ex-wife and tell her about the safe deposit box.

He wasn't sure how fast things moved, but if the police were not on it yet, his lawyer could get her to come to see him tomorrow. She could get to the bank; that was not a problem. What happened next was the question.

Ninety Two

Branchik was alive and an ambulance was coming. The second shot had hit him in the neck, about one inch from his carotid artery.

One of the state cops applied sterile compress gauze to the neck wound and put tape on it. Branchik was conscious and grimacing, but he did not speak.

Before the second state police cruiser arrived, Ragsdale shot out the other three tires on the Pontiac, which puzzled both Frankie Sullivan and the two state cops at the scene.

"Old score," Ragsdale said. He walked back to the truck with the shattered windshield.

The word went out rapidly – a ten-95 on the radio – that the suspect was in custody. Porter and his FBI agents were at the scene just as the ambulance arrived.

Colonel Richard Quincy got the call on the incident in Pelham and that Branchik had been apprehended.

Relaying the information to the Attorney General gave him a momentary sense of relief, much like the end of a bloody shootout in the small town of Colebrook many years ago.

Quincy and AG Kelly Alexakis were extremely grateful that no officers or citizens had been injured in the process. Both knew the story would get a lot of play in the media.

Ragsdale was leaning against the hood of the truck, his arms folded. Sullivan had been talking with Porter, the other FBI agents and the state cops.

"Sully," Ragsdale said. Frankie looked over and Louie made a motion with his head for Sullivan to join him.

Ragsdale took a small notebook and pen from his jacket and wrote something. He tore off the sheet of paper and handed it to Frankie.

Sullivan read it, then looked at Louie, who just nodded and pointed at the EMTs about to load Branchik into the ambulance.

Frankie walked to the back of the ambulance and read from the piece of paper in his hand.

"Good luck in the ER, scumbag. Hope the blood supply doesn't run out."

The EMTs closed the doors and moved out.

Later, on the slow drive back to the Pelham Police Station, Frankie asked Ragsdale why he just didn't give Branchik the message himself.

"Afraid I'd shoot the fucker again."

Frankie nodded at the answer.

Ninety Three

It was early Wednesday morning when I got the call from Louie.

In what I suspected was a sanitized version of what really happened, he told me about the chase and the shooting the night before.   As I listened to him describing the events, a thought occurred to me.

"It'll be on the news later, but I'm going to call the Farrands. And the Turners," I said, referring to the families of the two women who'd been kidnapped by Branchik a year ago.

We talked about the fact that the state of New Hampshire had reinstated the death penalty, but had not executed anyone in more than 75 years.

Louie said that only one man was currently on death row in New Hampshire. So, what was likely to happen to Arnie Branchik was not certain.

"He's going away for the rest of his sorry life. And then some," Louie said.

On Friday morning, Attoneys General Kelly Alexakis in Concord, and Jane Tarleton Miller in Augusta, Maine, had sufficient information that connected Warren Lapierrre to Robert Lazzelle, and Robert Lazelle to Arnost Branchik.

The case adding Charles Reilly's murder to Branchik's long list, as well as the killing of John Dervil in Pelham, were both looking inevitable. How many others might be charged and with which offenses was still undetermined.

Lazelle's attorney was getting close to the end of his bargaining abilities. The name of Richard Marco had not yet surfaced.

Charles Wehner was the first person to call Margaret Reilly to relay the preliminary news about her son's killer.

The same information was being shared with Blair Watson by Kelly Alexakis.

The news, and any trial later with a conviction, would not bring Charles back.

Nothing would change, nothing would get better.

In what was a relatively minor side note, police finally were able to locate the owner of the stolen Airstream.

Steve Fagula, a retired coal miner, had parked the trailer at his sister's home in Tewksbury, Massachusetts. While Fagula and his sister were visiting friends in Nova Scotia, the trailer had been removed from the driveway of the rural home and its absence only discovered upon their return two days ago.

Ninety Four

By the middle of November, many phone conversations and hours of speculation later, and with appreciation to Bruce Lyndon, Virginia Jackson and Louie Ragsdale , I was closer to finding my direction.

All the waffling over working in the media versus getting serious about my newest effort to become a professional private investigator was about to end.

At least that was my thinking at the moment. There remained a kernel of uncertainty that suggested further discussion might be required. Probably with a bottle of wine to help the process along.

After watching just a couple of weeks of the campaign silliness, it was hard to imagine that one reporter, maybe not even a whole bus load of good reporters, would really make a difference. God bless them for trying and a sincere wish that they would all get their stories and get them right. It simply was no longer something for me to be doing.

Then a phone call from Bonnie was a surprise.

We carefully talked about what each other had been doing for the past two weeks. She knew all about the nastiness in New Hampshire and wondered if I'd spoken with John O'Neil. I filled her in that yes, I had.

She politely asked about my time watching the primary campaign and was somewhat curious if I was reconsidering going back into radio. My quick response felt right.

"No. It's all different and much the same. I think that I would just be going through the motions. No real interest, no real effort."

Then Bonnie threw another surprise. She said that she was going away for Thanksgiving with 'a friend'. Would I take care of her dog, Rocco.

Are you kidding?

"Bring that boy up here."

Acknowledgements:

- *Midnight* – Grace Potter (8/15 – Hollywood Records)
- *Song From M*A*S*H* – Johnny Mandel and Michael Altman (1/70-Columbia/CBS)
- *Did You Ever Have to Make Up Your Mind* – The Lovin' Spoonful (4/66 – Kama Sutra Records)
- *Born in The USA* – Bruce Springsteen (4/84 – Columbia)
- *MacArthur Park* – Richard Harris (4/68 – Dunhill Records)
- *Ain't No Sunshine* – Bill Withers (5/71 – Sussex Records)
- *It's Still Rock And Roll To Me* – Billy Joel (5/80 – Columbia)
- *Money For Nothing* – Dire Straits (7/85 – Warner)
- *We Can Work It Out* – The Beatles (12/65 – Capitol)
- *The Tracks of My Tears* – Smokey Robinson and The Miracles (7/65 – Motown)
- *The Tears of A Clown* – Smokey Robinson and The Miracles (10/70 – Motown)

Thank you for the music.

- ROLEX (since 1905 - www.rolex.com)
- *Snow White and the Seven Dwarfs* (1937, Walt Disney Productions)
- Chris Craft Boats (since 1874 – www.chriscraft.com)
- Vermont Law School (since 1972 – www.vermontlaw.edu)
- NH Department of Safety MARINE PATROL (www.nh.gov/safety/divisions/nhsp/fob/marine-patrol)
- Lowell, MA (since 1653 – a lot of history – www.lowell.com)
- NH Presidential Primary (since 1920)
- *Zoobiquity:The Astonishing Connection Between Human and Animal Health* – Natterson-Horowitz/Bowers (2012, Knopf)
- Rolling Rock (since 1939 – www.rollingrock.com)
- Airstream (since 1936 – www.airstream.com)
- YouTube (since 2005 – www.youtube.com)
- ORVIS (since 1856 – www.orvis.com)

ABOUT THE AUTHOR

The author is a former broadcaster living in Vermont. He began his radio career as a news reporter covering municipal and state government meetings and political campaigns.

While some characters, conversations and real life experiences have inspired much of what you will read in these books, the stories are fiction.

www.nemysteries.com

Two NEW mysteries coming –
preview on the following pages.

- *A Pizza Night in THE BAHAMAS*
  (Fall 2016)

- *A Hot Afternoon in MASSACHUSETTS*
  (Spring 2017)

Excerpt from *A Pizza Night in THE BAHAMAS* –

"**Ah, mon! Dey got us,**" said Atty Gilbert. He leaned back against the wall, buried his face in his hands and hunched his shoulders forward.

The siren stopped quickly. Atty knew that in a matter of minutes he would be in police custody.

"No, mon. Be still. Dey don't know we here," Joey Aberle whispered. He stood with his ear pressed to the door, gripping the handle.

Atty slumped to the floor and went limp as a rag doll. He sat motionless and looked up at Joey. "You shoot dem boys. Dey know dat," Atty said, tears now welling in his eyes and his voice choking.

Joey glared at him. He thought for a second maybe he shoot Atty. In contrast, Joey's voice was deep, slow and deliberate as he scolded his partner.

"Dey don't know who shoot dem boys. Dem boys stupid. Dey cheat us, mon." He looked down as Atty rolled his head from side to side still covering his face with both hands.

Having just entered deluxe suite 214, the two men thought they were about to score some serious jewelry and maybe some cash. They'd watched the American couple for two days. Now inside the resort suite for less than a minute, they heard the siren.

Joey was cautious, Atty was scared. This was not what they imagined.

Excerpts from

A Hot Afternoon in MASSACHUSETTS –

By the time they would clear the beach I knew that my evening plans were about to change.

Walking back to the car to check on Rocco, I told the cop where I was going and that I would return.

The Sandwich Police Chief had arrived. His guys on the scene had been there for nearly an hour. It was obvious that I would have to go through the story again. Maybe I should start carrying my little digital recorder with me all the time.

Wait, Hanlon. Breakthrough! People actually use their smartphones to record these days.

The chief was headed in my direction.

"Look it up, hotshot. Nobody ever has – and nobody ever will – do a better version of that song. Period," Louie said.

Ragsdale was never shy about his opinions when it came to pop music. Never mind the inconvenient fact that his taste in music, kind of like mine, was slogging around in another era.

"You know, I once heard this local band at a club in Morgantown, West Virginia. They were pretty good," I said.

"Oh, I'll bet they were. Made the cover of *Rolling Stone*, right?"

74056238R00205

Made in the USA
Middletown, DE
19 May 2018